SONS OF IO

by Alain Medel

For Alba, Gabriel, and Jazmyn

CHAPTER ONE

Purgatory - AE 2086

"Hurry, Virgil, Numeyer's coming," said Haley, frantically running back to the bookshelf.

"It's ok, Haley, we've never been caught before," Cameron said, waving off her concern. Then, just as he looked away from her, the doorknob began to turn. A half-second later, Haley and Cameron were fifteen feet in the air, hovering over a short pudgy man, staggering to his bedroom door, completely drunk.

Numeyer, even drunk, sensed something was off in his massive library. He stumbled to his desk, but didn't seem to see anything out of place. He then made another attempt to his bedroom door, which seemed like a hundred feet to him, but was really only ten. He successfully turned the knob and opened the door on his third try. It would have been comical, if it wasn't so sad. He made one final glance around his library before going into his room and locking the door.

"That was close," said Cameron, with a huge smile. Haley gave him an evil stare that would have burned through any normal person. But Cameron just smiled even bigger. He was used to Haley being annoyed with him, so naturally, he found ways to annoy her even more. She was the closest thing he had to a sister.

Just as Cameron was pushing the thought from his mind, both he and Haley began to turn in mid-air toward one of the bookshelves. As they turned, they met the eyes of their best friend, Virgil. He stared at them for a moment and then smiled and shook his head. "When will you two ever give it a rest?" he said, with the voice of a parent disciplining whining children. Slowly, Virgil slid from the top of the bookshelf to meet the other two fifteen feet above the floor. "When I put you two down, will you promise to behave," he said with a smirk on his face.

This time, Haley and Cameron shared the same annoyed expression that was directed at Virgil. Slowly, all three were on the floor and headed to the back of Numeyer's library. It had always been called that since the only person ever allowed into the space was Numeyer. He was gifted the collection in a will left by his estranged parents years ago. All four walls, with the exception of a door to Numeyer's room, were filled with bookcases fifteen feet high and ladders to reach the books on the higher shelves. In between the walls were a dozen other freestanding bookshelves of equal height, in two rows of six. In the front to the massive room was Numeyer's beautiful mahogany desk with several rare books and his notebook that he was always seen with. An antique-looking lamp was always on at the right back corner, illuminating the student reports for that week.

Virgil always figured that such a poor excuse for a human being should never have been allowed such a beautiful piece of furniture. Some years back, he had thought about scratching the desk up as retribution on a beating he did not deserve. However, Numeyer was a vicious drunk, and Virgil knew they all would suffer if he did, so he thought better of it.

The three teenagers went as they always did, to the back right corner of the library to read their latest find. "So, what do we have for tonight?" Haley asked in a whisper, even though there was no way Numeyer would be able to get up from his drunken stupor. Virgil learned a few years back that Numeyer had been abused as a child and abandoned by his parents at age thirteen, to fend for himself on a foreign planet. For a long time, the three of them understood and pitied the man. But after years of the abuse being reciprocated on them, they lost that pity.

"Tonight we have *Dante's Inferno*," said Virgil, with a triumphant look on his face.

"Oh, come on, you've read that one a hundred times," said Cameron, snatching the book from him. He held out his own personal favorite, which wasn't really a book, *The Slang Dictionary*. "Now this is a book you two need to read. You two dudes will love it."

As usual, Haley gave him a blank stare and turned back to Virgil. "Come on, Virgil, I don't want to read a book that we can read in our common room, I want to read something that is off-limits."

Virgil gave his usual sigh and offered up, *Purgatory: Layouts & Blueprints*.

Cameron punched him in the arm. "I thought we agreed to no more Dante."

"This isn't Dante. Purgatory is the name of this place. These are the blueprints."

"Purgatory? I didn't realize they named this place after Hell. That's just sick," Haley said, suddenly not feeling well. "Does that mean that this place is underground?" she asked with genuine curiosity.

Virgil kept both eyes glued to the blueprint. "Yes, it appears that this place was built fifteen years ago at a depth of 333 feet."

Haley and Cameron followed Virgil's finger as it went down the first page of the blueprint. He turned the page to find a bunch of pipes and service tunnels that were hard to understand.

"Look...here," Virgil said, pointing to the left side of the page. "An air duct that leads to the surface. There's one on either side of the complex. We can use one of those to escape."

Haley and Cameron snapped their heads up immediately and looked at Virgil. The thought of escaping had crossed their minds in the past, but they had thought better of it. Once, five years ago, a boy named Dylan had tried escaping, but did not make it twenty feet past his bedroom door. When one of the guards grabbed him, he was found with his clothes and some food he had been hiding in his pillowcase. He was never seen again.

It was at that point that they realized the entire facility was monitored at all times and in all locations.

"No way, it's too risky, dude," said Cameron.

Virgil cocked his head at his friend. "Dude, please don't call me dude...it sounds idiotic."

Haley gave a silent chuckle in the affirmative.

"*Dude*," Virgil said with a grin. "It'll be just like we do now, sneak out in the middle of the night, read some books, and sneak back into our rooms."

They weren't convinced.

"How many times have we snuck out of our room?" Virgil asked.

"A few hundred," Haley whispered.

"And how many times have we been caught or anyone noticed?"

Cameron raised his head to look up and stare blankly at Virgil. "Uhhh...none."

They both knew Virgil was right, but they still did not want to risk it.

"Ok, how about this? I will work on an escape plan, and then run it by you two and see what you think?" Virgil said in a calm and reasonable voice.

"Deal. Now can we read something more enjoyable, like rainbows and unicorns?" said Cameron, batting his eyes rapidly toward Haley. She dismissed his attempt to provoke her and went to find herself a book. A few minutes later, Haley was absorbed into a romance novel and Cameron was silently talking to himself, practicing some slang words to use the next day on some of the other students. Virgil kept to his blueprints and took notes. They sat there for hours and occasionally, Virgil would smile at the blissful expressions of his closest and only friends reading the forbidden books.

If they only knew the truth about this place, they would think of nothing else other than escaping. But how can I tell them their life is a lie? He looked down at his blueprint again, more determined than ever.

CHAPTER TWO

History Lesson

"Ok, everyone sit down, sit down," said Ms. Boscombe from behind her podium.

Once everyone was seated and quiet, she continued, "As you all know, today we begin our studies on history."

An audible sigh came from behind Virgil; no mistaking Cameron. Ms. Boscombe snapped her head in their direction, and he immediately looked down at his desk. The kids knew better than to mess with Ms. Boscombe. She was as mean as she looked. She was a tall, lanky woman of sixty-five with the rage of a teenager. She once slapped Cameron across the face with her wooden ruler when he commented about a math problem he did not understand. They had learned very quickly never to question her, as they would later regret it.

"Is there something you would like to add to our discussion Mr. Leah?" she asked, with such venom in her tone that it made for an uncomfortable answer from Cameron. "No, Ms. Boscombe, I love history. It's my favorite subject," he said, knowing full well that he hated everything about our history class, since they found out some of the real history years back in Numeyer's library.

She gave him an evil sneer. "In that case, why not regale us with a history lesson of humans prior to IO."

"Of course, Ms. Boscombe, I will get to work on a report tonight and give it to you tomorrow before our lessons."

Haley looked at him with her eyes wide, knowing that was not what Ms. Boscombe meant.

The lanky woman made her way to Cameron's desk and towered over him as he stared at the book on his desk. "You will get up and give us a lesson now, Mr. Leah!" She smacked her thick wooden ruler across his forearm. He winced from the pain, and after a moment, stood and walked to the front of the room. As he made his way to the front, Virgil and Haley gave each other a worried look. They both knew that Cameron would have a difficult time recalling what was taught to them and what they learned from the library. It was evident that Cameron shared this anxiety, as he gave a quick glance to both Haley and Virgil.

"Where would you like me to begin, Ms. Boscombe?" Cameron asked, with a timid voice, as to not upset the instructor and receive another hit.

With an air of annoyance in her voice, she said, "From the *Year of Destruction*, of course."

Cameron was momentarily relieved. This part of the history lesson was real and taught to everyone from the earliest of ages. "The year was 2025, and the world's population could not be sustained by the massive under-production of food due to droughts and water shortages." He looked up, as if trying to retrieve memories form the back of his mind and continued, "After seeing massive famine and starvation throughout Africa and Asia, the United States, on orders of the President, launched a pre-emptive nuclear strike on the Eurasian continent on May 1, 2025, taking out China and Russia's military capabilities in a single day…thus assuring neither country would attempt an invasion for resources."

He paused to catch his breath and continued, as if reciting a lesson taught many times over and memorized. "Although crippling the nuclear powers was achieved, so was the unintended consequences of nuclear winter. It was a lose-lose situation, as the United States knew it would eventually be invaded for its natural resources, but it would ultimately destroy the planet in its own defense. Had they worked it out diplomatically—"

"Please stick to the facts, Mr. Leah, not opinion," Ms. Boscombe said, abruptly cutting him off.

He rolled his eyes, away from Boscombe, of course, and proceeded. "Once the damage was done, the countries that had underground bunkers were forced to use them. Only three months after the bombs were dropped, all farming and agriculture efforts were ruined. All farm lands and cities were rendered uninhabitable."

He paused for effect on the weight of those words. "After only a year, if you were not living underground, you were not living. It was only after much deliberation that the government came to the conclusion that the Earth would be a nuclear wasteland for thousands of years to come and decided to seek refuge on another planet." He looked at Virgil, and with a nod, continued, "As part of the secret space program, there had been site surveys done on every celestial body in the solar system for over seventy-five years."

Virgil glanced over at the only pupils in the room who seemed even somewhat interested in the dissertation. A group of five children had recently joined the facility. No doubt kidnapped by the people in charge. Their only crime…having light purple eyes. It was the common thread between all of the students. *Students?* Virgil had always thought of themselves as prisoners. He and he alone knew the real truth. Virgil was snapped out of his reverie by a loud slap to his desk. He was not immune to fear whenever she used her ruler. She appeared to take joy in the sight of the kids' terror when she wielded her stick. Even more so when she struck a kid with the implement in question.

"Please do pay attention, Virgil," said the old woman. It always bothered Virgil that he was the only pupil ever addressed by his first name. It could be due to the fact that he came into the facility without a last name. He had tried on several occasions to find his name in his file in Numeyer's library, but that page was missing.

Reluctantly, he turned to face Cameron, who was still reciting his assignment.

"It was known long ago that the best shot at a new home would be here on IO, as it had breathable air and water to sustain life. Over the next fifteen years, the collective intelligence on Earth completed a series of spaceships, capable of carrying a couple million people each, along with what was left of the world's treasures. Of the seven ships, one was used solely for the transport of raw materials not seen on IO, to be used for construction of a new civilization. In total, just over ten million souls were able to flee Earth, most of which were society's wealthy and elite."

Cameron gave a cautious look at Ms. Boscombe to make sure he did not overstep with his remarks. Luckily, she had been paying attention to one of the new pupils and had not heard his comments. Relieved, he continued, "The refugees fled Earth in the year 2040, on a two-year journey to their new home."

"That is enough, Mr. Leah," said the instructor, waving her hand dismissively in his direction.

Quickly, Cameron went to his desk before the old hag changed her mind.

"Ms. Hawthorne, you're up." Ms. Boscombe said, catching Haley by surprise.

"Yes, Ma'am." Obediently, Haley made her way to the podium and started from where Cameron had ended. "Once the refugees arrived on IO, they were immediately tasked with building numerous colonies on various parts of the moon. This was in order to take advantage of the water and mineral resources located at each of the specified locations. The volcanic activity all over the moon made for rich farm land, but also has a very unpredictable surface. The tides move up and down by some sixty feet, depending on— "

"Please, Ms. Hawthorne, we do not need a geography lesson. What happened shortly after arriving to IO? Specifically, what happened to law and order once the population was acclimated to their new home?"

As if reading from a prompter, Haley recited what she had been repeatedly told, "Without the rule of law, anarchy ensued and the self-appointed rulers had to implement strict laws to regain order." It made her gag, spewing this propaganda when she knew the truth. *The elite had power on Earth and they intended to do the same on IO.* She could not say it. "Through the continued efforts of the ruling few, law and order were restored to the nine colonies. The anarchists were either jailed, killed, or banished from the cities to fend for themselves."

Virgil looked at Cameron, knowing that the truth was much more complex than what they were taught. A few years back, they had read from one of Numeyer's manuscripts that a small group of refugees wanted to just be left alone. They did not want help form the new government and wanted to survive and thrive on their own, as they knew they could. This did not sit well with the leadership, and they decided to smear them and make them look like a bunch of crazies. They succeeded and had the power and control over the people that they so desired.

"And tell us now of the plague, please," said Ms. Boscombe.

As instructed, Haley went on, "In the year, AE 2066, a plague of unknown origin tore through the colonies. Thousands were killed in the months following. It was later found that the earliest indication of the virus is found in childhood." Haley looked around the entire room. "At an early age, once a child develops light purple eyes, they are quarantined here, at the school, until a cure can be found." She gulped hard. "And so it is, that we stay here, day after day, until a cure is found. And as part of our treatment, we are given a shot monthly to prevent any adverse effects to the virus."

At that, Virgil looked down and closed his eyes. He knew that eventually, he would need to admit to his friends that there was no virus. But not yet, he had to wait for the right time. *Was there ever a right time?* He tried to forget, for now.

CHAPTER THREE

Happy Birthday to Me

"Happy Birthday!" screamed Haley and Cameron right in Virgil's ear.

With the sudden shock of being awoken and screamed at, Virgil promptly sat up, then fell on the floor. Haley and Cameron laughed so hard, they too almost fell on the floor. No one was ever told how old they were in Purgatory, but some years back, the three of them found their student records in Numeyer's study. Haley found out she was almost a year younger than Virgil and Cameron, which they loved to tease her about. They decided to keep whatever they found out from the forbidden files to themselves, as they did not know who to trust.

Virgil found out that he had an off-the-charts IQ. Upon learning this, he quickly started acting as if he were a mediocre student, while secretly reading everything he could get his hands on in Numeyer's library.

All three found out when they arrived in Purgatory and were not surprised to find out that Virgil had been the very first occupant. Virgil knew he had been alone for a while, but could not remember the details, as he was so young when he was brought to the facility.

"Ok, you have to make a wish," said Haley, handing him a drawing of a cake and candle. She memorized as many details as she could from a children's book she had read a few months prior. It showed a family singing to their child and watching him blow out a candle on a cake.

"Ha! If you can blow out that candle, I'll kiss Haley," said Cameron, laughing at Haley's impromptu cake.

"Deal!" said Virgil. He erased the flame with his finger and smiled triumphantly at Cameron. "Well, go on then," he said, knowing full well that Haley would throat-chop Cameron before he ever got close enough.

Seeing his defeat, Cameron conceded, "Ok, best two out of three."

They all laughed and sat on the floor for the next hour, talking about the few good times they had enjoyed here in Purgatory. Then, as if on cue, they all realized that this was their one free day of the week. All they needed to do was get their monthly shot and the rest of the day was theirs.

"What better way to spend a birthday than with a day off?" said Haley, as they made their way to the common area from Virgil's room. As they walked down the corridor, they were joined by several dozen other pupils on their way to the same place. The eight-foot high corridor opened up to a twenty-five-foot high dome-shaped space. The common area was large enough to fit all 124 pupils comfortably, with enough area in the center for each to work out and get their required exercise. A three-lane jogging track encircled the space. On either side of the inside of the track were a series of benches that faced a large field with fake grass. At various points along the walls were climbing obstacles and apparatus that each pupil was required to learn as part of their physical activities.

As usual, four tables were set up, side by side, at the back of the space where nurses stood, poised to administer the injections. Four at a time, the students walked up and got a shot in the arm. The needle stung for only a second, but the contents of the syringe were not as temporary. Everyone knew that their arms would feel like they were on fire for about two hours. After taking it for so long though, everyone was quite used to it.

This day always bothered Virgil, as it always reminded him of the secret he kept from his friends. When they split from the rest of the group, deciding to claim the seats on the left side of the dome, he knew that this was the time and turned to his friends.

"Hey, I need to tell you two something, but you have to promise not to get mad." He waited for their response, scared senseless. He had decided long ago not to share what he knew, as he thought it would only depress his friends, because there was nothing they could do with that knowledge. *Yes, they will understand,* he said again to himself.

"Well, don't look so *cray cray*. Spit it out," said Cameron.

As usual, Haley could not resist. "*Cray cray?* You sound like a moron."

Virgil's laugh was a momentary respite, as he knew they would most likely not talk to him after he told them what he knew. "Ok, do you guys remember that time like three years ago when I went to Numeyer's library on my own?" He waited for their nods, seeing confusion in their eyes. In truth, Virgil had been to the forbidden library countless times by himself, but they didn't need to know that. He was already feeling like a total liar, no need to make it worse. *This is harder than I thought.* "When I went there by myself, I found something. Something that I think you two should know."

The concern in their eyes grew to anticipation. "Just spit it out already," said Cameron.

Virgil took a deep breath, and—

BOOM!

A wooden table at the back of the dome hit the wall twenty feet away with such force that it splintered into a dozen or so pieces. One of the newer pupils ran from the nurses and guards. He was grabbed by a guard but with barely a flick of his wrist, the guard was thrown twenty feet in the opposite direction. He hit the ground with a thud and slid another ten feet. The child then proceeded to pick up a bench nearby like it was a toy car. He let out a blood curdling scream and dropped the table, falling next to it shortly after. The medication had taken effect. His *Gift* had been repressed. In a day or two, the Warden would label the incident a fluke and forget all about it. And in the meantime, Virgil's secret was still his to bear.

"What the hell was that?" asked Cameron.

"Never mind, I'll tell you guys later tonight," said Virgil, as he ushered them towards the corridor.

Virgil thought back to the first time when he learned of his *Gifts*, he was only seven years old. He was reading in his room and accidentally dropped his glass of water from his desk. As he reached for it, he was amazed at what happened next. It hovered in midair just a few inches off the ground. He stared at it for a moment and then reached for it. At that moment, it dropped to the ground and shattered. From that day on, every night he practiced what he later found out was called telekinesis; the ability to move objects using only his mind. After years of practice, he got so precise with his *Gift* that he was able to thread a needle with almost no effort.

Then, at age eleven, he figured out that he had the ability to cloak objects, also just by thinking it. He experimented with random objects in his room for months. Some no larger than a pencil, and others as large as the chest at the foot of his bed. One day, he decided to try it on Cameron. The only problem was, he hadn't mentioned anything to him first. While in the common room, Cameron and the other pupils were doing their mandatory exercises while Virgil took a break on the benches to the right of the room. *Don't worry, nothing bad will happen.* That's what Virgil kept repeating in his head. Then, he went for it. He stared at Cameron, with the intention of cloaking him completely, to give the illusion that he had suddenly disappeared.

The first scream came from Haley, who was closest to him. "Help! Someone, help! Cameron lost his legs!"

Cameron looked down at his legs and screamed like a girl. It took everything in Virgil to not crack up laughing. Cameron fell on the floor and began grabbing at where his legs should've been and was partially relieved to feel them there. "They're here, I can feel them!" he said, exasperated.

By the time one of the adults made their way to his side, Virgil had released the illusion and Cameron looked like a crazy kid grabbing at his legs. He looked down and was speechless. The nurses were wide-eyed and for a while, Virgil thought they were going to medicate Cameron.

Later that night, Virgil had both Cameron and Haley come to his room to reveal his secret Gifts. Of course at first, they didn't believe him. It wasn't until he picked

Haley up a few feet off the ground without touching her and made her disappear that they were sold.

"Cool! Can you pick her up again and hang her upside down?" asked Cameron with a straight face. They were amazed anyone could do what he could. They promised to keep his secret, and for the next few weeks, they practiced sneaking out of their rooms. They started small, walking to the bathrooms, then the dome. And after weeks of consideration, they thought they were ready to sneak into the library.

Just after lights out one night, Virgil concentrated and formed a cloaking field several feet around his body. When he was confident he could hold it, he walked out of his room and then two doors down to Cameron's room. He stood in front of Cameron's door, to camouflage anyone coming out of the room. Once Cameron was next to him, they proceeded down the corridor to Haley's room. As soon as Haley's door was closed, they proceeded to the end of the corridor. To the left was the dome, and to the right was Numeyer's study. When they reached the door, they turned it, only to find it locked.

After what seemed like an eternity, Cameron found a solution. "Hey, why don't you try moving the locking bolt with your mind?"

I'm the genius, I should've thought of that. Virgil quickly scrubbed the thought from his mind and started trying to unlock the bolt. Surprisingly, it was rather simple. With only a slight nudge of his mind, Virgil was able to unbolt the door and grant them access to one of the only restricted rooms in Purgatory.

Once inside, the three were in awe of what they saw. From outside, the door could easily be confused with a broom closet. But once inside, the room opened up, much like the dome. Only this room was filled with books and manuscripts.

From that night on, just as tonight, they were in the library. Tonight however, they were free to be as loud as they wanted because Numeyer was out of Purgatory tonight on business.

The three sat at his desk, all with their legs kicked up, reading. Then suddenly, as if reading Virgil's mind, Cameron closed the comic book he was reading. "Oh yeah, so what was it you wanted to tell us earlier in the dome?"

Haley sat up as well. "Come on, we don't have all night here. Well, we do, but...whatever, just tell us what you wanted to tell us."

Virgil hesitated. "It's nothing, really. Forget I said anything."

This only made Haley and Cameron more curious. "Stop trippin', bro," said Cameron, a bit too seriously to be taken seriously.

Virgil and Haley both looked at each other and just shook their heads.

Haley leaned over the desk and picked up his slang book. "Ok, you're done." She threw the book halfway down the room between two bookshelves. "Seriously, Virgil, we're not going to leave you alone until you tell us what's bothering you."

I guess it's time.

Shifting uncomfortably in his seat, he took a deep breath. "There is no virus."

Haley and Cameron looked more confused now than a few seconds ago. It was Haley who broke the silence. "What are you talking about Virgil? Do you mean the one that landed us down here?"

"Yes," he said, staring at his hands on the desk. He was shaking, but he was unable to stop it.

Then it was Cameron's turn to chime in. "What do you mean there's no virus? We get that shot for it every month. Trust me, a day or two before we get our shots, I start feeling light-headed and groggy. If that's not the virus, then what could it be?"

Without looking up, Virgil answered, "It's the side effects of the drug wearing off. They only give it once a month because any more than that would kill us." He looked at both of them for any sign of understanding, but it was clear in their faces that they still didn't get it. Virgil stood up and walked toward a nearby bookcase. "The shots they give us are to suppress certain *Gifts,* that's the best way I can explain them. We all have some type of special metaphysical ability that is suppressed by the drugs."

"Like what you can do?" Finally...Haley was starting to see. "Wait, but if that's the case, then why can you still do what you do?"

"I have no idea," said Virgil. "I get the shot every month like everyone else, but it doesn't seem to suppress anything. It's been that way since I first realized I had these powers." He waited again for a comment or remark before he continued. "Do you remember the young boy today in the dome? He had an adverse reaction to the drug, and it caused what we all saw with the table. Every child in this facility is being held prisoner here because the people in power are afraid of what we could do if we were not on their side."

Cameron shook his head in disbelief. "No way, man. They feed us, they house us, and they give us the best education possible. Prisoners don't get that kind of treatment." He began to pace back and forth, not wanting to believe his friend.

Then, Haley looked up, as if she had just solved a puzzle in her head. "They teach us to brainwash us." She looked for a nod from Virgil as confirmation of her thought. "They indoctrinate us on a daily basis. After a long enough time, you will believe anything they tell you." The sadness in her voice was undeniable.

Still confused, Cameron said, "I don't get it. If we're that dangerous, why not just kill us all? It would save a lot of time and money."

"They want to use us, if possible. A weapon in the right hands can be a very powerful form of control over others," said Virgil. "The ones who are too much trouble are disappeared and never seen again."

They all sat there for a moment, remembering the kids that were taken away and never seen again.

After a while, Haley asked, "How long have you known about this?"

"About three years now."

Haley and Cameron looked as if someone punched the air out of them. They looked as one would expect a close friend to look after being betrayed.

"How could you keep that from us? I thought we were family." Haley's eyes began to well up with tears.

"It wasn't my intention to keep it from you guys, but I knew it wouldn't do any good telling you something you had no power to change." Virgil looked at them for reassurance, but their looks of betrayal pierced through him as sharp as a dagger. "But it's different now. We're older and more capable of taking care of ourselves. That's why I've been working so hard on an escape plan. I was going to tell you two just after we escaped."

They weren't at all convinced. "I can't believe that after all we've been through together, that you wouldn't trust us with the truth. I think I'm going to be sick. Please just take me back to my room," said Haley. She had heard enough.

Virgil looked at Cameron, but there was no sympathy in his eyes, "Just take us back to our rooms, man."

"No, wait, we can talk about —"

"Now!" Cameron said, with so much pain in his voice that it made Virgil's heart drop. Without another word, he cloaked the three of them and proceeded down the corridor, first to Haley's room, and then to Cameron's. It was the most uncomfortable evening of Virgil's life.

Afterward, alone in front of his door, he decided to go back to the solitude of the library. He worked his way back into the space and sat in the corner of the library nearest to Numeyer's desk. He was alone now. Completely alone. He couldn't blame Haley or Cameron for their reactions. *I would've done the same thing to you, dumb-ass.* He reached into his pocket and pulled out the folded piece of paper with the drawing of the birthday cake. *Huh, some birthday this turned out to be.* And with a tone of pure defeat, he mumbled, "Happy Birthday to me…"

CHAPTER FOUR

It's All an Illusion

I'll just give them some space. Soon enough they'll see my side of it and come around. The thought did little to reassure Virgil. The three of them had been like peas in a pod for as far back as he could remember. He had never seen them so angry. Not even angry, they felt betrayed. He knew it would take a while to regain their trust.

He was so caught up in his thoughts that he did not hear the door unlock. Just as the door opened, he shot his head up.

Numeyer swung the door open and saw someone sitting on the floor by his desk. He blinked, and they were gone. "I must be going crazy," he said, wiping the sweat from his forehead with a small towel.

That was too close. Wait till I tell...

He had no one to tell. He was all alone for the foreseeable future. In attempt to drown out his thoughts, he thought he would watch Numeyer for a while. He had done this many times before and rather enjoyed it. He recalled once seeing him drunk at his desk, staring at a book from across the room. He stood up and walked as drunkards walked, straight to the book he fixated on. He stumbled back to his desk and sat down, only to stare at the book for another fifteen minutes. He appeared to be daydreaming. His expressions ranged from tranquil to angry, then depressed. Finally, he picked the book up, and Virgil was able to make out part of the title, *Peaceful Parenting.* In a sudden fury, Numeyer tossed the book into the trash bin next to his desk.

He then stood up and did something that absolutely shocked Virgil. He stood in front of the bin and began to urinate on the book. This appeared to give him great pleasure. "Take that, you bastard," he said, followed by a loud burp.

Virgil knew Numeyer was referencing his parents. One of the many personnel files Virgil went through some time back happened to be the warden's. *Ha, something else I neglected to mention to Haley and Cameron.* He knew it would be wrong to read Numeyer's record, but at the time, all he wanted was to know the truth. Virgil read for hours about how Numeyer was constantly beaten by his father and on several occasions, forced to watch his mother take the same abuse. When he was only thirteen, he felt brave enough to confront his father and save his mother from a drunken beating.

It didn't work out so well for him. He suffered a broken nose and fractured a rib. He ended up in the hospital for a couple of weeks. After the second day, a nurse came in and told him that they were not able to locate his parents. The authorities went to their home, but it was empty. They had abandoned him. He was sent to a home for unwanted children, where he suffered for years at the hand of other kids with emotional issues who had someone to take their rage out on.

A loud ring came from the warden's desk, snapping Virgil back from his reverie. Numeyer's eyes opened wide. Apparently, this was a surprise to him as well. He quickly hid the bottle and combed back his thinning hair behind his ears. After a few seconds, he took a deep breath and pressed something underneath the desk. Suddenly, a holoscreen appeared two feet in front of the desk. Fascinated with what he was seeing, Virgil made his way a few feet behind the warden so that he could get a better view.

With a click, a picture of another room came up. Lit up in the background was what looked like IO, with eight stars in a circular pattern within the moon. At the center of the circle of stars was a central star, slightly larger than the rest. Then a tall man, covered by shadows, stepped into the picture. He sat at what appeared to be a desk and waited for the warden to respond.

"Good evening, sir. I was not expecting a call at this late hour," Numeyer said, shifting uncomfortably in his chair.

Sir? People only addressed *Numeyer* as sir. This only fueled Virgil's curiosity, and he stepped a little closer and—

"What's that behind you?" said the man on the screen.

Virgil froze. *They see me!*

The warden turned around and studied the area behind him. After a moment, he reached…straight in Virgil's direction. Virgil tried to move, but he was paralyzed by fear. *This is it.* He could feel his heart ready to explode out of his chest.

Then, at the last second, the warden moved his hand slightly to the left and grabbed a bottle on the shelf, missing Virgil by a fingertip. "It is a very old bottle of brandy," he said. "Left to me by my father. It's two hundred years old."

"Come now, John, you don't have to be cordial with me," said the man on the other end. "Everybody knows your parents left you as a boy. The only reason you got all of this is because your pitiful excuse for a mother left it to you before she died."

The rage in Numeyer's eyes looked as if he could kill the man through the screen. But his response was most surprising. "Yes, sir, that is correct. My father would have sold it all rather than leave it to me. Luckily, he died some years before my mother." The pain in his voice was undeniable. Yet, the man in the shadows did not care in the least.

"I hear there was an incident today with pupil number 124, and his injection." The man's voice held no compassion. This was clearly an interrogation.

"My nurses tell me the boy had a negative reaction to the drug. It was his first time. It has since kicked in. They have made their notes and his dosage will be raised accordingly, so that this does not happen again," Numeyer responded.

"See to it that it doesn't, because if it does, you won't be around to make another mistake," the other man said with such venom that it made the warden stutter when responding. "Yes, sir, I understand. It won't happen again."

"Are there any other issues that I should be made aware of?"

"This is still my facility, is it not? If I had something to report, it would have been reported, sir." The alcohol had clearly given the little man his liquid courage. This however, was short-lived.

"What did you just say to me?" snapped the man on the screen. "Don't forget your place, you maggot." The man stood up and moved closer to the screen. "You may have those *children* down there thinking you're a god, but up here, everyone knows just what a drunken degenerate you really are." Seeing that it was starting to affect the warden, he continued, "Even your wife left you…knowing what a loser you were. Why do you think you got the job as babysitter?" Then the man's face, still in the shadows, smiled wide so that the dim lights shined on his teeth. He was obviously enjoying this. "Now, think carefully before you answer me again." He sat back in his chair, regaining his composure. "Are there any other issues I should be made aware of?"

"No, sir, no issues," Numeyer answered quickly. "The indoctrination is functioning as designed. You will have fine soldiers when the time comes."

"Good. That's what I want to hear. By the time we're done with them, they'll be so brainwashed that they'll kill their own parents in the name of the government." The man leaned back in his chair, the satisfaction in his voice apparent.

Soldiers? What is he talking about? Virgil was thoroughly confused. *We're just kids.*

"That will be all, John. Go get some sleep. You look as if you've been drinking again," said the shadow man.

"Yes, sir, I—"

Click. The man at the other end disconnected their call before the warden finished his sentence. Numeyer sat, looking at his desk, for what was only a few seconds, but felt like an eternity. Then, he banged the top with his fist with such force that Virgil thought the desk would break in two. He pounded again. And again. Then he smacked his hands down and slid everything on his desk right to the floor. Tears started streaming down his face, as all bodily control had gone. He was letting out all of his emotions in what he assumed was an empty room.

Virgil couldn't help feeling sorry for the man. He understood his reasons for treating everyone like dirt. He understood why this man spent all of his free time drunk. He even understood his rage. All of the yelling and shows of force with the children…all of his power…it was all an illusion. To the kids, he was a god, but to this man on the screen, he was a mere drunk. Even as small as the warden was, he commanded great fear from all of the kids. To Virgil, the illusion was destroyed. He would never see the man the same way again.

After a few minutes and some bloody knuckles, the warden retreated to his room. Virgil wondered if the man would take his own life, but then realized that if he were able to, he'd have done it a long time ago.

CHAPTER FIVE

Can't We All Just Get Along

A little more than a week had passed, and still, neither Haley nor Cameron were talking to Virgil.

It wasn't for a lack of trying. Every time Virgil approached the two of them, they would whisper something to each other then walk away. He'd known they would be upset with him, but just not to this extent. He also stopped going to Numeyer's office. *What's the point? Why plan an escape when my friends aren't involved?*

He found himself swiping his hand back and forth on his holo-desk. By far, the best part of being in these classes were the desks. The entirety of the desk's surface was a touchscreen learning tool. "The world's collective knowledge at your fingertips," Ms. Boscombe called it. But on this particular day, it was nothing more than a distraction for Virgil.

"Did you hear me, Virgil?" Ms. Boscombe said.

"Yes, ma'am," he replied, slightly annoyed.

"Did you now? Well, ok, what were we just discussing?"

He honestly had not a clue in the world. So he improvised, taking a cue from Cameron's playbook. "How unbelievably awesome I am?"

She narrowed her eyes at him. "Not quite. We were discussing the rise and fall of civilizations. Care to provide a little insight?"

He shrugged his shoulders. "Not really." This time, her face turned red and her stare made him shift uneasily in his seat. He knew he was treading in shallow water, but he didn't care. He let out a big huff and said, "Fine. What would you like to know?"

She took several steps toward his desk. "Before the United States launched the missiles in 2025, it had already ceased being a super power years earlier. What led to the collapse?" She straightened her back and slightly raised her chin at him, a sign he took to mean that he was beneath her.

"That's easy," he said, in a very point-of-fact tone. "Personal responsibility."

Everyone in the class, with the exception of Haley and Cameron, cocked their heads to the side in clear confusion. Haley and Cameron knew what he was going to say. They'd argued it a hundred times over the years. Virgil was always adamant in his position of this issue. "When the people who have nothing can vote away the rights and money of the people who are working, a society will inevitably collapse, as the takers very rapidly outnumber the producers."

She rolled her eyes and gave him a dismissive look. "Who on Earth taught you that? That government fell because of the greed of a small few who owned the majority of the world's wealth." She straightened her shoulders as she spoke.

He always loved hearing that argument, always regurgitated by the mindless drones in the seats next to him. "They were but a symptom of a bigger issue. Let me ask you..."

Haley's eyes widened. *This is not good.* She knew never to talk back to the instructors...as doing so would certainly result in consequences. She knew how seriously Virgil regarded philosophy, human nature, and politics...and was nervous to see how far he would push this.

Virgil continued, "Why was it that these corporations never went to one another when they wanted a tax break or competitive advantage? Because the only ones who had the guns and power to change the laws were the politicians they bought." He slouched down in his chair. Clearly, he did not care about what the instructor thought about him. "It worked the other way as well...when the politicians wanted the poor and middle-class vote, they would simply bribe them with the future earnings of the unborn." His apparent lack of regard for the consequences seemed to dwindle as the realization of what was to come finally sunk in.

"That is quite the imagination you have, V—"

"And furthermore," Virgil cut her off mid-sentence.

Ms. Bascombe's eyes burned red as if she were strangling him in her mind. She closed the distance between her and Virgil in a few steps...standing over him as if giving a veiled threat to be quiet.

And still, he persisted, "Using force to solve complex social issues will always get you the opposite of what was intended—"

Smack! Ms. Boscombe said nothing as she backhanded Virgil in the face. "That will be enough out of you," she said, cursing under her breath.

Virgil looked at Haley and gave her a smirk, as if pointing out his correctness. "Thank you for proving my point," he said to Ms. Bascombe. And with that, he received another slap in the face.

Haley quickly looked away. She couldn't bear to see her friend being hurt.

"Guards, take him to the detention room. Let him stay there until the warden has a word with him," Ms. Bascombe instructed.

All Haley and Cameron could do was stare at their friend as he was being dragged away.

Damn, is this what it takes for my friends to look at me? Virgil laughed silently to himself, knowing that laughing out loud would welcome more unwanted abuse, but this time by the guards.

He was led down the corridor past all of the sleeping quarters to the far side of the facility. When the guards opened the door, Virgil looked inside, but saw only the left side of the entrance, as the rest of the room was on the right of the door. The rest of the room was hidden by the shadows. He was pushed into the room and had the door shut before he could get his bearings. He took what must have been two steps and smacked his head into the wall. *What the Hell!*

Not wanting to make that mistake again, he raised his hands in front of him and began to sweep them from side to side to get an idea how big this space was. He was able to easily touch two sides at once while also having his elbows bent. *This can't be good.* He turned in the opposite direction and was able to fully extend his arms, but was able to touch the other wall with only a slight bend sideways.

He had never actually been in a detention room, but he'd heard about it from a pupil that sat in one for a few hours. *That was seven years ago. And the kid was so much smaller than me.* This room was a coffin for someone of Virgil's size. He laid down, only to find that he could not straighten his legs completely. He had no idea where the door was either. It was a very disorienting feeling to him. *No bed...no toilet...no books? Way to go, dumb-ass.* He figured he would be fine. It would only be a few hours, a day at the most.

With nothing better to do, Virgil stayed on the ground and laid his head on his arm. There was no concept of time in this room. What felt like a lifetime may have been just a few minutes. Virgil tried his best to try and keep track of how long he was in there, but after just a short time, he was lost. Giving up, he curled up on the cold floor.

Then, the voice of an angel spoke. "Had to open your big mouth, didn't you?"

Not a very nice angel.

It was Haley. She sat on the floor on the other side of the door. "Did they beat you?" She sounded really worried, which for some reason, made Virgil's chest tighten ever so slightly.

He dismissed that feeling. "No...at least not yet. Have you heard anything about how long I'll be in here?"

She was quiet for a long moment before she answered. "I heard Ms. Boscombe talking to the warden. She told him that you were insubordinate and that you threatened her."

"Threatened her grasp of history, maybe," he said, in a tone that would normally make Haley laugh. He always knew what to say to make her smile.

"This is serious, you idiot," she said. Apparently, it wasn't going to work today. She went on, "Numeyer is leaving the facility for two days, and he just told her to leave you here until he gets back."

All the blood drained from his face. He knew that he would be able to get out if he really wanted to, but he did not want to risk getting caught and them finding out about his *Gifts*.

"They can't do that," he huffed.

"They can do anything they want, remember?"

She was right. He was caged like an animal, and there was nothing he could do. "How long have I been in here…seven, eight hours?"

"Ha, you're close…three hours."

"Will you at least come see me when you can?" He was hoping that she would say maybe, possibly forgot the little details about him lying to her.

"Of course I will."

He was quiet for a moment. "I'm so sorry I lied to you, Haley. It was never my intention to hurt you or Cameron. I just figured the truth would be worse than not knowing."

She let out a huff and said, "I know you didn't. It's just…we only have each other in here, and I don't want us to have any secrets between us."

"I know, and it will never happen again, I promise." He waited eagerly for her response.

"Ok, then I guess all is forgiven...with me, that is. I'll talk to Cameron and see if he will stop by here. Maybe you can call him "dude" like a hundred times and you two will kiss and make up." He heard the smile in her voice as she spoke through the door.

"Thanks, Haley...I don't know what I would do without you."

He heard her catch her breath before she spoke. "Umm...ok, I'll...I'll come back later on when it's safer. We were told not to come down here too much or we'd get in trouble. Talk to you soon." And then she was gone.

Damn, I hope he didn't hear that. What's gotten into me? Haley couldn't shake the fact that her breath caught when Virgil said he didn't know what he'd do without her. He had always said things like that before, but she never thought anything of them. *It's because of what's happening. Yeah, that's it.* Her reassurances were not working.

Determined to get out of her own thoughts, she walked back to the sleeping quarters to find Cameron. He was reading some comics on the holo-desk in his room. She went in without knocking and plopped down on his bed.

"You could knock, you know," Cameron said, without turning his head.

"It was open. Besides, when do I ever knock?" She knew that he was worried about Virgil, but he was too stubborn to say anything. "So, I went to see…I mean talk through a door, to Virgil."

Cameron said nothing, just continued with his comic. She knew he wasn't actually reading it because he was flipping the pages entirely too fast. "I don't have anything to say to him." He wanted to go see him, but his pride got in the way. Honestly, he just wanted his friend back. "Did he say anything?"

"Yeah, he asked how you were doing."

Liar, liar, pants on fire. Well, if I don't make something up, these clowns won't talk to each other for months.

"He did?" This time he turned around to look at her.

"No, not really…but I figured it would get you to turn around?"

He rolled his eyes and turned back around to his desk.

"Ok, you're both pretty," she said, sounding exasperated.

"What?" He turned around to face her again. He had no idea what she was talking about.

"He lied...we got upset...now it's time to forgive and move on."

"So, you're just going to forget what he did and move on? Sorry, I'm not built that way."

"No, I didn't say forget, I said forgive. He apologized to me, and I forgave him. You need to do the same. He needs us right now more than ever." She looked at him for any sign of conceding.

Finally, he caved. "Do you ever think about it?"

"Think about what?" She was completely lost.

"Think about what you can do...without the inhibitors, I mean?"

She exhaled in relief. *Good, I'm not the only one thinking about it.* "All the time," she said.

"I almost hate to admit it, but I kinda wish he hadn't told us."

Her eyes widened at his response. "What, you're admitting that you were wrong?" Now she was just torturing him.

"I didn't say that. I just can't help but think about it all the time. What if I can fly? What if I have super strength?" He pointed to a picture of Superman on his desk. "Look at what Virgil can do. And we always thought he was just different. Now, knowing what we know...it makes me mad that I can't do anything to change it." He sat there, shaking his head.

"I know. And that's exactly what Virgil thought would happen. I think about it all the time. I keep thinking that I can read people's thoughts, or maybe walk through walls. I'm annoyed that I don't know what I don't know."

"If it makes you feel better, I don't know what you just said." He cracked a smile.

"You're such a moron," she said, displaying a wide grin.

"Alright, I'll go with you later to talk to your door. But I'm still not saying sorry."

"Deal." She stood up and held out her hand, signifying his agreement with her.

He shook her hand and at the same time, pushed her out of his room. "Ok, now leave me alone. Superman is going to change into his tights."

She rolled her eyes. "You're such a dork." And then she was gone.

A few hours passed and Cameron found himself staring at the slop on a plate they claimed was dinner. He looked at Haley, who apparently was thinking the same thing. "Feeding this to us is cruel and unusual punishment," he said, while making a puking gesture.

She moved closer and whispered, "Hey, wanna go see if Virgil's awake?"

"Of course he's awake. Why wouldn't he be?"

"He's in a pitch-black room with no concept of time. When I saw him earlier, he thought he had been in there for half the day. It may be good for him to hear some friendly voices."

He hesitated, but only for a second. "Fine, but if we get in trouble, I'm blaming you."

The two of them made their way from the dining hall to the corridor that led to the detention room. But, as they turned the corner, they stopped short, seeing a guard sitting in a chair in front of Virgil's door.

"Great, what do we do now?" Haley asked.

"We can use our newfound powers on them...oh wait, that's right, we don't have them yet..." His tone dripped with sarcasm. But even through the snide remarks, Haley could see the tension in his eyes. He was worried for his friend. "Ok, come on...we'll come back later before lights out. The guard will be gone by then." He sounded confident but looked as unsure as she has ever seen him.

As fate would have it, the same guard was there when they came back before lights out. "Well, I guess tonight is out of the question," Haley said. "I hope he doesn't think I'm going back on my word."

Seeing the worry in her eyes, Cameron tried to calm her. "He knows we would get in trouble if we tried to see him. Of all people, *Mr. Logic and Reason* himself will understand."

Haley laughed, but she wasn't any less upset. "I'll try again tomorrow after class."

"What is he's out by then?" he asked abruptly.

She narrowed her eyes at him. "He's in there until Numeyer gets back, genius."

He shrugged his shoulders. "I knew that."

* * *

"Can I have some water, please?" Virgil asked. He hadn't had anything to drink or eat for what felt like an eternity. All of a sudden, a small slit opened up at the bottom of the door. He quickly sat up in time to see a teacup-sized glass and a bowl of something he figured was food slide under the door. Before he even reached for either of the items, the small hole closed, plunging him back into the darkness. He slowly moved his hands to where he last saw the items and picked up the water glass. He took two gulps and the water was gone. That made him even thirstier. The lack of water made him anxious for what was in the bowl. He reached for it a little too fast and spilled most of the contents on the ground. "Dammit." *I guess I'm not eating today.*

Virgil tried to find any semblance of comfort in the small space, but it was not to be. He finally settled on laying on his back and staring at the ceiling. *They're trying to break me, but this will only strengthen my will.* He kept trying to keep his spirits up, but it was no use. Slowly, he drifted off into sleep. He figured that maybe if he slept long enough, he would wake up and it would all be over. But before long, he found himself dreaming, something he rarely did.

He was standing on a ridge, overlooking a vast arid plane. In the distance, he saw smoke rising from a small building. He walked toward the building, but for some reason, he never seemed to get any closer. He fell to the ground from exhaustion and dehydration. Just as he was on the verge of passing out, a beautiful orange and black Monarch butterfly landed on his right hand. He stared at it and it stared right back, unmoving. A silhouette behind it caught his eye. He looked past the butterfly to see a beautiful woman approaching. Delirious from heat stroke, his eyes began to close just as the woman reached down to touch him....

Virgil jumped up to the banging of the door. They banged on the door several times before he heard their footsteps. *Wow, that felt so real.* He spent most of that day trying to figure out what it meant. He knew dreams were symbols of your subconscious mind, but he had not the foggiest idea of what this meant. Even though he hadn't seen the woman's face, he felt as if she knew him. He was sure this was his mind playing tricks on him. *This never happened before I was locked in the death trap.* And even that was not enough to put his mind at ease.

Shortly after the knocks on the door by the guards, another set of knocks rang out. This time, it was to announce that the warden would be here shortly to discuss his punishment. *Has it been two days already?* He was stunned. He had been in and out of sleep for nearly two days.

With that thought, the door opened and the warden appeared.

Virgil towered over this puny little man, and yet he was scared to death of him. Numeyer sat in a chair in front of the door and spoke in a calm voice, which scared Virgil even more. "What exactly was it you thought you were doing in Ms. Boscombe's class the other day? She tells me you threatened her and that she was forced to hit you to subdue you. Is this true?"

"Yes, sir, it is true," he said with his head down. Not because he could not look at the man, but because the light hurt his eyes after so long in the dark. He also figured that it would be pointless to tell the truth, as he would just be called a liar anyway. "I talked back when I shouldn't have and raised my voice. She had every right to hit me."

Numeyer shook his head. "You wouldn't lie to me, would you, boy?"

"No, sir."

"Very well," he said. "For your insubordination, you will be confined here for the entirety of the week."

Virgil shook his head, in denial. The warden began to stand up, but Virgil grabbed his shoulder. "Please, sir, I'm begging you...don't leave me in here."

The Warden shrugged off Virgil's hand. "Very well, then let's make it two weeks, shall we?"

Virgil didn't say another word. He was in a state of shock. "Two weeks in this box? You can't do that. You can't do that..."

Oblivious to Virgil's objections, Numeyer turned to a guard, instructing him to bring a larger container for

Virgil's waste. "You are to empty his waste daily. Is that understood?" The guard nodded and returned to his post.

The door slammed shut again. He could do nothing more than sit on the ground and cry like a baby. *When I leave this place, I will make him pay for this.*

* * *

Meanwhile, somewhere on IO, a woman emerges from a cave on the side of a mountain. "He's alive! My God, he's alive," she said, falling to her knees and crying.

CHAPTER SIX

Light in the Darkness

Days had passed, and Virgil remained in his hole. Cameron and Haley were now not allowed anywhere near the detention room. And it wasn't for a lack of trying. Each day after their classes, they would attempt to walk near the door, even just to say hi and that they didn't forget about him. But each time they did, they were stopped short by a guard near the room. They even went as far as to try and distract the guard so that Haley could get to the door, but that too proved unsuccessful. They were resigned to the fact that they would be waiting the full two weeks.

While sitting in the dining hall eating their lunch, Cameron looked up at Haley as if he just had an epiphany.

"I didn't even realize it...Virgil is going to be elated when he gets out of the detention room."

"Of course he is, you idiot...he will have been trapped in a hole for two weeks," she said.

"No, I mean that a few days after he gets out, it'll be my birthday." He smiled from ear to ear.

"Were you dropped as a baby? You couldn't be this dumb on your own...could you?" She tried to muster as serious a face as she could without laughing, but that lasted all of three seconds.

Then, as if having a similar epiphany, she said, "Hey, maybe that's your *Gift*."

The look of confusion on his face gratified her. "Your *Gift*...maybe when you use it, you go full moron." This time, it was her smile that went from ear to ear.

He shook his head with his lips curled in. "When are you going to stop being a hater and stop drinking all that hater-ade?" His knack for slang grew every day.

She smacked her hand on the table, laughing. "See, you're going full moron right now. The Force is strong with you, sir," she said, referencing one of his favorite books. She wouldn't admit it to him, but she was also rather fond of the stories of a galaxy far, far away.

Again, he could do nothing more than nod. "You got me. I'm going to stop now because you're going to make me cry." He puffed out his lower lip and bowed his head.

"Fine, you big baby...I'll leave you alone...for now," she said, with a devilish smile.

After they were all through laughing, he leaned forward over the table and motioned Haley to do the same. "We can't do anything for Virgil where he's at, but we can maybe spend our time trying to figure out a way to escape once he is out."

She nodded in agreement. "We'll meet in my room every day after dinner to start going over some ideas."

"Why does it have to be your room? Mine is way cooler than yours," he said, arrogantly lifting his chin as he spoke.

"Because all you'll do is ignore me with your comics while I make plans."

He couldn't refute her logic. She knew him too well. "Fine, but I don't want to hear about any plans to escape on unicorns, or fly away using pixie dust."

All she could do was shake her head. "You know...the entirety of Earth's written texts from throughout all recorded history is at your fingertips. You are allowed to read things other than science fiction and comic books."

He shrugged his shoulders. "That's no fun. I leave that stuff to you and Virgil. When you want a laugh, you let me know." He smiled and started to get up. "Ok, so I'll meet you in your room after dinner. Should I bring flowers?" He didn't turn around to see the grin on Haley's face.

"What are we going to do with you?" She followed after him to their next class.

* * *

Meanwhile, back in the detention room, Virgil sat with his legs crossed and his palms on either knee. He had read all about meditation and other metaphysical phenomenon a while back, but never actually tried any of it. *Now is as good a time as any.* Clearing his mind, he started to concentrate on his breathing. He had a singular purpose...he was going to meditate on his childhood, prior to coming to Purgatory. He remembered nothing of his very early childhood and thought that meditating may be his answer.

Concentrating on his breathing, he began to relax his body until it felt like putty. He began to see swirling colors on the insides of his eyelids. Then, beautiful bright colors began flashing from side to side. Caught off guard, he opened his eyes abruptly and saw only darkness again. Frustrated with his lack of concentration, he started again. And after a short time, the bright beautiful kaleidoscope of colors reappeared. The surge of emotions hit him hard, as tears began to fall from his eyes. *This is so beautiful.* Only moments ago he was surrounded by darkness.

Finally, he was able to figure out how to control his emotions. He took a deep breath and concentrated on his inner-self. *Show me what I wish to see.* A few breaths later, he began to see flashes of images in front of his eyes. He could not see them clearly, but at the same time knew exactly what the scenes depicted. A torrent of memories started to come to the forefront.

Flash after flash, he saw scenes of his childhood that he had no memory of. Crawling on the ground, toward someone's leg. Being thrown in the air and caught by a man with his back to him. He had jet-black hair and was built like one of the guards. He was massive compared to baby Virgil, but at the same time as gentle as a teddy bear. Virgil then felt the memory of that flash in his mind. He could see the man throwing him in the air over and over again until he couldn't throw him anymore. He then hugged him so tight that Virgil lost his breath. *I was loved. Why did they send me here?* He let the thought go and took his focus back to the images.

He saw a flash of him running to a blonde woman near his father. He crawled up to his mother and sat on her foot. She laughed and started walking with Virgil still sitting on her foot. He held on tight as she walked back and forth.

The rush of emotions was too much, and he found himself back in the darkness of the detention room. He reached for a glass of water and was shocked to feel three glasses of water and three food bowls.

He was stunned. *How long was I meditating?* Days had passed and it felt like only a few minutes. He spent the remainder of the time in the room determined to find out what happened to him when he was younger. Unfortunately, all of the subsequent times he meditated were much shorter and he saw only images similar to the ones he saw the first time. He was never able to see his parents' faces or hear their voices. But he did feel the love between the two of them and with him. He felt the happiness in his life, which made this part of his life all the more painful.

On top of all of that, he continued to have the same dream he had the first night. The woman in the valley. And the butterfly. Each time was the same….the butterfly would land on his hand and he would see the woman coming toward him. The only thing that changed was that he did not look up at her face, but saw what appeared to be a tattoo on her ankle. He thought his anxiety blocked the rest of the images in his dreams and meditations. He was grateful, however, for the opportunity to see things where he would otherwise see only blackness.

* * *

Finally, the day came for Virgil to be released from the detention room. Cameron and Haley were waiting just around the corner, peeking at the guards. This was their day off, so they had an excuse to be wandering about. One of the guards opened the door and the other went in. After a moment, Virgil was pushed out of the room and fell on the floor.

Haley gasped and put her hand on her mouth. Cameron watched with clenched teeth as they closed the door behind Virgil. They were kicking him to stand up, but he didn't appear to have the energy to do so.

Without saying a word to Haley, Cameron stepped from around the corner and ran to his friend. "I'll take him to his room."

The guards looked at each other and stepped aside. Then Haley appeared and they both picked up Virgil, their shoulders under each of his arms, and carried him away.

The long walk back to Virgil's room was a silent one. Cameron was filled with anger and concern for his friend.

"How could they do this to him?" Haley said. Tears welled up in her eyes.

Virgil looked as if he had lost ten pounds. They had starved him. As Haley moved the hair in his face behind his ear, she could see the dark rings around his eyes. He was emaciated and lethargic as they reached his room. They laid him on his bed, where he groaned but did not open his eyes. Cameron sat right next to him in a chair, and Haley sat on his bed at his feet.

"Just rest, man. I'll get you some food and water at lunch," Cameron said.

Virgil mumbled, "Thanks, dude." He cracked a smile after he said it.

That only made Haley cry even more. Even in such pain, he was being his old self. "Cameron, go see if you can sneak him something to drink," she said.

Cameron nodded and was off. She watched as Virgil lay there on his side, shivering through the blankets. Without thinking, she moved up his bed and laid behind him, hugging him. She held his hand as the shaking subsided. She had never been this intimate with her friends, but felt the need to do so at that very moment.

"I'm so sorry they did this to you, Virgil," she said.

He gently squeezed her hand to acknowledge her.

Cameron came back into the room with a glass of juice, but stopped short when he saw Haley laying behind Virgil. He raised an eyebrow and smiled at Haley. She gave him a look that would burn through him if she had Superman's heat vision. Naturally, he ignored it, "I can come back later if you like. You know, give you two some time alone."

Virgil smiled and murmured, "We'll see you later then."

Haley felt the heat in her cheeks as they reddened.

Cameron saw the awkward look on her face and said, "I have some comics to catch up on anyways. I'll see you two at dinner." And with that, he left the juice next to the bed and was gone.

Haley saw him smile as he walked out. *Do Virgil and Cameron talk about me when I'm not around? Why did Cameron smile like that?* She was pushed from her thoughts when Virgil squeezed her hand again.

"Thank you for staying with me, Haley," he said.

She reached to turn off the light next to his bed, but was stopped short by Virgil's shaking hand. "No, please, leave the light on. I've been in pitch black for two weeks. I would like to sleep with the light on for a while."

A wave of hate surged through her at his words. She wanted to find everyone responsible for hurting him and make them pay. "I'll never let them hurt you like this again," she said, as she hugged him tighter. She laid there with him for hours.

"Ok, time to get up," said Cameron as he walked into the room.

Haley jumped, instantly embarrassed, as she saw how intimately she had been holding Virgil. "Oh, shut up," she told Cameron.

He smiled. "What, I didn't say anything."

"Alright, alright, you're both pretty," said Virgil as he sat up in his bed.

Cameron and Haley both smiled. "It's about time you got up," Cameron said. "You look like crap."

"I love you too, man."

"Ok, let's go get you some food. You look like you haven't eaten in weeks."

Haley and Virgil cocked their heads to the side and gave Cameron a wry look.

"Too soon? Ok, I'll wait a few days, but that's it," Cameron said as he walked out the door.

Virgil and Haley looked at each other, shaking their heads, and followed Cameron.

As the three of them entered the dining hall, all eyes went to Virgil and an eerie silence swept the room. No one said a word as they made their way to the serving station.

In an attempt to break the silence, Cameron said, "Please, everyone…must you do this every time I walk into a room?"

Virgil grinned as everyone gave Cameron the same look he and Haley always had.

The three of them got their food and sat at their usual table, away from the other pupils. They were never fond of sitting near the other kids, as they were always afraid of who they could trust and of accidentally letting a secret slip. They sat quietly until everyone stopped staring and went back to their conversations.

Virgil picked at his food while the other two inhaled their plates. He was afraid to eat too quickly and get sick. He took twice as long as he normally did, but he finished his food. He even went back for seconds.

As Virgil was finishing up his second serving, Cameron leaned close and said, "Me and Haley have been working on some things. Make sure you go to her room after dinner."

Haley nodded at him for confirmation.

After dinner, the three of them made their way back to Haley's room. Upon entering, Haley pulled out some drawings that she and Cameron had been working on.

"What is this?" Virgil had no idea what he was looking at.

"It's our escape plan," Cameron told him.

Virgil studied the drawing and then remembered the blueprint they saw in the warden's office a few weeks back. "You guys drew this from memory? That's pretty good. Have you guys thought of any ideas on how exactly to get out of here?"

"Hey, we got this far. That's what you're here for," said Cameron.

"Yeah, we weren't sure the extent of your *Gifts* and if you'd be able to lift us the length of the air ducts to the surface," Haley said with a shrug.

Virgil had never lifted them more than twenty feet, which took a little toll on him. But that was also while cloaking the three of them at the same time. Maybe, if he did not have to worry about cloaking them while they were lifted, they could cover the distance.

"I say we go the night of the riots," said Virgil.

Looking at the completely lost looks on their faces, Virgil elaborated. "It will be a few days after getting our shot. Little will they know that the shot they will be giving us will be water."

Slowly, Haley and Cameron's gears started spinning.

Virgil grinned. "If we change out the solution with plain water and they inject that into every pupil, they will be none the wiser. But after a couple of days, everyone will mysteriously start having abilities they never had before."

Haley understood and smiled as she continued his thought. "These kids would have no idea what is happening or have any ability to control their *Gifts*."

"Exactly," said Virgil.

Then Cameron chimed in, finally understanding their logic. "And in the midst of the chaos, we will quietly slip out one of the exhaust vents?"

"Yeah," said Virgil. He looked much better and more attentive after eating his fill of dinner. "The rest of this week, we can monitor the service doors to the exhaust systems and see when they are most vulnerable."

With a look of concern, Haley interrupted, "You can also take the week to get back to your normal self and build up your energy."

Virgil nodded, while looking at the plans. He was hoping that the heat he felt on his cheeks did not translate to blushing that they could see. He couldn't explain it, but his feelings toward Haley changed the night he was released from the detention room.

Feeling the awkwardness in the air, Cameron said, "Ok, so there's kind of a hole in this plan."

Haley and Virgil waited for the snide comment, but instead Cameron said, "With everyone freaking out about things that are happening to them, won't Haley and I be in the same situation?"

To that, Virgil replied, "The advantage we have is that we know it's coming. You'll just have to try and control the effects as best you can until we can get out.

Once we're out, I think it would be in our best interests if we all try and learn the full extent of what we can do. That way, we can defend ourselves against them when they come looking for us."

Cameron and Haley nodded in agreement.

"We kinda' have to figure out *where* we are once we get out, don't we?" Cameron asked.

"Details, details," said Virgil, waving his hand dismissively. "When we get to the surface, we'll have to look at a map and see where the closest city is."

"Ok. The next issue is going to be swapping out the inhibitors for water. How exactly are we going to do that?" Haley was running though the scenarios in her head.

Virgil thought for a second. "The same way we get into Numeyer's library. We'll go to the infirmary after lights-out the night before the injections and swap them."

Cameron interrupted, "But won't they be able to tell the difference?"

Virgil started to answer, but was cut short by Haley. "The liquid is in a metal syringe. They won't be able to see what's inside once they set them up the night before."

"Yeah, what she said," Virgil agreed. "Ok, so tomorrow night, we'll start in the library, then head to the infirmary when there are less guards."

Cameron's face darkened, as if remembering the last time they were in the library together.

Virgil winced. "Hey, Cam, about the lying. I'm really—"

Cameron cut him off. "No worries, dude. You were right."

Virgil and Haley looked at each other, astonished at what they were hearing.

Seeing their expressions, Cameron said, "I know what you're both thinking. Cameron is actually admitting he was wrong. As it turns out, I thought I was wrong about something once, but I was mistaken about being wrong."

They all started to laugh.

Cameron continued, "No, seriously, dude…all I've done since you told us has been think about what I can do. It's been driving me crazy. I mean, obviously I don't need a *Gift* to be awesome, but I would certainly like the ability to fly." And with that, Cameron was a few feet in the air. "Very funny, dude," he said to Virgil.

"Your wish is my command."

CHAPTER SEVEN

Things Will Never Be The Same

Each day that passed, Virgil was feeling stronger and stronger. The three of them did exactly as planned and each night scoped out a different location in the Purgatory. They would sit in silence, cloaked from view for hours on end by a particular door to see when would be the most opportune time to exit. They felt that they needed Plans A, B, and C in the event that one exit was blocked and not another. It had begun to take a toll on them in the classroom, as they would spend all night up and all day trying to stay awake. It was especially hard today, as they were being bored to tears by an astronomy lesson by Ms. Boscombe.

"Can anyone tell me why we have two distinctly different calendars?"

Not wanting to raise suspicion on their lack of attentiveness, Haley raised her hand. "Yes, Ms. Hawthorne, because one calendar…the one that is used to track our age and maintain our link to Earth, is tracked by 365 days in a year."

The instructor nodded, indicating her desire for Haley to continue. "The other calendar is the IO Lunar Calendar, which makes a complete rotation around Jupiter once every 1.77 days. Which translates to 646 Earth days in the year."

"Very good, Ms. Hawthorne," Ms. Bascombe said. "You may be seated."

Relieved, Haley quickly took her seat and went back to concentrating on keeping her eyes open.

Later in the afternoon, they sat at their usual table at lunch. All three could have fallen asleep right there in their chairs.

"We have to think of something else," said Haley. "If we keep this up, we won't have any energy to get out of here when the time comes."

"Ok," Virgil said. "Starting tonight, let's go to sleep right after dinner. That way, we'll have a couple of hours before lights-out."

"Perfect. I'll leave my door unlocked so you can come in and wake me up," Haley said.

Smiling, Cameron said, "Fine, I'll leave my door open too. Good luck waking me up though. I feel like I haven't slept in days."

"You haven't, you moron," Virgil said, laughing. "Don't worry, I'll think of something."

Cameron gave him a tired, scornful look. "I hate you right now, dude."

Virgil responded, "I love you too, dude."

* * *

That night, Virgil woke up just after the announcement for lights-out. He waited until he was sure everyone was in their rooms before he headed out. His first stop tonight would be Haley's room instead of Cameron's. His room was next door to Cameron's, but he wanted to give his friend a little extra time to sleep. He very quietly went into Haley's room and closed the door behind him.

As he reached for her shoulder to wake her, he stopped short. He had never really taken time to notice her the way he did on this night. Her skin looked silky smooth. She was beautiful. He loved the way her mouth twitched ever so slightly when her chestnut-colored hair tickled her nose. He brushed a strand of hair from her face and tucked it behind her ear. And with that, she began to move. Quickly, he cloaked himself, not really knowing why. He watched silently as she opened her eyes and smiled before going back to sleep.

He sat there next to her for a few minutes before he finally touched her shoulder. "Haley, it's time to wake up."

"No, baby, just a little while longer," she said.

"Baby?" He was at a loss for words. *Is she dreaming?*

Haley's eyes flew open wide, and she realized what she had just said. "Oh…uh…I said maybe…*maybe* just a few more minutes." She was mortified. *How embarrassing to have a dream about him and then have him wake me up? Way to go, Haley.*

Not knowing how to respond, Virgil said, "Alrighty then. Ready to go?"

Still looking down, she said, "Can we just forget the last couple minutes ever happened?"

"What last couple of minutes?" He understood completely.

She relaxed her shoulders and stood up. "Ok, let's go get SuperDork...I mean Superman," she said, trying to change the subject.

Luckily, she couldn't see that Virgil felt the same exact way. He came to the decision that he did not want to jeopardize their friendship for some feelings he wasn't all that sure of. He cloaked the two of them and they made their way quietly to Cameron's room.

"Hey, Cam," whispered Virgil.

Cameron opened his eyes to see Virgil staring up at him. It took him a minute before he realized that he was on his stomach eight feet above his bed. His eyes went wide with surprise. "Are you crazy! Put me down, stupid."

A sly grin formed across Virgil's lips. "Your wish is my command." He released Cameron, who fell to his bed, bouncing ever so slightly.

Cameron, still looking at his pillow, said, "You're a real jerk-face, you know that?"

Haley said nothing. All she could do was bite down on her fist to keep from laughing.

"Oh, I see how it is, Haley." Cameron was starting to smile now. "Just wait till I get my super strength...I'm going to toss you guys a hundred feet in the air and scare the crap out of you before I catch you…if I catch you."

Virgil was snapped into the memory of his father throwing him in the air. He wanted to lose himself in that moment.

"Earth to Virgil…are you ok?" Cameron asked, pulling him back.

"Uh, technically…it's IO," said Haley.

Cameron sneered, "Whatever, jerk-face number two."

She sneered right back at him, sticking her tongue out at him.

"Alright, let's head out," Virgil said.

They made their way down the corridor.

"Where to tonight, oh fearless leader?" Even whispering, Cameron was obnoxious when he was tired.

Ignoring his comment, Virgil said, "Exhaust room two."

As they approached the door, they noticed a guard standing a few feet from it. Virgil motioned to Cameron and Haley that they were close enough. One by one, they each sat on the floor against the wall. And there they sat, for what seemed like all night. They came up with a system where one of them would sleep while the other two stayed awake. Virgil was stuck always being awake, as they needed the cloaking. Haley and Cameron would take turns to stay up and make sure Virgil didn't dose off.

Cameron gestured to Haley, and moved his mouth, being careful not to speak. "Ladies first."

She nodded and laid her head down on Virgil's leg. Cameron looked at Virgil and smiled. Without opening her eyes, she raised her arm in Cameron's direction and stuck up her middle finger. Virgil's eyes opened wide. He'd never seen her do that before. He saw a smile on her face before she passed out.

After an hour, Virgil gently woke up Haley. She got up and patted Virgil's leg, motioning Cameron to lay down. Virgil gave Cameron a look of warning, as if he would punch him if he attempted to lay down. Cameron puffed out his bottom lip at Virgil and then laid on his side, with his hands between his head and the cold floor.

Haley and Virgil sat there, staring at the guard and then at each other. They silently played rock, paper, scissors and almost blew their cover when they wanted to laugh.

Cameron suddenly sneezed, but stayed asleep. Haley and Cameron looked at each other in terror as the guard glanced in their direction. He stood up and made his way toward them. The guard's boot came to within a foot of Cameron's nose before he stopped. Any closer and he would be inside the cloaking and see them all. But he did not come any closer. He stood on his toes and looked into the vent above Cameron.

"Damn rodents," he said. He leaned back on his heels and went to sit back down is his chair.

With long sighs, they both looked at each other in relief. If Haley could, she would've punched Cameron in the kidney. After another hour, Virgil put his hand over Cameron's mouth before waking him.

Cameron sat up and looked at them and moved his lips without saying a word, "Did I miss anything?"

"I'm going to kill you!"

Cameron wasn't positive, but that's what it looked like Haley said.

After a total of four hours, the guard only moved one time to go the restroom. Slowly, they got up and headed back to their rooms. They all convened in Haley's room.

"I'm really not sure what the point of all of this is," she said. "If the rest of the kids in here start going crazy with the powers that they cannot control…why are we going to assume that the guards will be on watch the same way afterwards?" She was right. There were only two days left before the inoculations, and her words put everything into perspective.

"She's right," Virgil said. "I guess the only thing we can do is be ready for whatever happens and improvise."

"Fine. We already know all of the exits out of this place. We'll find the one that's the least guarded and head that way." Cameron's logic was sound.

"The tricky part is going to be maneuvering around them if they're running all over the place." Haley looked worried.

Virgil touched her shoulder. "We'll figure it out."

She smiled at him.

Cameron and Virgil made their way out of her room and toward theirs. Cameron turned to look at his friend. "You should tell her how you feel, dude."

Caught off guard, Virgil hesitated before he answered. "What are you talking about?"

"Don't play dumb with me, dude. I've known you way too long. I see the way you look at her when you think no one is looking. She does the same to you."

"She does?" Virgil said before he could think about it.

"Yeah, dude…and honestly, the more dodging you do with each other, the more annoying it gets. There are all of five girls in this entire place and the prettiest one has googly eyes for you," he said, trying to lighten the mood.

"I don't know, man," Virgil said, after a moment. "I have feelings for her, but I don't want to jeopardize what we all have here."

"Lose what you have here?" Cameron was now mocking Virgil's reasoning. "You're two prisoners in a facility 333 feet underground. I don't think that's the kind of relationship anyone wants to hold on to."

"You know what I mean, dummy. I don't want to screw our friendship up. You two are all of the family that I have."

"First of all, you have your family out there somewhere," Cameron said, pointing up. "And second…even if you two didn't work out, do you honestly believe she would stop being your friend? We all grew up together…through thick and thin. We're not going anywhere."

"Thanks, man," said Virgil.

"That being said, if you try to kiss me or pinch my butt, I will do extensive harm to you, my friend." They both laughed. "Remember, in a few days, I'll have my super strength, so watch out."

With that, Virgil left Cameron's room and went to his own. The morning alarm would be going off in a couple of hours, and he needed as much rest as possible.

* * *

The alarm rang loud throughout the facility. At the same time, in different rooms, the three of them climbed out of their beds. It had felt like they slept for only minutes. But that would not be their biggest hurdle today. This would be the day they snuck into the infirmary and swapped out the inhibitors for water. *Today is the day we take our lives back,* Virgil said to himself.

They all met for breakfast as usual. After that, they spent the day in their classes. They were nervous for what was to come that evening. They had no experience with what they were planning. They had no idea what to expect in the infirmary. The only thing they knew was that no one was in the infirmary past lights-out.

After dinner, they met up in Virgil's room.

"Ok, I'll stop by your rooms just past light-s out, like usual," he said. "From there, we'll make our way to the infirmary. There should be 124 inoculations set up somewhere in that room. We'll find them and split them up into three piles equally. We'll all switch out our own pile. As soon as we're done, we'll put everything back the way we found it. Are there any questions?" There were none. They knew what they had to do. It was relatively straightforward. "We'll get it done fast and get back fast. We're going to need all of the sleep we can get the next few days."

They all went their separate ways, waiting for lights-out before they met up again.

After the lights-out alarm rang, Virgil waited until after everyone was in their room before making his way out. First, he stopped at Cameron's room and then they made their way down the corridor to Haley's room. She was soon in tow and they went to the infirmary. It was a little too easy, which made them more uneasy. But they waited a few minutes while the infirmary cleared out and there was only a guard traversing the corridor. Virgil motioned to them to head toward the door as soon as the guard was down the hall. Once the guard was far enough away, Virgil used his *Gift* to turn the deadbolt to the unlocked position.

Unfortunately, it made a loud popping noise. Virgil never took into account that they may not have greased the door hinges. The guard stopped pacing and turned around. Virgil hurried them into the room and quietly closed the door behind them. He was not able to lock it, because doing so would certainly put the guard on them.

As the guard approached the origin of the noise, he pushed on the infirmary door to make sure it was secure. What he could not see was the three kids on the other side of the door pushing with everything they had to make the door appear locked. Once they were sure that the guard had moved on, Virgil quietly turned the dead bolt to the closed position, this time careful not to make any noise.

He turned to see Haley and Cameron already searching the room. They eventually found the inoculations in a clear refrigerator. The four cases had tomorrow's date on them, along with thirty-one syringes. Each syringe was marked with a number ranging from 1 to 124. Each number corresponded to a pupil in Purgatory.

"I'll take these two, you guys each take one," Virgil said. "When you both finish yours, come help me with mine."

They nodded and went to retrieve cups of water. Once they each had their water, they began. One by one they squeezed the inhibitor solution out of the syringes and sucked water back into them. They were careful to make sure the labeling and packaging looked as if they were not tampered with.

"Ok, last one," Virgil said.

They all looked at each other, understanding what this would mean. Their lives would never be the same. Then, just as Virgil picked up the last syringe, number 124, they heard a voice in the corridor.

"I just forgot my comm device on my desk," said a female voice to what must have been the guard. The three of them looked at each other in horror. They had no time to empty the last syringe. They quickly placed it back in the box, and Virgil opened the refrigerator while Haley and Cameron quickly put the cups back. Just as the refrigerator door quietly clicked closed, the infirmary door opened.

The woman walked right by them, to the point where they felt a breeze of air as she walked by. She grabbed the comm device and started making her way toward the door, where the guard was waiting. Suddenly, she stopped in front of the refrigerator door and began to stare at the cases of syringes.

Damn, we screwed up, thought Virgil.

Alain Medel

She stood there, not looking at anything in particular.

Then, the guard came forward. "There's nothing you can do, Lisa. If you don't do it, they'll just find someone else who will," he said.

She responded, "Yeah, well, at least I wouldn't have to live with it if someone else does it." With that, she walked out and the guard closed the door.

Once they heard the lock click into place, they looked at each other in utter confusion. "I thought these people didn't have souls," Haley whispered.

"Most of them don't," Cameron said. "She still has no problem giving it to us, does she?"

They waited several minutes before they made their way to the door. They listened for the guard to be down the corridor and then quickly exited the room and locked the door behind them. They all made it back to their rooms and promptly went to sleep.

The next morning, they all sat in the dining hall for breakfast. All they could do was pick at their food. They kept looking at each other, then looking down at their plate.

"Is anyone going to say anything?" Cameron broke the silence.

That was enough for Haley to finally speak up. "Do you guys really think this is a good idea?

"You're not having second thoughts, are you?" Virgil looked at her wearily.

"No, I mean…" She struggled to find the words that would convey her thoughts most clearly. "Do you think it's fair to the rest of these kids to knowingly expose them to something that will most certainly transform their lives? We're not even giving them a choice in the matter."

Virgil took a breath, but before he could start speaking, Cameron spoke up. "Do you honestly think they would choose anything other than what we are offering them?" He said it as if it were a rhetorical question. "If anything, I think if we told them now, they would be rioting by lunch."

"Cam's right," Virgil said. "In a small way, we are setting them free. To now see the chains, is to be free of the chains." He let that sink in before he continued, "At this point, it's a win-win. They're going to start going crazy in the next few days, and that will provide us with the distraction we need to finally get out of here."

"I know," Haley said. "It's just…after seeing the look on that lady's face in the infirmary last night…I just don't want anyone to get hurt."

"Karma's a bitch," said Cameron, shrugging his shoulders. He saw the look on Haley's face, but he was unmoved. "I'm sorry, but they *all* had a hand in what this place is. I don't feel sorry for any of them."

Virgil and Haley said nothing to that. Deep down, they felt the same way.

"It's just the nerves kicking in," Virgil said. "We've never done anything like this. We have no clue how it's going to play out. That's going to cause a lot of stress. We just have to make sure we're here for each other."

They all nodded to each other.

"Ok, hands in." Cameron moved his hand to the middle of the table. "Ok, let's all say, 'Cam's super, crazy, awesome,' on three."

Haley chuckled and looked at Virgil. "Can we accidentally leave him here when it's time to go?"

Cameron's smile turned into a gap with a tongue sticking out. "Don't be cray-cray, Hay-Hay."

Virgil squinted his eyes, "Hay-Hay? What the hell is that?"

Cameron bit into a piece of bread and spoke with his mouth full. "It's all I had at the moment. Haley...Hay-Hay." The remark was met with the usual shaking heads. "Whatever, dudes...you're just jealous you aren't this awesome," he said while wiggling his fingers from his forehead to his chin.

Virgil patted Cameron on his back, while at the same time looking at Haley. "What on Earth would we do without him?"

"True," she said. "How on Earth could I feel so amazingly smart without having Cam around?"

Virgil grinned and Cameron just snickered. "Jerk-faces."

Haley only answered by pretending that she was blowing up her thumb, much like a surgical glove, to make her fist expand. However, the only part of her fist that expanded was her middle finger.

Shaking his head back, Virgil said, "Well, that's not very lady-like of you."

"You're right," she said. "I brought this to breakfast with me. Can you hold it for me?" She reached into her pocket and withdrew another middle finger. Cameron and Virgil looked from Haley and back to each other, their mouths wide open. This wasn't like Haley at all. They all started laughing, not realizing that the guards started to stare at them. Finally noticing their stares, they calmed down.

"Ok, we just have to get past the next couple of hours, and we'll be in the clear." Virgil was all business again.

They gave each other a nod and finished the breakfast they were unable to eat a few minutes earlier. Then they made their way to the dome. They wanted to get there as the room was being transformed for their monthly inoculations. They wanted to make sure that the syringes were brought out as usual and that no one realized what had been done.

To their relief, everything was going as they planned. Nothing seemed out of the ordinary. Feeling like he was floating, Cameron looked over at Virgil to see if he shared his emotion. But rather than relief on his face, Virgil looked as if he were lost in thought, staring at the ceiling. He bumped his arm. "You alright, dude?"

"Yeah, I'm fine. Just thinking about some things."

"Anything you want to share?" Haley had noticed it as well.

"I'll let you know." Virgil was rather cryptic with his response.

With their minds on more important issues, they let him be.

A few moments later, the overhead speakers blared, "All pupils, please report to the common area for your inoculations."

Cameron rubbed his hands together. "Here we go…"

CHAPTER EIGHT

Adverse Reactions

Within a few minutes, the dome was filled with the 124 pupils who called Purgatory home. The three of them were already in the room before any of the other kids, so they were the first ones in line. They got their water shots and quickly went to sit down in the stands. They watched as the kids moved through the four lines.

The kid who had the violent reaction to his first shot the month before stood pressed up against one of the walls. He looked as if he was hoping that they would forget about him and not give him the injection.

In that instant, all three of them looked at each other, they quickly realized that his was the one syringe that they were not able to replace. "Don't worry," said Virgil, sitting back in the chair with his hands behind his head. "We get the shot every month, and we're just fine."

Haley shook her head. "Yeah, but you also said that they were going to increase his dosage to counteract his *Gift*."

Virgil forgot that he had told them everything he witnessed in the warden's study when he spoke to that mystery man.

"She's right, Virgil," Cameron said. "When's the last time you heard of anyone's dosage being increased? What if he's allergic to it somehow?"

"There's no way to know," Virgil said. "What if I hadn't been in that study when that conversation took place?" They knew he was right, but it just didn't feel right.

As two of the lines cleared out, the infirmary nurses looked around to see if there was anyone who had been missed. As expected, one of the nurses turned and looked at the kid. With a stern look, she waved him over.

Slowly, he stepped away from the wall and walked toward the nurse. She walked to the last table and grabbed the syringe marked 124. He closed his eyes before the nurse stuck the needle in his arm. She emptied the contents into his tricep.

"See…nothing to it," she said, looking down at the ground, unable to meet his eyes. Haley saw her trembling hands as she returned the needle to the table.

He walked away, rubbing his arm and wiping a tear that began to run down his right eye. He was so little. They felt horrible that they weren't able to change out the liquid in his syringe in time.

"Ok, it looks like we're in the clear," Cameron said.

The three of them let out a huge sigh of relief.

Unfortunately, at that moment, pupil 124 let out a scream and began convulsing on the floor.

The nurse who administered his injection was the first to his side. She sat him up and he vomitted blood all over her. By reflex, she inadvertently jerked away and dropped him back to the floor.

Do they also think that we have a deadly virus? Virgil pushed the thought from his mind. He wasn't sure who knew the truth.

Another nurse was quickly at his side. She held him, this time with his back to her. She was making sure she was not going to have a repeat of the previous nurse. She held his head to the side until the convulsions finally subsided. When the shaking ceased, she checked him for a pulse, then placed his head gently down on the floor. She plopped down next to him, rubbing her hand on the back of her neck, mumbling inaudibly.

It took the three of them a full minute before they realized what just happened. "He's dead?" Haley had her hands to her mouth, tears falling down her face.

Virgil leaned over and hugged Haley, trying to block her view of the floor in front of her.

"Let's get out of here," Cameron said.

Virgil nodded and held Haley while Cameron led the way out to the corridor.

Haley shook them off. "We killed him, didn't we?" She wrapped her arms around herself as tight as she could.

"No, we didn't…they killed him," Virgil said.

She clenched her jaw. "We changed everyone's but his…he'd be alive right now if we did."

Virgil and Cameron knew there would be no winning this argument. So they all went back to Haley's room and closed the door. They were not going to say a word until she did. Eventually, she would realize that it wasn't their fault.

After what seemed forever in an awkward silence, she sniffed. "I know you guys don't think it's our fault…and I mostly agree with you…we did what we could. Obviously, no one thought he was going to die." She slouched in her chair, unable to look up from her hands. "But I just keep coming back to what that nurse said to the guard about not having to live with what she was doing." She looked up at the two of them with puffy red eyes. "We didn't kill him, but we were in a position to prevent it."

Cameron and Virgil could do nothing but sit and blankly stare at the floor.

* * *

Meanwhile, back in the dome, the nurses were frantically running around, trying to keep order with the other kids who were still there. Some had started to hyperventilate, thinking that the same thing would happen to them. The nurses and guards had tried to reassure them, but they looked as clueless as the kids did.

Hearing all of the commotion, the warden made his way to the dome. He saw kids running in the opposite direction. He yelled at them to walk, but they did not listen. He walked into the room and saw most of the nurses standing together. "What in the hell is going—"

He stopped in his tracks when a nurse moved to the side to show the small limp body of pupil number 124. He took out a handkerchief and wiped away the sweat on his brow. He tried to be as calm as possible before he spoke. "What has happened here? Did someone do this to this boy?" He looked around the room for answers, but no one said anything.

Finally, one of the nurses stepped forward. "He collapsed to the ground shortly after receiving his injection." She swallowed hard to prevent the tears from streaming down her face.

He dismissed her comment with a flick of his wrist. "Lisa, please…there hasn't been a single death in this facility, since its inception, as a result of that shot." He left out the part about the other deaths that were not part of the inoculation program.

She lifted her arm and pointed it in the direction of one of the corners of the dome. "Please, sir…we need to speak in private."

He nodded and walked to the corner, where they were out of earshot of the other people in the space. She turned her back to the room so as to not let them see what she was saying. "Pupil 124 was the one who had the allergic reaction last month." She looked over her shoulder before she spoke again. "We increased his dosage this time around, thinking that it would mitigate the effects." Tears began to well up in her eyes again. "But it didn't...we killed him."

His face turned instantly red as he grabbed her jaw with his hand and held it there, forcing her to look at him. "Now listen very carefully...we did not kill this boy. He had an adverse allergic reaction to the inoculation and succumbed to the effects. That is what you will write in your report. Do you understand me?" He searched her eyes for understanding.

She said nothing, but nodded her head while staring at the ground.

That was not good enough for him. He met her gaze and said, "I want to hear you say that you understand me."

"I...I understand, sir," she said, lowering her voice to a whisper.

A slow smile crossed his lips. He let go of her jaw. "Good...now get these kids out of here so that this mess can be cleaned up."

She motioned to the guards to clear the room. In less than a minute, the space was vacated. The warden gave the staff a quick, disgusted snort and walked out of the room. As he was leaving, a nurse made her way in with a gurney. One of the guards put the boy on it, while another covered his body. The nurse then rolled the gurney out, while the others stayed behind to clean up the massive amount of blood covering the floor.

The dome was off limits for the rest of the day.

Shortly after the events of the morning concluded, everyone found themselves in the dining hall for their afternoon meal. No one seemed in the mood to talk after what transpired earlier. Suddenly, the warden came walking into the hall. Haley and Virgil looked at each other. It was most unusual for the warden to come into this room. He never liked being in it at the same time as the kids. His eyes moved from side to side as he walked to the raised platform in front of the room and made a grunting noise to clear his throat.

"As you all may know, there was an incident earlier today involving one of our new pupils." He looked around the room to make sure that all eyes were on him. "He had a severe allergic reaction to the antivirus he was administered. He went into shock and subsequently passed away." His voice was calm, yet cold.

Virgil held onto Haley's arm, making sure she stayed calm. He and Cameron kept looking at her, then to each other…hoping that she could hold it together.

She did, but it took everything in her to do so. *I hope this prick burns for this,* Haley thought. She was not a mean or hateful person, but at this moment, she hated this man who was looking down on them as if they were ants to be squashed. She had thought that knowing what she knew, she would have a little compassion for him, but that proved to be false.

"If any of you find you are in need of grief counseling, please get with one of the nurses and they will make sure you receive the proper attention." He rolled his eyes at all of them as he spat the words. "Does anyone have any questions?" He looked around for a second and then nodded to one of the nurses. Once the warden was through, he stalked off of the stage and through the room, back the way he came.

Then, out of nowhere, something shiny went flying through the air. It flew by so fast, Virgil was not able to make out what it was. That is, until the hilt of a knife stuck out of the warden's back.

Virgil and Cameron went pale. Haley's eyes widened. None of them could move. They all stood and openly stared.

"Everybody stand back!" One of the guards came rushing to the warden's side, but it was already too late. His eyes were wide open...the shock of it frozen on his face. He took one last gasp of air...

"Haley," said Virgil, pausing to examine her state of mind.

Holy cow, it was all in my mind... Wow, I really do hate him. Finally realizing that she was being stared at, she turned around. She tried to play it off as best she could. "What? Haven't you guys ever heard of daydreaming?"

"That didn't look like daydreaming," Cameron said. "When Virgil bumped you, you looked like you had seen a ghost."

"I'm fine," she lied. She felt now more than ever that they needed to get out of this place.

"Fine, be that way," Cameron said, folding his arms across his chest. "But if you're going to dream about me...at least do it in the privacy of your own room where no one else can see you." He gave her a wink and a smile.

"Dude, seriously...had she been dreaming about you, she'd be in the infirmary right now with uncontrollable vomiting." Virgil gave an even bigger smile, smacking his friend on the shoulder. Without a witty retort, Cameron was left shaking his head.

They finished their meal and were making their way back to Cameron's room to hang out when Virgil caught sight of something out of the corner of his eye. It was a maintenance worker coming out of one of the maintenance shaft rooms. This was a normal occurrence, but what he hadn't ever noticed before was the nose aperture the maintenance worker had just taken off after entering the corridor.

"Hey, have you guys ever seen one of those guys with that?" Virgil pointed to the device the worker had just clipped to his side.

"Oh, that," Haley said. "They use that when they go topside. I overheard Ms. Boscombe talking to one of them about it a few months back."

Becoming suddenly still, Cameron looked at her. "Don't you think that would be something we might need to know if we happen to…I don't know…go topside?"

Virgil was thinking the same thing.

"With everything going on…I guess it hadn't really occurred to me." She shrugged her shoulders and kept walking.

"Ok, when we get into the room, let's go over what our plans are. We need to factor this into the equation," Virgil said, opening his mouth to criticize her, but stopped short. He thought the plan they had conceived was rock solid. Now, they may have to rethink their entire strategy.

They made their way back to Cameron's room. As soon as the door closed behind them, Cameron spoke his mind. "What the French, toast?" he said, taking a breath and holding it.

Virgil looked at Haley, his head tilted to the side. "What did he just say?"

Haley shook her head.

"No, seriously, I have no idea." Virgil knew exactly what Cameron meant…he had just wanted to emphasize the point of just how idiotic he sounded. "Dude, I think that you should be grounded from that book." He pointed to Cameron's favorite piece of literature. "I think it's making you stupider than you already are."

Haley eyed Cameron, knowing Virgil's joke wasn't going to blunt his aggravation with her.

Cameron was all business today. "Seriously…that one little piece of information could've been enough to get us killed. We have no idea what it's like up there. And if they have to wear those things on their noses." He made his hand into a fist and used it as a prop against his nose while he spoke. It wasn't at all necessary, and only made it harder for the other two to take him seriously. They gave each other an inconspicuous nod of understanding. They knew if they even cracked a smile, Cameron would be all over them.

"I'm sorry, ok. I didn't think about it." Her eyes began to water.

Virgil and Cameron didn't know if this was a ploy to have them forgive her, or if she was truly being sincere. They went with the latter. Once she saw the aggravated expression on Cameron's face fade, she continued. "Don't you think if I had thought about it, I would've told you guys? I'm trying to get out of here, the same as you two." She briefly clenched her fists.

Virgil waved his hand at them. "Alright, let's move on already."

Haley gave him a thankful smile. "Ok, so how do we go about getting our hands on a few of those?" She shook her hand across her face, clearly mocking Cameron's earlier gesture.

He smiled at her jab, while not providing one of his own. He wanted to pick his battles, and he felt this wasn't the most opportune time to bless them with his comedic genius. Then again, he couldn't resist annoying her. "Quick show of hands...who wants to punch Haley in the kidney?" He raised his hand high in the air, moving his head up and down while having his mouth wide open.

"I can't take you two anywhere," said Virgil. "Seriously though," he was suddenly serious. "We need to get those tonight. We don't know how much time we actually have before this place starts going crazy. The only problem is…where do we find them?"

They all sat quiet and tried to think of a solution. Then, as if a light bulb had gone off in his head, Cameron said, "I bet the guard office would have them." They cocked their heads sideways, staring at him blankly. Seeing their expressions, he sighed and then continued, "Think about it…if all of the people who work down here have a home up there, then it would stand to reason that they too would need one of those inhalers." He stuck his tongue out at Haley. "That's just in case you were thinking about making fun of me.

"The thought never crossed my mind," she said, with a devilish grin.

"Anyways," said Virgil. It seemed that the older they got, the more childish his two friends became. "What were you going to say?"

"So, like I was saying…we've never seen anyone walk in here with one of those things or any of their personal belongings. It would stand to reason that since they walk past the guard station before entering the facility—" He motioned his hand in a circular motion, prodding them to complete his thought.

Then it clicked. "You're not as dumb as you look," Haley said.

Virgil put his hand up before Cameron could respond to her barb. "Ok, so our next problem is going to be getting in there."

Cameron shrugged his shoulders. "I can't come up with everything."

"That's easy," said Haley, dismissing their concerns. "Which of us is the best actor?" Haley and Virgil said nothing, but turned their heads at the same time to look at Cameron.

He looked up at the two of them in bewilderment and said, "Me? What are you talking about?" He really had no idea. "I mean, if you had asked who was the best looking…then fine, you can look at me. But, I can't act to save my life."

She ignored him and looked back at Virgil. "If we can create a diversion…like say, oh I don't know…having a seizure near the guard station."

Virgil's eyes lit up. "That should work…Cameron can pretend to have a seizure while you come over to help him. And with everything that happened this morning, everyone will be on edge."

Haley continued with the plan, "And when all of the guards come out to help, you'll be standing near the door cloaked...and just walk right in."

Cameron was now nodding with understanding.

"And once I'm inside, I'll need a couple of minutes to search the room for some spare masks."

Cameron looked at him and asked, "Why not just grab the first few you see?" But right after saying it, he realized how dumb the question was.

"We don't want to raise any suspicion with the staff if they are missing their own breathers." Virgil knew Cameron understood now, but wanted to clarify the point, just in case there was any doubt. "I will try and find at least six to take...maybe more if there's a bunch."

"Six or more...we flying back to Earth?" Cameron did not understand Virgil's logic.

"How long do they last?" Virgil raised his eyebrows as he asked Cameron the simple question.

He cocked his head and said, "I haven't the foggiest idea." Virgil waited...and then Cameron realized, "Ah...right. If they only last a little while, we'll need extra."

Haley continued, "Ok, so we can probably buy you two or three minutes tops. Anything more than that and they'll be putting needles in Cam's butt. On second thought—"

"Ok, that's enough out of you," Cameron said, putting his hand over her mouth.

"Let's plan for just after dinner," said Virgil. "Everyone will still be awake and it will create a bigger scene."

"Sounds like a plan," said Haley.

Looking worried, Cameron cut in, "So what happens if my spectacular acting skills land me in the infirmary? What if they want to run tests on me?" They hadn't thought of that. "What if they take blood and test it? Are they going to see that I have none of the inoculation in my system?" He was right, they would have no way of knowing what they would do.

"We'll just have to hope for the best," Haley said. "We'd be taking an even bigger risk if we didn't get those breathers. Besides, it'll take them time to run your blood. By then, hopefully all hell will have broken loose." Her logic was sound.

"Great...now that that's settled, can we get to the more important stuff?" Cameron said. Then he tapped his desk and up popped the last comic he had been reading. Haley and Virgil just looked down and shook their heads.

CHAPTER NINE

A Change in Management

At dinner, the three of them sat quietly…rehearsing in their minds what would be transpiring in just a short while. Haley twirled her hair in her fingers, while moving her food from one side of her tray to the other. Cameron kept dropping his fork and cursing under his breath. His palms were sweating so much that he had trouble holding onto his utensils. Virgil seemed to be the only one who was unfazed as to what they were about to do. Haley figured that it was because he had the advantage of not being seen. She and Cameron, on the other hand, would have to play a much more prominent role.

Cameron dropped his fork a fourth time and looked over at Virgil, flicking his gaze up and down. "How can you be so calm?" he said, looking over his shoulder. "I'm about to pee myself."

Virgil put his hands on his chin and moved his eyes from Cameron to Haley. "Because it doesn't do any good to freak out. It's better if you think about something other than getting caught." He leaned in closer. "Try thinking about what it's going to be like *after* we get out of here. This is only a single step in our plan. There are more to come, and we need to be clear-headed to succeed."

That was enough to make the creases in Haley's forehead loosen up. Cameron rocked his head back and forth slowly...the tension relaxing in his shoulders.

If they only knew that I am probably more scared than they are... Virgil had always been the strength in the trio and knew he had to be strong for his friends at this moment. If he lost his nerve, they would inevitably lose theirs. He took the opportunity to get their minds occupied on other things. "So, what do you guys think it's going to be like when we get up there?" he said, looking toward the ceiling.

Cameron looked at the two of them with all of the seriousness he could muster. "I don't care...as long as they have edible food and comic books, I'll be fine." He smiled, then took a bite of his food. *When we get out of here, I'm finding my parents.* He dismissed the thought and heaved another forkful into his mouth.

Haley put her fork down and looked warily at the two of them. "If it's anything like what I've read, we'd be safer here."

Cameron and Virgil scrunched their eyes at her.

"What are you talking about?" Virgil said. "There's nine different colonies up there. We're bound to be near one of them."

Haley tilted her head and raised her eyebrows. "Don't be so sure. Half of this moon is erupting volcanoes...the other half is smelly, hard-to-breathe air. The only safe places are in the colonies, where the air barriers are in place." She looked over her shoulder, "And once we're out of here, those will be the places that they search for us."

Virgil saw her point, but thought differently. "Even if you're right...which I'm sure you are...anything beats staying down here."

Cameron agreed, "Virgil's right...and maybe there's more people out there like us...willing to help us."

"I know, I'm just saying." She tilted her head and shrugged her shoulders. "It would just be nice to know what we're going up *to*. If we're near a colony, then great...but what if we're on the other side of the moon near all of the active volcanoes? We won't survive for too long." She let the weight of her words sink in, then picked up her fork and took a bite.

Virgil exhaled completely. "You know...I was changing the subject so that we could think of something more positive." He squinted his eyes accusingly at Haley.

"What?" she said, shrugging her shoulders. "Am I the only realistic one in this group?"

Cameron gave her a smirk. "Yeah, and thanks to you...now I'm thinking about what we're doing later *and* suffocating to death. Much appreciated. Next time, why not just say that it's going to be nice up there? Or heck...maybe that we're going to live happily ever after..."

At a loss for words, Haley just bobbed her head and stuck her tongue out at Cameron.

As usual, Virgil pulled them back to the task at hand. "Ok, people are starting to leave the dining hall. This is as good a time as any." He looked at the two of them and waited for their agreement.

Haley cocked her head toward the corridor. "Let's go."

Virgil stood and walked out first. He needed to be at the guard station well before Haley and Cameron, to make sure he was cloaked and in position to sneak into the room. A full minute after Virgil left, Cameron and Haley made their way out.

Once Virgil was just around the corner from the guard station, he stopped. He peeked around the corner and saw a single guard near the door. He then saw the silhouette of another guard inside the room. He looked around to make sure no one saw him, and then created a cloaking field around his body. He concentrated to make the field as small as possible, cloaking only his body and nothing else. He was not sure how close to a guard he was going to come and didn't want to take any chances.

Once cloaked, he made his way around the corner. It took everything in him to control his breathing. He felt as if his heart were pumping hard enough to leap from his chest. He made his way past the guard outside of the door, to stand within a few feet of the entrance. *Hurry up, Cam...I'm freaking out here...* Virgil shook his head and pushed the thought from his mind. He needed to concentrate on the objective at hand.

At last, Cameron and Haley were visible in the corridor that intersected the guard room corridor. Not knowing if Virgil was ready or not, Haley winked at Cameron. He nodded and took a deep breath. He then collapsed to the floor. Haley let out a scream that should have alerted the entire facility. "Somebody, please help!" she screamed. "Please don't die!" She began to cry.

Damn, she's good. Virgil almost forgot he had a job to do.

Upon hearing the screams, the guard in front of the door and three others in the room ran over to Cameron, who was convulsing on the floor. As the last of the guards left the room, Virgil grabbed the door, just as it was closing. Unfortunately for him, he hadn't grabbed it in time. The door slammed on his hand, but rather than scream and draw attention to himself, he bit his lip...and in doing so, drew blood. He now had pain shooting in two parts of his body, and for a split second, his cloaking disappeared. Luckily, everyone was too preoccupied with Cameron to even notice. Virgil got himself under control and quietly opened the door just enough to slide in.

While all this was going on, Haley was kneeling over Cameron, frantically calling to the guards to get the nurses. The guards attempted to reach for Cameron, but

Haley was having none of that. She knew that it would take time for the nurses to come running…and she needed all the time she could get. She began to lightly smack Cameron in the face, in an attempt to calm him. He opened his eyes while convulsing and glared. She bit her bottom lip to stop from smiling.

Just then, one of the nurses was at their side. Haley tried to stall as much as possible, holding onto Cameron's hand.

The nurse grabbed Haley's arm. "I'm going to need you to step aside." Her voice cracked as she spoke. She looked as if she was going to see a repeat of this morning.

It's working, Haley thought. She moved aside to let the nurse work on Cameron. He had stopped convulsing and was now panting heavily, as if his breathing was becoming labored.

Meanwhile, Virgil was quickly looking through the guard room for the breathers. He found the staff breathers right away, under the front counter…but was going to stay away from them at all costs. He searched all of the drawers and cabinets, but there were none to be found. Then he made his way to the last spot he could check…the closet. Only when he opened the door, he realized that it wasn't a closet at all. It was another office within the guard room. Most likely a supervisor's office.

He went inside and smiled broadly. *Jackpot!* The office was half of the size of the outside room, but it was filled almost entirely with equipment. The office barely had room for the desk in the center. All four walls were lined with shelves, filled floor to ceiling with what appeared to be riot gear. One of the shelves was filled with battle helmets. Another with batons.

Maybe this is what they meant by soldiers, Virgil thought as he ran up to the shelf with the breathers. There were several shelves worth of them in boxes. Carefully, he reached in the back of one of the lower shelves and grabbed a few boxes. He then removed the breathers and replaced the boxes in the same place. He grabbed another three boxes and did the same. Once he was done, he had six breathers and it appeared as if he hadn't touched a thing. *The shelf is too low for eye level, and the boxes appear to be intact.* He reveled in his cleverness for a moment before moving on.

As he was getting ready to exit the office, a backpack caught his eye. On the outside tag it read, *Three-day Survival Pack*. He looked closer and saw that there were dozens of them, neatly piled on top of each other.

Again, he reached for the back of the pile and pulled three out. It would be highly unlikely that they would notice one of these missing before he and his friends made their escape. He quickly stuffed the breathers in one of the bags and made his way out of the office.

Just as he closed the door behind him, two of the guards walked into the room. *Dammit…can't anything ever go as planned?* He shook his head in frustration. He figured that Cameron must have gotten up or been taken to the infirmary by now.

* * *

As luck would have it, he was not. Cameron was being held down by two of the nurses while they waited for the head nurse, Lisa.

"I'm ok now…really," said Cameron, trying to squirm out of their grasp to stand up. It was no use. They were scared to death that he was suffering the same reaction as the boy from this morning.

Haley was equally unsuccessful. "Look at him…he's fine," she said, waving her hands dismissively. Sweat had begun to drip down the side of her face. She felt helpless.

Finally, the head nurse came around the corner. "What is his condition?" She looked at the other nurses around Cameron.

"He's stable," said one of them. "He stopped spasming shortly before we got here. We wanted to keep him here until you arrived."

They stepped aside as she knelt down next to Cameron. "How are you feeling son?"

Cameron waited a moment before he spoke. "A little dizzy, but I'm fine," he said, blinking his eyes hard. He had partially been telling the truth. He had not received his monthly shot, and the disorientation that came a day or two before the shot were kicking in. "I think I just need a little water and some sleep." He began to stand up.

"Just as soon as we run some tests on you," she said, giving him a reassuring smile.

Cameron slowly nodded his head and looked at Haley. The blood rushed out of his face.

* * *

The guards in the guard room had made their way around the counter and were again staring at what was going on not far from them.

"Do you think this one's gonna die too?" said one to his co-worker. His monotone voice held no concern for Cameron whatsoever. The second guard said nothing, only shrugged his shoulders.

Virgil saw no way of getting out without another guard walking in. Feeling that it would be too risky to tiptoe across the room, he closed his eyes and raised himself toward the ceiling. Once he was able to touch the ceiling, he lightly pushed off and oriented himself so that it was as if he were flying. Once his back touched the ceiling, he lowered himself a few inches. As he was maneuvering himself toward the door, he neglected to pay attention to the backpack strap as it slipped from his shoulder.

At the last second he felt it slipping off, but it was too late. It slipped off of his shoulder and was caught by the inside of his elbow. The abrupt stop of the bag created a clanging sound. It was not loud, but it still drew the attention of one of the guards.

"Did you hear that?" he said, tapping the other guard's shoulder as he scanned the room.

"Hear what?" he said, not even turning around.

The guard took one last look around the room. "Nothing…guess I'm hearing things." He turned back to the show in the corridor.

Virgil closed his eyes and took a deep breath. He then floated toward the door, hoping that the third guard who was in there earlier would come back in soon. He wasn't sure how long he would be able to keep himself in the air. Securing the backpack on his second arm, he waited. The sweat bubbles began to build up on his face. Every muscle in his body ached. Even though he was mostly immune to the shot, the side effects that came days before still affected him.

After several minutes, the muscles throughout his body began to burn. He figured that the show was over, as the guards went back to their normal duties. All except the guard who was in the room previously. *If this guy doesn't hurry up, they're going to get quite the ghost experience in here.* He knew that they would freak out if they saw their door opening by itself, but he would soon have no choice. He then looked out the window, never so thankful to see a guard approaching him. He got into position with his feet on the wall by the door, ready to push off and through once it was open.

The guard opened the door, but rather than walking right in…stood there talking to someone down the hall. "Yeah, make sure you log this in and report it to the warden."

Virgil was hovering two feet above the man's head. The door was not high enough to squeeze between it and the guard. A drop of sweat grew on his nose. His eyes went wide and he caught his breath. As he watched in horror, the drop made it to the size where gravity would shortly be taking over.

It left the tip of his nose and fell. As if in slow motion, it made it's descent toward the guard's bald scalp. He closed his eyes and concentrated on the drop of sweat. The drop came to a stop just a fingertip from the guard's scalp and flew toward the window. It hit the glass with a splat. The guard scrunched his eyes as he saw the water on the glass in front of him. He looked at the other guards as he let go of the door. "Did one of you wipe your sweat on the glass?"

The two guards looked at each other, then to him.

Shaking his head, he dismissed it. "Never mind."

Virgil didn't have time for relief, as he was concentrating on filling in the space no longer occupied by the guard as he moved away from the door. With a solid push off of the wall, Virgil squeezed through the door just as it was closing. Then he let out a gasp, as he had been holding his breath for over a minute. He quickly made his way around the corner and lightly landed on the ground. He let out a whimper. All of his muscles were on fire, and he was still cloaked. He couldn't chance being seen with the backpacks. He ran to his room and hid the bags under his bed. Ignoring the pain, he finally uncloaked and then made his way down to the infirmary.

When he arrived, he saw Haley sitting on the floor just outside of the door. When she saw him, her face lit up. She had never been so happy to see him. She ran up to him and hugged him tight, as if afraid she would lose him.

Realizing what it looked like, she leaned back and grabbed both of his shoulders. "Are you ok? Did you get what we needed?"

"And then some," he said, smiling…while bouncing his eyebrows up and down. "They had more than I had imagined. It's like they were in preparing for war." He quickly changed the subject. "What happened with you and Cameron?"

"Apparently," she said, looking to the side. "Cam did such a good job that they're running a bunch of tests on him to make sure he's really ok."

Virgil frowned. "He thought this might happen. We'll just wait here for him until they're done."

Haley nodded. They both went and sat down near the door. She leaned on him as they waited.

* * *

Inside the room, Cameron was having a much harder time. The head nurse had pulled several vials of blood from him and set them in a centrifuge. "You should be fine, but we'll know in a couple of days. We don't have the proper equipment down here to analyze this, so we'll send it to a place that does."

Cameron smiled and closed his eyes, thankful for the good news. *They won't know for days. We'll be long gone by then.*

She smiled back at him, not knowing that he was happy for other reasons. "You're free to go. If you have any issues or feel strange, there is always a nurse on staff. In the meantime, don't exercise or exert yourself in any way until we get your results back." She went to her desk and wrote him a note. "Here, give this to your instructors. You are to do nothing physical until I say so…is that clear?" She gave him a stern look.

"Crystal," he said.

The nurse put a small bandage where the needle went into his skin and then escorted him out. Holding his arm, he stepped into the hallway. Once the door closed, he saw Haley and Virgil sitting on the floor. When they saw him, they both jumped up, looking suddenly uncomfortable.

Cameron chuckled as they came toward him. They looked guilty enough as it was and he didn't feel the need to tease them. "See, I told you my acting skills would land me in there. You guys never listen to me when I tell you how awesome I am." He twiddled his fingers down the front of his face as he said awesome. They both gave him a hug and headed to his room. Once inside, he asked Virgil, "Were you able to get what we needed?"

Haley cut in before he could answer, "He hooked us up," she said, smiling.

Virgil gave her a fake blank smile. "That only sounds good coming from Cam." He turned his eyes to Cameron and said, "Saying something that dumb only sounds good coming from a dumb person."

They all started to laugh, but Cameron stopped almost immediately and gave them a sour look. "Jealousy will get you nowhere, my friends." He crossed his arms and made a pouting noise.

"Alright, let's get some sleep," Virgil said. "I think the next couple of days are going to be very interesting."

With that, Haley and Virgil left Cameron alone in his room. He promptly laid down and was out cold in a matter of minutes. He hadn't even bothered staying up and reading his comics.

Haley followed suit. She was asleep well before lights out. The stress of the day had finally caught up with them. Virgil was the only one of them that was unable to sleep. He kept running through all of the possible situations that would arise over the next few days. He knew there were things that they would not be able to foresee, but that did not stop him from trying to figure them out. After what seemed like forever, he was finally able to allow his body to sleep. He knew he would be waking up to a world of soreness in the morning, but he would deal with that tomorrow.

* * *

That next morning, Virgil was awakened to a banging on his door.

"Go away," he said, with his face under his pillow.

A manly voice came through the door. "Excuse me! You will get up now, dammit!" The banging got louder.

This made Virgil jump out of bed. He wasn't positive, but it sounded like the warden. He quickly put on a pair of shorts and ran to the door. Looking down, he opened the door and said, "My apologies, sir, I didn't realize—"

Haley stood there, biting on her fist, until she wasn't able to hold it anymore. She let out an obnoxious laugh that left Virgil scratching his head. "Sorry...that was too funny," she said, catching her breath. "You should've seen the look on your face."

He began to laugh, but stopped short, now looking serious. "How did you do that? You sounded just like Numeyer."

She shrugged her shoulders. "I don't know...I just thought of mimicking him to scare you and, voila..." She motioned her hand away from her mouth as she spoke.

"That was amazing," he said as he turned back to his bed. "Now go away, I'm tired." He put his hands on his bed, ready to lay back down.

"Oh no, you don't," she said, putting her hands on his waist to pick him back off of the bed. He froze. She had grabbed him countless times in the past, but never once when he had no shirt on. Finally realizing his discomfort, she quickly let go of him. "I…I'm sorry…I didn't mean to…"

"It's ok," he said. "You just caught me off guard." He stood up and changed places with her so that he could retrieve a shirt. She plopped herself on his bed while he rummaged through his drawers for a shirt.

As she sat there, she noticed him in ways that she never had before. He was much taller than her, which was fine by her, since her head fit comfortably in the crook of his neck when she hugged him. *Oh my God, look at that body.* She closed her eyes tightly, trying to force the thought out of her head. But as he put on his shirt, she couldn't help but notice his perfectly cut abs and his shoulder-length blond hair. She felt the blood rushing to her cheeks. *He's going to be mine someday*, she thought.

She felt an arm on her shoulder and let out a yelp. She quickly covered her mouth as she saw Virgil looking at her.

"Are you ok?" he asked.

She quickly regained her bearings. "Yeah…sorry, I was just thinking about how surprised Cam's going to be."

Virgil tilted his head.

Haley sighed. "Ugh, you two never remember anything. It's his birthday today."

"Oh yeah, I totally knew that," he said.

"Figures," Haley said, heading toward the door. "Whatever you do, don't say you forgot when you see him...even though he didn't remember yours either."

They left his room and went next door to wake up Cameron. Vigil had a mischievous look on his face and turned to Haley. "Hey, do what you just did with the voice thing, but this time, try and imitate one of the nurses."

She smiled at him as she knew exactly what he was thinking.

"He's going to love this," she said, as she began to pound on his door. When she stopped banging, she began to speak, sounding exactly like the head nurse. "Mr. Leah, please, wake up. We got the results back from your blood work. It's worse than we thought." She leaned on Virgil as she spoke, almost unable to finish.

They heard a loud thump, followed by some inaudible cursing. Then, the door flew open. He was still too groggy to notice it was them. "Is it bad? Am I going to die?"

Unable to take it anymore, Virgil said, "If stupidity was lethal, then yes...you most certainly would be dead."

Cameron's eyes flew open then narrowed in on the both of them. He turned around and slammed the door.

Haley looked at Virgil and said, "Oops."

Virgil opened Cameron's door and they let themselves in and closed the door. "Dude, get up…it's time to celebrate."

Cameron rolled over. "Go away…for the love of all that is sacred, please let me sleep." He put his pillow over his face. Haley was amused at how much Cameron and Virgil were alike. She could see how they got along so well.

"Fine, then I guess you won't be wanting any presents," she said, heading back to the door.

He took the pillow off of his face. "It's my birthday." He sat up and swung his legs off of his bed. "So…what did you get me?" he said, eyeing Haley.

She smiled. "Oh…nothing. I just figured it would get you out of bed."

He snickered and looked toward Virgil. He cocked his head upwards. "How 'bout you, dude…what did you get me?"

Virgil showed his teeth and raised his hands up to his shoulders, palms up.

"You forgot, didn't you?" he said dryly.

"Yeah…but hey, I'm here now."

"Come on, get dressed...we've got a special breakfast set up for you," said Haley, impatiently motioning to the nonexistent watch on her wrist.

He narrowed his gaze on her. "Dining Hall?"

She chuckled. "Well, yeah...but you get to eat in the presence of us," she said, while gesturing to herself and Virgil.

"Get out...I need to get dressed." Cameron ushered them out of his room and walked to his drawer. Just as he reached it, he tripped on his slang book and fell forward. He was going to hit the corner of his dresser and only had time to position his forearm to blunt the hit. The hit sent a jolt of pain up his arm. By the time he looked at his forearm, blood was running down his arm. He cursed as he reached for something to wipe the blood.

"Everything alright in there?" said Virgil from the other side of the door.

"Yeah...I'm fine." Cameron grabbed a worn shirt and patted the wound lightly. He didn't feel any pain, so he looked at his arm to make sure he was applying pressure in the proper location. He pressed a button on his desk and the wall in front of his dresser turned into a mirror. While wiping the blood from his elbow, he looked up at the mirror and went slack jawed. *That's impossible.* He still was not quite sure what he was looking at. He knew he had a gash on his arm, but he did not see the source of the blood. He grabbed another shirt and frantically wiped away the rest of the blood on his arm. He looked at his arm, then at the mirror, then back at his arm. Nothing was there. *I think I'm losing my mind.*

He finished wiping his arm and changed his shirt. Once he composed himself, he walked out of his room. For the time being, he decided to keep this to himself. He figured that not taking the inhibitor was causing him to hallucinate.

"You alright, dude?" asked Virgil.

"Yeah, I just tripped on my book and hit my dresser, but I'm good."

"Great, now let's go eat," Haley said, bumping his shoulder with hers. "You can have the best birthday breakfast you've ever had. All you have to do is imagine that you're not in here and that the food tastes good."

Cameron shoved her right back...so hard in fact, that she fell right into Virgil's arms. Cameron cocked his head toward Virgil and said, "You're welcome."

For some reason, Virgil couldn't help but to blush as he helped Haley straighten up. She gave him a quick glance, then looked away. She couldn't remember at what point it started to become so awkward between them. *Just kiss him and get it over with.* But she knew better than to try anything when they had so many other things to worry about.

Once she regained her bearings, she punched Cameron in the arm. "Fine…no birthday cake for you."

They made their way into the dining hall. Virgil came to an abrupt stop and was subsequently bumped into by Haley and then Cameron. "What the hell dude," said Cameron. Virgil motioned his head toward the raised area near the front of the hall.

There, at the top of the stairs, was a tall, skinny man with his hands behind his back. He was quietly scanning the crowd. He looked so familiar to Virgil, but he couldn't put his finger on it. The man waited for everyone to sit down before he spoke. "As all of you may know, a pupil passed away in this facility yesterday."

Virgil froze. *He's the guy who was talking down to Numeyer a couple weeks ago.*

"From what I am told…this was the result of an apparent allergic reaction to the monthly inoculations you children receive to counteract the effects of the virus you carry within you. As a result, the warden has been relieved of his duties."

Everyone in the hall began to look around in disbelief, quietly muttering to one another.

"Quiet down," said the man.

The room fell instantly quiet. He continued, "Until a replacement is named, I will be in charge of this facility." He waited a moment before he continued...giving the pupils time to digest the information.

"My name is Desmond Hersch...but you will address me as Mr. Hersch. And if any of you have any questions or concerns, please locate a staff member and I will address it when I am available." He then stepped down from the platform and walked out of the room. As soon as he was gone, the room erupted into numerous separate conversations.

Virgil sat with his hands clasped together, analyzing the situation in his head. Realizing that he was being stared at by Haley and Cameron, he nonchalantly said, "This changes nothing...even he can't stop what's getting ready to happen." His words did little to change the dull look in their eyes. To them, it was yet another variable that they had to add to their equation.

"I'm starting to think that the universe is trying to tell us something," Haley said, twirling her hair with her finger.

Cameron let his fork drop out of his fingers, letting it clang on the plate. He threw up his hands up in the air. "I give up, man…seriously, the universe has thrown everything short of a neon sign at us. At what point do we take a hint?"

Virgil shared their frustration, but not their resignation to do nothing. He stuck his hands out in front of them, gesturing them to calm down. "Ok…what would you guys suggest? You guys don't realize it, but we passed the point of no return when we swapped out those inhibitors." He waited for the full weight of those words to settle in with them. "We have no idea *what* they're going to do to us when everyone starts *changing*."

"We know," Cameron huffed.

"It's just frustrating…that's all," Haley said, rubbing her temples with her right hand.

Virgil shook his head in agreement. "Let's just try and pay extra special attention the next couple of days…any changes to security, personnel, or staff behavior. Maybe it'll give us an idea of who we're dealing with."

"Who knows," Cameron said, shrugging his shoulders. "Maybe he's a nice guy…I mean, compared to Numeyer, anyone would be an improvement."

Virgil stayed quiet…knowing deep down, that Cameron's assertion was way off the mark.

* * *

Back in the warden's office, Numeyer sat at his desk, clutching his knees with both hands. The door opened and Numeyer promptly stood up. Hersch walked into the room and motioned Numeyer to step aside. Without breaking stride, he sat in his chair while gesturing Numeyer to pull up another chair.

"This chair is for the warden of this facility," Hersch said coldly.

Numeyer stopped short of sitting in the chair and stared down at the man in front of him. He straightened his back and puffed out his chest before speaking. "The death of that child was not my fault. No one could have anticipated that —"

"Maybe," said, Hersch, quickly cutting him off. "Just maybe…if you didn't spend the majority of the time inebriated, you would have been able to see something sooner."

Numeyer's face boiled over with rage. "How dare you talk to me like this…I'm the warden." He began breathing heavy, overwhelmed by his anger toward the man in front of him.

With his salt and pepper hair, Hersch looked as old as him, but was in fact twenty years his junior. He wasn't going to be talked down to when he was two decades his senior. "You will have some respect for your elders," Numeyer said, wiping the sweat from his brow and the small bits of drool at the corners of his mouth. Never had he held so much contempt for anyone, even his own father.

Hersch wiped his fingers across the top of the desk, as if checking for dust. The casual demeanor only fueled Numeyer's rage. He stood up and walked out from behind the desk to stand directly in front of the former warden. Numeyer was unfazed by this, squaring his shoulders and raising his chin in defiance.

Hersch swept his hand down the front of Numeyer's suit as he spoke. "You know...I think this is the most sober I've seen you since we met." He then grabbed a handful of the man's suit jacket and lifted him off of the ground, with almost no effort.

Numeyer's eyes opened wide in disbelief. He suddenly realized that Hersch was one of the very people that he spent his career hunting...and now guarding. As he reached out to grab Hersch's arms and steady himself, he was thrown fifteen feet in the air, slamming into a bookshelf. He fell to the floor with a thump. Several dozen books had also fallen off the shelves on top of him. He was pulled to his feet by the back of his jacket. Once on his feet, Hersch pushed his back against the bookshelf. He then reached up and wrapped his hand around the old man's neck.

Numeyer stared into Hersch's vacant eyes. "You'll never get away with this," he gurgled, fighting for air through the hand collapsing his windpipe.

Hersch looked blankly into Numeyer's eyes as he spoke. "Your services are no longer required." He tightened his grip on his throat and squeezed. Understanding that this was the end, Numeyer did not struggle…he simply closed his eyes, waiting for the final moment.

Crack…

Hersch quickly shifted his thumb to the right, snapping the warden's neck. He released his grip, allowing his limp, lifeless body to fall to the ground. He stood over the man for a moment, then made his way to the door. He ushered in one of his personal guards who had come with him earlier that day.

"Take care of this," he said, as if he were asking for the trash to be taken out.

Without hesitation, the man picked up the body and laid him on a rug near the table. He placed the body at one edge and rolled it up completely to the other side. Clearly, this was something he was all too familiar with.

"Wait until everyone is asleep…then take that piece of trash to the incinerator." He spat on the corpse now inside the rug. He held no compassion for the drunkard…and even less so for the occupants of the facility.

The man nodded, again not saying a word.

CHAPTER TEN

Look What I Can Do

"Are we done yet?" Cameron whispered, bored out of his mind. Today's classes were duller than normal, as there was a new warden checking in on the classes. From time to time throughout the day, the kids noticed Mr. Hersch standing near a window with his hands behind his back. He would glance at each pupil in the class for a brief moment, and then turn his attention to the instructors...his face unreadable. After a while, he would walk away, to what they could only assume was another classroom. They had not recalled a time when the previous warden would even bother to see their progress in their classes.

Haley usually found ways to entertain herself while she waited for the classes to end. Her favorite was spinning her holo-desk pen as fast as she could and counting the rotations. She was never really sure how many times it spun, because it would initially spin very fast before slowing down enough for her eyes to be able to make out the end of the pen and therefore count the revolutions. For some reason though, today was different. She spun her pen and instantly saw the end and was able to count the rotations. *Twenty-nine*, she said to herself. She was amazed with her newfound talent. As she continued to spin the pen, she found that she was able to watch it as if it were spinning in slow motion. She would spin it as fast as she could, and yet had no problem keeping count. Just as she began to spin the pen again—

Smack!

Ms. Boscombe had slammed her ruler on Haley's desk. Haley's eyes opened wide…but not at the sudden snapping of wood on her desk. She watched in amazement as the sound ripples from the ruler were fanning out like a pebble in a pond. She was *seeing* the vibrations as they slammed into the nearby walls and bounced off like water hitting a rock. She followed the sound frequency waves until they finally dissipated a few seconds later.

She was shaken out of her state by a sharp pain in her shoulder. Ms. Boscombe had dug her thumb into Haley's arm in order to get her attention.

Haley blinked hard for a second and then saw that everything looked normal again. Quickly, she composed herself. "I'm sorry, ma'am, I did not sleep well last night and—"

"That is not my problem, Miss Hawthorne." The woman was now directly over her. "However, if I catch you day dreaming again, you are going to make it my problem…and that will not work out well for you. Am I making myself clear?"

Haley clenched her jaw. "Yes, ma'am, I understand."

"Good…now open your books to chapter seven," Ms. Boscombe said, staring out of the corner of her eye for any sign of Hersch. Luckily, he had not seen that exchange. *I can't afford to lose this job. Without it, I have nothing,* Ms. Boscombe thought to herself as she made her way back to her desk. The woman was slightly older than Numeyer, but was not married and had no children. She gave her life to her career and ended up wasting away in a school for kids with a rare disease. *If I could do it all over again…* She stood up and continued with the lesson.

* * *

At lunch, Haley couldn't help but play with her newfound *Gift*. She kept trying to let her eyes relax...but every time she did, she would see the various kids in the room changing colors. She couldn't quite understand what she was looking at. One moment they appeared normal...in the next, the area around their bodies would explode into a beautiful palette of colors. She also noticed that each time a color would abruptly change colors on someone, they would close their eyes and blink hard, just as she had done earlier. *Their abilities are starting to become unlocked...just like mine.* She was so happy she could barely contain herself.

She was snapped out of her reverie by a nudge on her side by Virgil. "I don't think I've ever seen you this happy. Is there something you want to tell us?" he said, raising an eyebrow. He thought that maybe she was starting to figure out that her *Gifts* were beginning to show since he was feeling the effects as well.

Her gaze darted from side to side...the excitement was too much for her to hold in any longer. "I can *see* things," she said, giggling.

He scrunched his eyes, leaning his head to the side. "What kind of things?"

She thought for a moment. "It's hard to explain." She looked up, as if searching her brain for the words. "I can *see* sounds…like the vibrations in the air." She waited for him to say something, but he sat quietly, taking in what she was saying. "I can see the ripples of sound waves as people speak, or bang things, or —"

"Ok, slow down," he said. "So that's why you were able to imitate those voices yesterday." He squinted his eyes as if he had just figured out what she could do.

"Uh, care to let me in on the secret?" she said.

"Oh, sorry," he said. "I think that your *Gifts* involve being able to see and manipulate frequencies."

Lifting a single eyebrow, she said, "I have no idea what that means."

"Well…since you can imitate voices…that means you can manipulate sound waves. And since you can see frequency waves…you may be able to manipulate those as well." He then looked at her quizzically. "Can you see colors around people?"

She folded her arms across her chest. "How did you know that?"

He shrugged his shoulders. "I don't know…I guess it stands to reason that if you can see frequency waves and colors…that you would also be able to see auras around people."

She shook her head. "Auras, huh? I'll have to remember that for later. I got a lot of reading to do."

"I'm starting to feel the effects as well," he said.

"You? But you've had your *Gifts* as far back as I can remember."

"I sneezed this morning and sent my chair slamming into the wall," he said, scratching the side of his head.

"You move stuff all the time…that's not a big deal."

"Yeah, but I've always been able to control it. It used to take me quite a bit of effort to move things. But now," he said, opening his eyes wide. "Now it feels like I could rip a door off the hinges and not think twice about it. There's no telling what we're capable of."

"We need to find Cameron," she said, suddenly looking around the room.

"I think he said he was going to his room before coming to lunch." He was about to bite into a forkful of food when she stopped him.

"What if he went back to his room because something was happening to him?" she said, twisting her hair in her fingers.

"You know…you do this thing when you're nervous—"

"Yeah, yeah, yeah…you can mock me later," she said, waving dismissively in his face. "Right now, we have to find Cam and make sure he's ok."

She grabbed his hand and started for the exit.

He slouched his shoulders and gave a huff before following her out. "Does this mean lunch is out of the question?"

She ignored him and kept walking.

When they got to Cameron's door, Virgil lifted his hand to knock. Before his knuckles could hit the door, Haley had swung it open. She gasped and took a step back at what she saw. It took Virgil a moment to see what had caught her so off guard. There were bloody clothes all around Cameron. She made it to his side in a couple of strides and grabbed his shoulder to turn him to face the two of them. When she did, she saw that he had a broken piece of metal in his hand and blood dripping down his arm. She tried to grab it from him, but he moved his arm away.

"This is all your fault, Haley," he said, weeping. "You made me do this." He brought the metal shard down across his forearm, opening a fresh wound. He winced in pain for a moment, but that was all.

Her eyes filled with terror, and she was suddenly unable to stand. Luckily, Virgil was behind her and saw that she looked as if she would fall. He held her up and sat her on Cameron's bed.

With his head down, Cameron brought his eyes level with the two of them, looking almost demonic. Then, as if unable to hold it in any longer, he let out a roar of laughter. "I had you two going, didn't I?" He took a fresh undershirt out and wiped his arm where he had cut himself.

Haley had her hand to her chest as she leaned in to see the laceration on Cameron's arm. The only problem was…there wasn't a scratch on him.

Seeing their slack mouths as they stared at his arm, he quickly ran the shard down his arm again. This time, their eyes did not move. Within a matter of seconds, the wound began to heal itself. In less than thirty seconds, there wasn't even a scratch to be seen. "It hurts when it happens, but only until it starts to heal." He spoke in such a giddy tone, that it made Virgil forget the last few minutes and smile.

Haley was not so forgetful...or forgiving. She shook her head. "You got me on that one." Her heart was still pounding. "So, you're telling me that you can get hurt...and then heal instantaneously?"

He straightened his shoulders and folded his arms across his chest as affirmation.

"Good," she said, and punched him square in his left eye. "Heal from that, you prick." She shook her throbbing hand as she walked out of the room and slammed the door.

Cameron cringed as he reached for his eye. "You think I pissed her off?" His eye had immediately began to swell, and then just as quickly went back to normal.

"Maybe a little bit," Virgil said, holding his thumb and forefinger barely apart.

"Dude, let me cut you," Cameron said.

"You can try...but I'll throw you into that wall behind you."

"No, seriously...I want to see if I can heal someone other than myself."

Virgil thought about it for a moment...then put his arm forward.

"Is this a trick?" Cameron didn't think Virgil would *actually* do it.

"No trick…you can try it, but only a little cut. We don't know the extent of your *Gift*, so let's lean on the side of caution." Seeing the hesitation in Cameron's eyes, he snatched the shard out of his hand and proceeded to cut his forearm. Unfortunately for him, he had cut a little too hard into his skin. As soon as the blood started flowing, he motioned for Cameron to heal it.

"What should I do?"

"Are you kidding me? You heal me…that's what you do."

"Maybe we should have thought this through before you cut yourself."

Virgil's eyes went red with anger, but he spoke as calmly as he could. "Dude…just come over here and put your hand on my arm…over the gash."

Cameron took a quick breath and put his hand on top of the wound. Virgil flinched as he did so.

"Ok, now try and visualize your power going through your hand and onto my arm…"

Even as he said it, he felt the burning sensation in his arm subside. When Cameron removed his hand, the wound disappeared. "There…see…never doubted you for a second," he said, waving his arm in front of him.

"Next time…try a paper cut or something," Cameron said, wiping the sweat from his brow.

"Ha…next time you can try it on Haley."

"Yeah right. She'd probably try cutting my arm off and tell me to heal *that*." Virgil quietly laughed, as he was not sure if Haley was on the other side of the door.

"Dude, she's going to get you so bad for this," said Virgil, giving his friend a cautious look.

"You've seen what I can do…I'll be fine."

"Who said anything about hurting you? There are worse things she could do to you that don't involve pain." Virgil let that sink in. "Can we go eat now, I'm starving."

"Ok, let me put on some clothes that don't look like I've butchered a village."

Cameron got dressed and they made their way back to the dining hall. As they sat down to eat, Haley came in. She stared at Cameron the entire way to her seat. Once she sat down, she cocked her head to the side. "I think I know how you can make things right between us."

Eager to diminish her wrath, he quickly said, "Name it."

"I want you to go up on that platform and start singing the Happy Birthday song."

Cameron scoffed at such a meager request. "That's it? You really want to waste this opportunity on something I would do anyways?" She ignored his comment. "Done!" He smacked his hand on the table and made his way to the raised platform. As he stepped up onto it, the kids in the room started to turn to see what he was going to do. As he began to sing, the rest of the eyes in the room fell on him. "Happy Birthday to you...Happy Birthday to you..."

As he sung, he stared at Haley with a big grin on his face, feeling that he had bested her again. After all, he lived for being the life of the party. As he watched her, he saw her lean in and whisper something in Virgil's ear. His eyes opened wide as she spoke to him. He then looked up at Cameron. He put his hands up and bunched up his shoulders. Cameron could not understand what was going on. He saw Virgil turn his head and cover his eyes. At that moment, his pants and underwear fell to his ankles.

It took him a full second to realize what just happened. The room froze...then burst out with laughter. He promptly pulled his underwear up, but not his pants. He tried running off of the stage, but tripped on his half-raised pants. From the floor, he managed to pull his pants up and walk off the platform.

He scratched the back of his head as he made his way back to his seat, directly across the table from Haley. She had her chin resting on her interlaced fingers, smiling triumphantly. "Ok, I think we're good here," she said.

Cameron was at a loss for words. He looked over at Virgil, but all he saw was him biting on his finger to keep from laughing. "You think this is funny, do ya? It's alright...you two got me. Just watch your backs from now on...when I get the two of you, it's gonna make this look like child's play."

Haley and Virgil just nodded in acknowledgement, while their bodies bobbed up and down from laughing on the inside. They knew that at some point, Cameron would exact his revenge...but this was the time to enjoy the here and now.

The three of them left the dining hall, en route to their afternoon classes. They had finally settled down with their laughter...but it was quickly replaced by the jeers of some of the other kids who were witness to the impromptu strip show. It didn't take long for Cameron to quiet them down though. He used his sizable physique to his advantage. He towered over most of the other kids and began bumping and pushing the smaller kids in an attempt to silence them all. After a few death stares and chest bumps, they relented.

Seeing that she had hurt her friend, Haley nudged his arm and said, "Don't worry...you'll only have to endure this for a few more days here. After a while, no one will ever remember this happened." She turned to look at Virgil, then back at Cameron. "Except me and Virgil, of course." She nudged him again and he laughed.

"Oh, I'm gonna get you so bad. I might even feel bad afterwards...that's how bad it's gonna be."

Virgil put his arm around his friend as they made it to their class. "Now you two behave in class or Daddy may have to punish you."

Cameron scoffed, "Please, Haley's going to cause a ruckus now...just so that you can "punish" her." He didn't turn around to see the looks on their faces. *Got em*, he said to himself.

Virgil didn't dare look at Haley, and vice versa. Their faces instantly turned red and they made it to their chairs without so much as a word. Haley sat two chairs in front of Cameron, but her eyes were on whatever happened to be right in front of her. Virgil sat to the left of Cameron and was giving him a silent earful. Cameron just smiled at him as Virgil had only moments earlier to him.

Understanding what Cameron was doing, Virgil squinted his eyes and faced forward.

Virgil realized that the only way Cameron would not be able to use his feelings against him would be to talk to Haley. He had wanted to wait until they were out of this place, but he kept feeling more and more uncomfortable as time went by. *I'll talk to her tonight*. Feeling a renewed sense of self, he turned his head to look at Haley. He wasn't sure why, but it appeared as if she were hypnotized. He watched her as she raised her forefinger in front of her face, as if poking at something...then put it down. She did this several times before he brought his attention to the instructor in the front of the class.

Haley sat quietly, observing the light show in front of her eyes. As she had sat down and concentrated on getting the redness out of her cheeks, she began to see flashes of colors. She let her eyes relax and then saw the flashes turn into a beautiful display of light waves. Each time a noise was struck, she would see a wave of sound energy propagate out. Occasionally, they would slam into her field of vision, prompting her to raise her hand. At one point, she reached out her forefinger to touch the wave. To her utter surprise...the moment she touched one of the frequency waves, it changed...almost as if she had the power to manipulate an existing frequency. She continued to experiment with this throughout the class...oblivious to what was going on around her. Luckily, the instructor had her back to her for the majority of the class.

Cameron turned his head, only to see Virgil motioning his eyes toward Haley. He looked over at Haley and then to the front of the class. The instructor had stopped midsentence when she noticed Haley blankly looking at the front wall. The instructor turned around to pick something up from her desk, momentarily taking her eyes off of Haley. That was enough time for Cameron to reach over the pupil in front of him and shove Haley in the back.

Cameron looked over at Virgil to make sure that it was enough to wake Haley from whatever she was seeing. It was. By the time the instructor turned around with a ruler in her hand, Haley was smiling intently at her. She smirked at Haley and stepped back to her desk to put down her ruler.

Haley turned her head slightly and looked at Virgil out of the corner of her eye. She mouthed the words "Thank you" and turned back around. Feeling left out, Cameron coughed a couple of times to get Haley's attention. He saw her shoulders collapse inward before turning to look at him with an annoyed expression. "Thank you, Cameron," she said, turning around before he could acknowledge her.

That was too close, she thought to herself. *From now on, I'll practice this with the boys or in my room.* She was too excited to concentrate on her lessons. She sat for the duration of the class…thinking of the possibilities.

Virgil spent the rest of their class time observing the other kids in the room…looking for any signs of their *Gifts*. He knew that at the rate that Cameron and Haley were going, the others would not be far behind…most likely hiding their abilities. He peered over his shoulder at one of the younger pupils and saw that his hand was disappearing and reappearing on his desk. The boy looked over and noticed Virgil looking at him and quickly stopped what he was doing.

He then turned to his left and saw one of pupils looking down at his desk. He looked up when he felt Virgil looking at him. *"What are you looking at?"*

Virgil was taken aback. The voice came from his head, but it was that of the kid looking at him. The kid's face suddenly went ashen, suddenly realizing that Virgil *heard* him. He shook his head, as if trying to get the voice out and turned to face forward. He had had enough for now. *It's only a matter of time now*, he said to himself.

Seeing the lost look on Virgil's face, Cameron began to scan the room. He stopped short when he noticed a boy staring at one of the lights. He turned his head up to look at the light and watched in amazement as the light dimmed and brightened. He noticed that each time the boy strained his eyes, the light would brighten. He glanced over to make sure that the instructor wasn't looking at the pupil. He then tapped the shoulder of the pupil next to the one messing with the light. Cameron gestured him to tap the boy. He did so…and upon being touched, the light went back to normal.

Once their studies were over, the three of them made their way to the common area. They sat on the fake grass, all facing each other.

"Ok, tell me you saw what was happening in there?" Virgil barely waited until after they were all seated.

"Yeah, sorry about that," said Haley.

"No, not you…the other kids in the class," Cameron said.

"It's happening," said Virgil, wiping his forehead. "We don't have much time."

"Yeah," Haley said, continuing the discussion. "We should also assume that one or two people are going to get noticed by a staff member and be turned in."

Virgil looked at Cameron, then they both looked back at her. "We need to be more careful...you were almost caught yourself, Haley. Anyone but us three can get caught." Virgil eyed the both of them, making sure they understood him clearly.

"I think we need to spend a lot more time practicing," Haley said.

"Practicing what?" said a voice from behind them.

The three of them froze. They looked at each other as if their secret had been revealed. Virgil took a deep breath and turned around. He was now staring up at Mr. Hersch. The silhouette of the man standing over them was intimidating.

Calmly, Virgil responded, "We're going to be practicing our rock wall climb."

Hersch looked around the space and located the rock wall. "For what?"

Virgil eyed Cameron...he hadn't thought that far ahead.

Haley quickly spoke up, "Because of Justin."

This time, all three men were looking at Haley…none of whom knew what she was talking about.

"He's almost beating us at that darn wall in our competitions," she said, looking exasperated.

Hersch focused his eyes on her, almost as if he was trying to read her, to tell if she was lying. After a long pause, he straightened up…"Very well…but it would help if you did less talking about it and more doing it." He motioned them toward the wall. As they made their way, he turned and walked out.

Once they saw he was gone, they let out a collective gasp, as if they had been holding their breath the entire time.

Cameron looked back and forth at the two of them and said, "Dude, I think I might have peed a little on myself."

That was enough to get them laughing and back to business. But before they could continue planning, they had to climb the wall a few times in the event that Mr. Hersch popped back in.

As Hersch turned the corner, he stopped just out of sight of the three of them. He watched as they stood up and made their way to the climbing wall. Once he was satisfied that they were doing what they said, he continued down the corridor. As he reached the intersection of the main corridor and the dorm rooms, his eyes caught a most strange sight. About twenty feet down the west corridor, he witnessed a pupil's arm disappear and re-appear as the boy shook his arm. The boy had been so focused on his new talent that he hadn't seen Hersch walk up behind him.

"How are you doing that?" barked Hersch.

The boy flinched hard and slowly turned around. He timidly looked up at Hersch, who was now standing directly in front of him. "I...I don't...I don't know, sir," he said, fighting to keep his voice calm and steady. "It just started happening this morning." He raised his arm and lightly shook it...getting his arm to disappear from the shoulder down. He moved his head slowly, still in disbelief of what he was able to do.

The sentiment was not shared by Hersch however. "Who else knows you can do this?" he said, nonchalantly.

"No one, sir. I just figured this out this morning."

"That is excellent news," Hersch said, suddenly grabbing the boy by his arm.

"Ow...you're hurting me."

"You will shut your mouth and come with me." Hersch spat the words at the boy as he pulled him back to the main corridor and down to the detention room. As they came to the room, the boy finally realized where he was going and began to resist Hersch. He tried pulling free of his grip, but it was of no use…the harder he tried, the harder Hersch clamped down on his arm.

Hersch motioned to the guard nearest the door. The guard quickly opened it and proceeded to grab the boy from the interim warden. He pushed the screaming boy into the room and promptly slammed the door shut. "He is not to get any visitors until I say so," said Hersch, barking the orders at all of the guards within an earshot. The guards nodded their heads and Hersch walked off.

He made his way to the warden's library and took a seat, facing forward. At the touch of a button, the screen appeared in front of him. After a moment, an older man turned to face him. "What is it?" asked the man.

"We have a situation…one of the pupils has the use of his *Gift*."

The older man leaned back in his chair. "You know the protocol," he said coldly.

"I understand, Father…I will handle it."

"Good…get it done." The man reached to turn off his comm device.

"Father, wait…how long must I suffer down here with these roaches?"

The man cocked his head to the side. "Don't forget, you *are* one of those roaches you claim to hate so much."

"I am nothing like them," he said, averting his gaze. "I never asked to be like them. I use my *Gifts* to my advantage…to rid this place of their kind."

"Nevertheless…you *are* one of them. The only difference between you and them is that you are my son. Had it not been for that…you would have been killed or locked up like the rest of them." He did not speak to him as a father would a son.

"How quickly you forget, Father…it was my plan and my teams that led to most of them being caught or killed." He looked up toward the ceiling. "I don't know what else I need to do to prove myself to you."

"There is nothing more you need to prove, Desmond. You are my son…my blood. What happened to you was not your fault. But that does not change what you are and why I cannot claim you as mine. You are the head of Security Services for all of the colonies…what more do you want?" The man let out an audible sigh.

I hate you, Hersch said to himself. "You're right, Father…you're always right. I will await your word to get out of this dump." With that, he turned off the screen and sat back in his chair. He sat for a long moment…with his hands folded across his lap. He then leaned forward and stood up. His lips flattened as he gripped either side of the table and squeezed until it began to crack. As the ends of the table began to get pulverized in his hands, he threw it with such force that it hit a bookshelf across the room and broke into a dozen pieces.

He yelled for one of his private guards. His head guard stalked into the room. His eyes went from the mess to his side and back to Hersch. "Sir."

"The boy in the detention room." He waited for the guard's acknowledgement before continuing. He had not mentioned the boy or the detention room prior to this moment, but the guard had already been made aware. "Tonight...when you are disposing of Numeyer's body. Make sure that the boy joins him."

The guard barked his obedience, "Yes, sir. Shall I come up with a story?"

"No, that will not be necessary. I will take care of it." Hersch turned back to face the mess he had created. "Tomorrow, get some guys in here to clear this place out. I don't want to be reminded of its previous occupant."

"Will do, sir. Anything else, sir?"

Hersch shook his head.

Without a word, the guard turned and walked out of the room.

* * *

Meanwhile, back in the dome, Virgil, Cameron, and Haley were finishing up with the climbing wall. "Any slower and you two would be going backwards," Virgil said, sneering at his friends.

"Says the guy who uses telekinesis to lift himself while we mere mortals have to use our finely toned muscles." Cameron was flexing his arm, kissing his bicep.

"Speak for yourself, meathead," said Haley. "I'm no mere mortal."

"Come on," Virgil said. "Let's go back to my room and practice a bit." They all headed out of the dome and toward Virgil's room.

Near the dorm rooms corridor intersection, they spotted another pupil looking from side to side, panic all over his face. He quickly walked up to the three of them. He grabbed Haley's arm and whispered, "Steven…he was taken by Hersch." His breathing became ragged. "Hersch took him to the detention room."

Virgil's eyes opened wide. "What did he do?"

"I don't know," he said, shrugging his shoulders. "I was coming out of my room and I saw Hersch grab him. I went back into my room and peeked my head out."

"Ok...we'll see what we can find out," Cameron said, attempting to reassure the boy.

They left the boy in the hallway and went into Virgil's room.

"Ok, this is not a big deal," Virgil said. "We'll make sure we get him out of there as we're escaping."

"How can you say that?" interrupted Haley. "Are you psychic now too?" She looked from one to the other. "None of us know what's going to happen when we try to get out of here...we'll try our best to get him out, but if it's between us getting out of here and that kid spending some time in the detention room...so be it."

Virgil took a breath. "Haley's right...we'll do what we can, but our first priority is getting out of here."

Cameron nodded in agreement.

"Ok...now let's see what we can do," Haley said, rubbing her hands together.

"I'll go first," Cameron blurted. He pulled the metal shard from his room out of his pocket and quickly cut Virgil's arm before he had a chance to react.

"Ow! Take it easy, you idiot," Virgil said, grabbing at the wound on his forearm.

Not paying attention to him, Cameron stepped back a few feet.

"Uh, hello…my arm is this way, not that way."

As soon as Haley figured out what Cameron was doing, she shifted her vision so that she could see their auras. With her mouth gaping, she watched in utter disbelief as a beautiful emerald green light emanating from Cameron made its way across to Virgil, covering him entirely. She watched as Virgil's bright pink aura blended harmoniously with the green. After only fifteen or so seconds, the emerald green made its way back to Cameron, until his aura returned to a subtle turquoise. She closed her eyes and took a deep breath…opening them back to her normal vision.

Virgil still did not know what had happened. "Are you going to do anything?" He looked over to Cameron, who was breathing heavy.

Haley put her hand on Cameron's back and turned to Virgil. "You didn't feel that?" She was sure he had to have felt something.

Virgil squinted his eyes. "I felt the top of my head tingle for a second or two, but that's it. What did you see?"

He moved closer to Haley, still holding his arm. She reached out and pulled his hand from over the wound. As he looked down at his arm, his eyes slowly widened with shock. "How did he—"

"I visualized myself pushing my healing ability to you," Cameron said.

"That's the most incredible thing I've ever seen," said Virgil, still in shock.

Cameron put his hand on Virgil's shoulder. "I know, dude, I know."

Haley and Cameron looked over at Virgil, as to let him know that it was his turn to try something. "Don't look at me…you guys have known for years what I can do."

Haley shook her head. "Not necessarily. You took the same shots we did, and you were still able to do what you do. Now that you haven't taken that shot, imagine how powerful you might be."

Virgil wasn't so sure. "Maybe I'm just immune to the inhibitors in the shot?"

"Maybe," Cameron said. "But you should try something…just to be sure."

"I don't feel any different than before. I wouldn't know what to try."

"Fine…my turn then," said Haley.

"Ok...so we know that you can see things that are not visible in our frequency range," said Virgil. "Have you tried anything else?"

She shook her head. "In class earlier...I was not only able to see every sound vibration as it traveled around the room, but I was able to touch them. I can't explain it, but it's almost like I can take those frequency waves and manipulate them."

Virgil looked up, rubbing his chin. "Ok, let's try something." He stepped aside so that the only thing in front of Haley was a wall. "Try and whistle softly and touch the sound wave."

Nodding, she relaxed her eyes and began to whistle.

"Ok, now reach out and touch it. See if you can stop it in place."

Again she nodded and reached for the edge of the wave and stopped whistling. As expected, once she touched the wave, it stayed stationary.

"Did you do it?" asked Virgil.

She nodded without turning her head.

"Good, now try and flick the end of it and see what happens."

She reached up again and flicked the edge of the wave with her pointer finger.

Instantly, the wave shot forward with terrific speed and slammed into the wall. The wave was gone, but in its wake was an inch-wide crack that ran the length of the wall.

"Holy Cow! Can you imagine what would have happened if one of you two were in front of that?" Haley was terrified of what she had just done.

"But we weren't," said Virgil, patting her back. "That was awesome."

"Yeah...I thought mine was cool," Cameron said. "Can you imagine what would have happened if you would've put more force into that? You would've brought that entire wall down."

Haley looked directly at Cameron, raising her right eyebrow slightly. "You may want to think twice now before you mess with me."

"I surrender," Cameron said, throwing up both hands while smiling.

"Good," she said. "I knew you'd see things my way." She jabbed him in the ribs as she walked toward the door. "Come on...all this work has made me hungry. Dinner is about to start." She opened the door without turning to see if they were following her.

The three of them made their way to the dining hall, which was already half full. "I guess some other folks had the same idea," Virgil whispered. With the effects of the inoculations wearing off, the changes that were hitting every one of them began to worry him. "You know…if all of these kids are reacting the same as the two of you…" He looked around the room warily. "What happens if one of them decides that they want to get out of here too? Or worse…what if they try to fight back? What if they put us on lockdown?"

The thought had occurred to Haley some nights ago, but she chose not to entertain it. "Even if that does happen…you can still sneak us out." Cameron nodded in agreement. "Besides," she continued. "If any of these other kids can do what we can do…we'd be smart to stay out of their way." She turned and headed for the food line.

Once served, they sat in their regular seats. Virgil watched as his friends ate as if they had been starved for days.

"Wow…you two are really putting that away," he said.

Haley shook her head. "I don't know what's gotten into me."

"Uh…that would be food," said Cameron sarcastically.

She sneered at him, then went for seconds.

Watching them eat nearly made Virgil lose his appetite. "Doing what we did earlier in my room probably took a lot of energy out of you. Try to sneak some back to your rooms." He looked at each of them to make sure they understood. "Each meal…from now until we're gone. Take a little something back with you. We may need it when we leave."

Haley and Cameron nodded.

Just as Cameron finished his second helping, on his way to thirds, the interim warden walked into the room. As before, the room fell instantly quiet. His walk was slow and deliberate. He made his way onto the raised platform and waited for everyone's eyes on him.

"As you know, the former warden was relieved of his post yesterday." He stood with his hands behind his back as he began to pace the length of the platform. "Upon hearing the news, he began to act erratically." Cameron, Haley, and Virgil each began looking at each other, then back at Hersch, all without moving their heads. "At the conclusion of your lessons today, I made my way back to his office. Before I entered I saw a note that he had left on the door." He continued to pace from one side to another. "When I entered his office," he paused before he spoke again. "He had taken his own life, and that of another pupil."

Whispering erupted throughout the dining hall.

"Quiet down, please," Hersch said immediately.

Virgil quickly turned his head and found the boy they had seen by his room earlier. The boy was looking at Virgil with terror in his eyes. Virgil looked away, as to not draw attention to the boy or himself. Haley looked as if she were in shock. She knew they were ruthless…but she did not understand just how much until this very moment.

"More details will be released as more information becomes available." Hersch once again stopped and looked around the room. He then made his way down the stairs and out of the hall.

As soon as he left, the three of them quickly got up and made their way back to Haley's room.

"Oh my God," Haley said, holding her hand over her mouth. "These people are insane. What are we going to do?"

"Stick to the plan," Cameron advised. "We've come too far now. If they figure us out, we're dead. Our only choice is to run." He nodded at Virgil for reassurance.

"He's right," said Virgil. "No matter what happens…the three of us need to get out of this place." He put his hand on Haley's shoulder and bent down to meet her eyes. She looked at him for a long moment, then nodded. "Ok, from this point on, we have to consider the fact that we may have to leave at a moment's notice. If we get put on lockdown…we'll plan on leaving an hour later, no matter what time it happens." He looked at Haley and then Cameron.

Haley took a deep breath and continued his thought. "That should give us enough time to —" She was suddenly cut off by the overheard speakers.

"ATTENTION….ATTENTION…Due to the events of earlier today, all pupils are instructed to go back to their quarters for the evening. Normal classroom schedules will be in effect tomorrow. You will have five minutes to report to your quarters, at which time a roll call will be taken. Thank you…"

The three of them looked to each other. Cameron and Virgil walked to the door, but it was Virgil who stopped just before walking out. "If anything happens…"

"I'll be fine," she said, trying to reassure him.

"But if anything does —"

Before he could finish, she leaned in and kissed him softly on his lips. She stepped back, watching him as he slowly opened his eyes.

"What was that for?" She had caught him off guard.

She shrugged her shoulders. "How else was I going to shut you up?" He gave her a warm smile. "I've been wanting to do that for a while. And seeings how I may not have the chance again—"

This time, it was Virgil who caught her off guard and planted a kiss on her lips. She melted into his arms as he moved his hand behind her neck as he kissed her.

"Dude, let's go we're …" Cameron stopped when he saw the two of them kissing. They had not even heard him. He smiled and quietly backed out and headed toward his room.

After a few seconds, Virgil slowly pulled himself away. Haley smiled softly. "I've been wanting to do that for a while too," he said to her as she opened her eyes. He put his hand on her cheek and met her gaze. "Seriously though…if they try to hurt you in any way, do what you did in my room." She nodded her head and he headed for the door.

"This isn't going to be awkward tomorrow, is it?"

He smiled as he walked out of the room, "Not at all."

CHAPTER ELEVEN

Damage Control

"It is done, sir. The children are in their quarters and the two bodies have been disposed of in the incinerator." The guard's monotone voice did not change as he informed the warden that a child had been killed.

"Good," said Hersch. "Make sure the boy's room is checked before we begin our roll call."

"Yes, sir." The guard turned and walked out of his office.

Hersch waited a few minutes in his office before he made his way into the corridor. He waved over another guard who had been stationed nearby. "Get me a list of all of the children in this facility." The guard nodded and was off. He returned a minute later with an electronic tablet that had a list of the occupants in Purgatory. "Very good…let's get started."

He began the roll call with the east wing of the facility. This side was reserved for the smaller children, as well as the female occupants. Including Haley, there were only a handful of girls down there. For some reason, the *Gifts* were not often passed down to girls.

One room at a time, Hersch spoke with each child. The smaller kids were given rooms together and once they were thirteen, they were able to have their own room. He would ask each child simple questions and move on. Little did they know, he was looking to make sure that there were no other children in the facility who were coming into their abilities. The last room in the corridor was Haley's, as she was the oldest of the girls.

"Hello, Miss Hawthorne," he said as she opened her door.

"Sir." She wanted to say as little as possible, as to not give herself away.

"I understand that you are the oldest in the east corridor."

"Yes, sir…I turned sixteen a few months ago."

"I see that you have been here for almost eleven years. In that time, have you had any side effects to the shots you've been administered?"

She shook her head. He stared at her for a long moment, almost as if looking into her soul. Her breathing began to speed up.

"Is there something troubling you, Miss Hawthorne?" His eyes were full of suspicion as he waited for her response.

"No, sir...I'm just still in shock about what happened today."

He turned his head to the side, staring at her. "Very well, Miss Hawthorne, have a good evening." He turned and began walking away before she could respond. She quickly but quietly closed her door. She leaned against her door and slowly slid down to sit on the floor. She put her hands to her face, sweeping them over her head. *That was close*, she thought to herself.

Hersch's next stop was the west corridor. His first stop would be Virgil's room. He opened his door and stepped out. However, before he could close his door, Hersch caught a glimpse of what he thought was a crack on his wall. "Hold on a second...what's that on your wall?"

Hersch pushed the door open and looked at the wall.

"I'm sorry, sir…I know that we are not permitted to hang things on the wall," said Virgil, pointing to a small piece of paper he had hung. It was the birthday cake picture Haley and Cameron had given him.

Hersch blinked hard as he looked at the wall. He could have sworn that he had seen a crack in the wall. He disregarded his mental error and turned back to Virgil. He tapped on the tablet in his hand and began to skim through Virgil's information. "I see that you are the longest serving resident of this facility."

Virgil nodded.

"What is your last name? I do not see it here."

"I do not know, sir…I did not come here with one."

Hersch looked at one of the regular guards, who gave him a nod as to the validity of Virgil's statement.

"Can't say I've ever seen that before," said Hersch, shaking his head. He then proceeded to ask Virgil the same questions as the other pupils. He received virtually the same responses. "That will be all Mr.…Virgil." He continued to look down at his tablet as he made his way to the next room.

Virgil nodded to Hersch's back and retreated back into his room.

As if knowing he was about to knock, Cameron opened his door. "How did you know I was going to knock on your door, Mr…" He looked down at his tablet. "Mr. Leah."

"I looked out earlier and saw you speaking with the other pupils. I was waiting by my door when I heard you coming."

"Very well," said Hersch, as he looked at Cameron's information. "Have you noticed anything different about yourself lately?"

"Actually, I have noticed one thing."

This got Hersch to stop tapping on his tablet and look at Cameron. "Such as?"

Cameron smiled big. "Each time I look in the mirror, I seem to look better and better." His smile quickly faded as he saw the Hersch was not amused.

The warden swiftly slapped Cameron on the side of the head. "Do you think this is some kind of joke?" He motioned to slap Cameron again, but stopped short. "The next time you think about sharing a joke with me…think otherwise." He gave Cameron a cold stare as he turned and walked away.

Once inside his room, Cameron felt as though his heart were about to jump out of his chest. *Damn, I'm a really good actor*, he thought to himself.

Once the warden was through with his roll call, it was well past lights out. The three of them laid quietly in their beds, running through what the next day would be like. After a short time, they were all asleep. The exercises in Virgil's room earlier had taken their toll.

* * *

The next morning, Virgil was the first of the three to awaken. As he stretched himself out, he opened his eyes to see his ceiling only inches from his face. With his eyes wide open, he slowly turned his head to see the entirety of the contents of his room floating several feet off the ground. *This isn't good.*

He closed his eyes, took a deep breath, and began to visualize the objects in his room slowly lowering themselves to the ground. He opened his eyes in time to see his dresser touching down softly on the floor. He then slowly lowered himself onto his bed. *Ok, this isn't telekinesis. This is something else entirely.* He decided to look into it after they left Purgatory, as he had too many things to worry about at the moment.

Just as Virgil had gotten dressed, Haley was waking up in her room. She rubbed her eyes as she sat up in her bed. When she opened her eyes, it took her mind a moment to process what she was seeing. There were dozens of cracks on her walls. Some were minute…others were the size of the one in Virgil's room. *What the…*

Her thoughts were cut short from a knock on her door. Her eyes flew wide open, as the thought of it being a Purgatory staff member frightened her into paralysis. Then, for some strange reason, she knew it was Virgil behind the door. She sighed with relief and said, "Come in, Virgil."

He poked his head in the room, looking at her sideways. "How did you know it was me?"

She shrugged her shoulders.

Virgil's eyes were instantly drawn away from Haley to the walls. He closed the door behind him. "Are you alright? What happened?"

"I don't know," she said, scratching her head. "I woke up and this was here. I think I'm losing control of whatever this is."

"You're not the only one." She squinted her eyes at him. "I woke up this morning, staring at my ceiling a few inches from my face." She plopped herself down on her bed. "And what's worse is that everything else in my room was up there with me."

She shook her head in bewilderment.

Just as she was about to speak, there was another knock at her door. Without looking up, she pointed to the door and said, "It's Cameron."

Not looking away from her, Virgil opened the door and Cameron walked in. "Ok...seriously, how did you know it was Cameron?" Again, she just shrugged her shoulders. Then, as if something clicked in his head, he said, "Bioelectricity?"

"Ok, clearly this is a conversation I don't want to be in," said Cameron, as he shoved Haley over to sit next to her on her bed.

"You can see frequencies...maybe you can feel the bioelectricity emitted by a person also." His question was rhetorical.

"Whatever, dude," said Cameron, waving off their conversation. "I had the craziest dream last night." He waited for them to ask about his dream, but they just sat there. "Ok, fine, I'll tell you. I dreamt that the three of us were in one of the colonies, fighting off a ruthless gang."

Haley and Virgil shot a glance at each other, then back at Cameron.

"Did you wake up to anything weird this morning?" There was an anxious tone to Virgil's question.

"Nope."

"What are you thinking?" Haley said.

Without responding to her, he asked Cameron, "Can you touch me when I tell you to?"

"Uh, no, dude."

Virgil shook his head, agitated by his response. "That's not what I mean, dummy. I'm going to use my telekinesis to lift that book," he said, pointing to a book on Haley's desk. "As soon as I start making it rise, I want you to touch my shoulder."

Cameron nodded, still not knowing what was going on.

Virgil looked at the book and it began to rise off of the desk. As soon as it was a couple of inches up, Cameron touched his shoulder. Without warning, the book shot up and slammed into the ceiling. Surprised, Haley jumped back on her bed and Cameron quickly removed his hand from Virgil's shoulder.

"I knew it," said Virgil, still staring at the book on the floor.

"Do you mind letting us in on what you know?" Haley still did not understand what had just happened.

"Cameron has the ability to boost our *Gifts*...even at a distance." It took a minute for Cameron and Haley to understand what he was saying.

"What are you talking about, dude? It was just a dream."

"Does this look like a dream?" Haley motioned her hand around her room.

Cameron hadn't noticed all the cracks on the walls when he walked in. "So, you're telling me that I can take what you can do and make it stronger?" Haley and Virgil nodded at him. "Do you know what this means? I am even more awesome than I thought I was...Boom!" He ran his wiggling fingers down his face.

They all burst out laughing.

Then, as if hit by a scary realization, Virgil's smile was gone. "Did there happen to be any other people in your dream?"

Cameron shrugged his shoulders. "Yeah, half the kids in this place...why?" Then, suddenly realizing what he said, his eyes were wide open. "You don't think..."

"Let's go find out," said Haley.

As they made their way down the east corridor toward the west corridor, they noticed a lot of the kids with worried looks on their faces. Some were pale with fear. They walked past one door that appeared to have charred black marks coming from inside the room to just outside the door. The door opened and a young boy popped his head out. He saw the three of them and quickly shut his door. They then saw his small hand under the door with a shirt, wiping the black marks off.

"Man, you really screwed us now," said Virgil, shaking his head.

"It's not my fault," Cameron exclaimed. "Do you think I meant for this to happen?" He gestured his arms in both directions.

"Ok...we need to figure out what we're going to do," Haley said. "Do we leave them alone, or do we help them cover up their messes?"

"We have to help them," said Virgil. "Otherwise, they'll want to go and check everyone's room...in which case, they will find out about Haley." They all nodded and proceeded to knock quietly on doors to find out if anyone needed assistance. The first few doors went unanswered. Obviously those children were too afraid of what they had done to get caught.

However, on the fifth door that was checked by Virgil, a ten-year-old boy peeked his head out to see who it was. His chest began to rise and fall quicker, as he realized that it was not one of his friends at the door.

Virgil saw his reaction and quickly asked, "Did you happen to have an accident last night?"

The boy let out a deep breath and let Virgil in.

He was temporarily blinded by the brightness in his room. By the time his eyes adjusted, he had to take a step back to take in what was in front of him. "How did you do this?"

"I don't know...I woke up and all of this was here."

He opened the door and quietly called over Haley and Cameron. As soon as they walked in, they had the same reaction as Virgil.

"This can't be real," Haley said. She could not help but stare at everything in the room. Amazingly, everything in the room, with the exception of the bed, were solid gold and silver.

Virgil needed Cameron's help with moving a golden chair.

Haley picked up a book that appeared to be silver. "This is alchemy, I think." She looked over at Virgil for his thoughts.

"I think you're right," he said. "I'll be right back." He ran out of the room and returned a minute later with what appeared to be several dozen plastic coins from a child's game and a deck of cards. He spread out the cards and all of the plastic coins on the desk and looked at the boy. "Ok, we're going to test something out." He gestured toward the items recently placed on the desk. "Put your hands on that stack of things and tell yourself in your head that you want them to be gold."

Not understanding, the boy still did as he was asked. He closed his eyes and put his hands over the items.

The three of them watched in awe as the coins and cards turned into solid gold.

After a few seconds, the boy opened his eyes and stared at what he had done. "What's wrong with me?" He began to cry.

Haley reached over to put her hand on his back. Her wrist was quickly grabbed before she put her hand on the boy. She looked up to see Virgil shaking his head. *Ah, if I touch him, I may turn to gold*, she thought to herself. She looked at Virgil, as if to tell him she understood. "There's nothing wrong with you," she said to him. "You have a beautiful *Gift*." She stopped to look at Virgil and Cameron before continuing. "But, just to be safe...you may want to keep this information to yourself." He gave her a confused look. "Older people will see what you can do and want to take advantage of you."

"When you grow up, you will be a very rich man," said Virgil. "But for now, you can't tell anyone."

The boy nodded.

"Ok, so how do we deal with this?" Cameron brought them back to their current predicament.

"They only do room inspections once a month…and we're not due for one for another couple weeks," Virgil said. "That should give us enough time to figure out a solution to our issue."

The boy quickly nodded his head. The last thing he wanted was to get in trouble.

Virgil went to the desk and grabbed all of the cards and gestured to Haley and Cameron to grab the now solid gold coins. Haley chuckled inside as she realized what Virgil had done. She looked at the boy as she stuffed the coins in her pockets. "We're going to take care of these…to make sure the staff doesn't find them." She looked at Virgil with a grin as she said it. He shrugged his shoulders and smiled as they headed out. Haley was the last one through the door. As she walked out, she looked at the boy and said, "When you go to class, act as if nothing happened."

The boy nodded.

The three of them made it back to Virgil's room. Once inside, Haley dropped her share on the bed and patted Virgil on the back. "Nicely done," she said.

"Did I miss something?" Cameron stood there, scratching his head.

"He showed the kid how to use his *Gift*, while at the same time getting us a bunch of gold pieces to barter with once we're out of here."

"Ah," Cameron said, finally seeing the ruse. "That was kinda sneaky of you, don't you think?"

"What...it's a win-win. He discovers something about himself, while at the same time helping us out." Virgil laid on the floor and reached under his bed in the far corner for one of the survival packs. Once it was in front of him, he pulled out a small pouch for the gold pieces. Before putting them into the bag, he separated all of it in equal thirds. "Here...we'll each take an even amount, just in case we are separated up there when we get out." They each took their share and stuffed it in their pockets. "Head back to your rooms and hide that for later. We'll meet up in the dining hall." They looked at each other and went their separate ways.

After a few minutes, they were all in the dining hall for breakfast. "I sure hope the rest of these kids can keep it together just a little while longer," Haley said.

"We go tonight, no matter what," Virgil said quietly, without lifting his head.

"He's right...we can't risk it." Cameron understood all too well what he was capable of doing now. He did not want to chance that he may have another dream and destroy the entire facility while they were still in it.

Haley agreed, "Alright...in between dinner and lights-out...we'll get everything ready to go."

They finished their breakfast and headed to their class. They spent most of their day looking around their classrooms...hoping that there would not be any incidents. They made it to lunch without any problems. Now they just needed to make it the rest of the day and dinner.

* * *

They were sitting in their last class of the day, when the unthinkable happened. One of the kids near the back wall stood up and was zapped by a power outlet. It was almost as if he were attracting the current to himself. He quickly pulled free of the current, but not before being spotted by the instructor. The sudden jolt of fear only made the situation worse. As his breathing began to quicken, a bolt of electricity flew from the opposite wall and into his right hand.

The instructor neared the boy, then froze in place, as the bolt nearly missed her head. The near miss turned out to be the least of her worries. Just as she had dodged the bolt of electricity, the boy instinctively raised his hands in front of him, as if to defend himself from an incoming blow from the instructor. With that movement, his hands lit up in a bright light and then released a surge of energy in the direction of the instructor. The current hit her with such force that she was thrown back ten feet in the air. On her way to a hard fall, she knocked down several other pupils who were unfortunate enough to be in her path. She crawled to her desk, wincing with pain with every movement. She reached up and pressed a button on the underside of the desk and then collapsed to the floor.

After only seconds, several guards converged inside the classroom. They quickly surveyed the damage. One of the guards turned to another guard and pointed toward the instructor. "Get her medical attention."

The other guard nodded and whispered something into his comm device.

"Who did this?" The head guard looked around the room, waiting for a response. He grew more irritated at the lack of an answer. "Tell me now, and I promise this will not end badly for all of you," he said sternly, while gritting his teeth. His eyes were met by one of the younger pupils in class. The boy did not speak, but he motioned his eyes toward the boy who had caused the incident. The guard's eyes immediately shot to a boy near the wall who appeared to be sweating profusely.

He pointed toward the boy, "You...come with us now," he barked.

Without looking up, the boy slowly made his way to the front of the room. Upon reaching the guard, he looked up to meet his eyes. The guard did not flinch, even while watching sparks of electricity leap from one eye to the other. He gestured his head at the third guard, who was now standing behind the boy. Without a word, the guard jammed a needle into the boy's neck, rendering him unconscious in a matter of seconds. The guard looked around the room, "This was for his own protection. We do not want him accidentally hurting himself or anyone else." He turned and walked out of the room, followed by the guard with the boy in his arms.

The last guard stayed by the instructor until a nurse arrived to tend to her. He then posted himself outside of the door to await further instructions.

Throughout the entire event, Cameron, Virgil, and Haley tried to keep as composed as possible. They were afraid that they may inadvertently trigger one of their *Gifts* if they were scared. None of the pupils were in their seats. They had all broken off into their little groups, as if they were in the dining hall. The three of them casually went to the corner of the room farthest from the exit. Haley and Cameron could barely stand still, their eyes moving wildly around the room to see how the others were reacting.

"This is getting out of hand," Cameron said, shaking his head.

"He's right," said Haley, looking at her hands, willing them to stop shaking.

"This doesn't change a thing," Virgil said. "No matter what happens, be ready to go the minute you are back in your rooms." His calmness was unnatural, given the situation. They had always looked to Virgil as the calm in the storm…a role which he did not wish to have. Inside however, he was holding back the same emotions that were affecting his friends. "We have no idea what they're going to do," he continued. "But we need to be ready for anything." He put a hand on each of their shoulders. "Are you guys with me?" They both nodded their heads. Their moment of calm was ended with a blaring of the loud speakers.

"ATTENTION....ATTENTION...ALL   PUPILS ARE INSTRUCTED TO RETURN TO THEIR ROOMS IMMEDIATELY. PLEASE CEASE AND DESIST FROM ANY AND ALL ACTIVITIES AND REPORT TO YOUR ROOMS. YOU WILL HAVE SIXTY SECONDS TO COMPLY."

The three of them looked at each other and took deep breaths, preparing themselves for the night ahead. They were the last to vacate the classroom, and were just in time to reach their rooms. Cameron and Virgil gave each other a silent nod before closing their doors.

* * *

"Sir...the children are in their rooms, as you instructed." The guard lowered his salute as he finished his remarks.

Hersch nodded. "Very good. See to it that none of them leave their rooms, unless they show signs of the illness. Place tables in the east and west berthing corridors.

They will be used for the pupils tonight for dinner. They are to come out of their rooms at dinner and grab a plate and return to their rooms. Until we know the extent of the infection, no one will be allowed into or out of this facility," Hersch ordered.

The guard nodded and headed out of the room.

* * *

Outside of Virgil's room, various people were walking back and forth in the corridor. As much as his curiosity was pressing him, he did not dare open the door. The fear of the consequences overruled his curiosity of knowing what was going on beyond his door. This would not have bothered him as much if he had something to occupy his time. The moment he closed his door behind himself, he quickly moved to pack the belongings he would be taking with him out of Purgatory later this evening. He finished much faster than he anticipated and was now playing a guessing game as to what was happening on the other side of his door. His best guess at the moment was that they were performing door-to-door interviews again to see if anyone knew what happened. His questions were answered by the wailing speakers above his head.

"ATTENTION...ATTENTION...ALL   PUPILS
WILL BE REQUIRED TO EAT IN THEIR QUARTERS
TONIGHT. PLEASE PROCEED OUT OF YOUR
ROOMS AND PICK UP A BOX ON THE TABLES
OUTSIDE OF YOUR DOORS. UPON RETRIEVING
YOUR RATIONS, PLEASE RETURN TO YOUR
QUARTERS UNTIL FURTHER NOTICE."

Cameron was already at the set of tables in the
middle of the corridor by the time Virgil came out. He was
quickly scanning the boxes to see what he liked best. To his
dismay, they all appeared to have the same contents...some
type of meat and a glass bottle of what appeared to be
water. He closed his box and looked up to see Virgil
standing next to him. Virgil leaned over and whispered,
"Don't eat or drink that." Cameron scrunched his face at
his friend.

"Dude, I'm starving," said Cameron, pleading with
Virgil.

Virgil almost imperceptibly shook his head. "You
have no idea what they put in that. It could knock us
out...giving them time to run tests on us."

Suddenly, the light bulb went off in Cameron's
head. He nodded to Virgil and took his box.

As they walked back to their rooms, Virgil whispered, "Be ready to go in an hour. I'm going to go warn Haley about the food." Cameron nodded and went to his room.

Virgil quickly went to his room and before shutting the door, he cloaked himself and stepped out. To anyone looking, he went into his room and closed the door. Little did they know, he was quietly making his way toward Haley, who had just opened her door and was entering her room. He barely made it into her room as the door was closing. Once inside, he saw that Haley had gone to her desk, where she had pulled out a fork to begin eating her meal. It took him only a couple of strides to make it to her side. As she brought the fork up to her mouth to take a bite…the fork flew out of her hand and hit the floor.

"Don't eat that," said Virgil, suddenly materializing in front of her.

"What are you doing?" She reached down for her fork, but he moved it with his mind toward her ceiling. She turned and gave him an annoyed stare. "Fine, keep the fork…I don't need it." She turned to grab her food, but found that the box was also floating near the ceiling.

"We can't take the risk that they put something in the food." He waited for the same realization that Cameron had to show in Haley's eyes. "Think about it…if we're knocked out, we'll have no chance of escape." She nodded her head and sat on her bed. "Be ready to go in an hour," he said. "We can't afford to wait any longer."

"Ok…but you better get back before someone finds out."

He smiled at her and cloaked himself, getting ready to walk out. Before walking out, he leaned over and kissed Haley on the cheek. She was startled, as she was not able to see him. "No fair," she said, smiling as the door opened and closed seemingly by itself.

* * *

Meanwhile, Hersch sat at a new desk in Numeyer's office, going through the footage from the classroom incident. He watched the entirety of the footage until the incident occurred at the end of the class. He watched as a young boy catapulted the instructor halfway across the room, and the ensuing aftermath. He watched as the rest of the pupils congregated in little groups throughout the room. His eyes were drawn to one of the corners of the room, where three of the older pupils had stood. He was curious as to why those three particular pupils seemed to not be as in shock as the rest of their peers.

"Sir."

He turned his head toward the guard coming out of Numeyer's bedroom. "What is it?" he asked.

"We found a safe behind a painting in the sleeping quarters of Mr. Numeyer."

He let out a sigh. "What's in it?"

"We don't know, sir. We will need to bring a safe cracker to open it."

Without saying a word, Hersch stood up and headed to the bedroom. To the side of the bed, he saw a two-foot by two-foot safe on the wall. He leaned his head from one side to the other, cracking the stiff joints. He then reached forward and effortlessly pulled the combination pad from the safe. He then pulled on the handle and ripped the door off of the hinges. He tossed the safe door onto the bed and proceeded to go through the contents within the safe. He pushed aside stacks of coins as if they were of no concern. He picked up a file marked *CONFIDENTIAL* and walked back to the desk.

He opened the file and began to skim over the pages. His eyes widened, as if in shock. He dropped the file on the desk and ran out of the door. He ran down the west berthing corridor and stopped at a door marked VIRGIL. It was the only door without a last name on it. Without knocking, he slammed the door open and went to the bed to apprehend its occupant. When he removed the blanket, his faced turned a bright shade of red. He turned and grabbed the guard closest to him and held him in the air for the rest of the guards to see. "You will find this child and bring him to me...do you understand?" He looked sternly at the other guards. "Sound the alarm...this facility is now on Level 1 lockdown!"

CHAPTER TWELVE

The Great Escape

The alarm rang out throughout the facility. Unsure of what was happening, a lot of the children opened their doors. They were quickly told to close them by the guards in the corridors.

"ATTENTION...ATTENTION...THIS FACILITY IS NOW ON LEVEL 1 LOCKDOWN. ALL PUPILS ARE TO REMAIN IN THEIR ROOMS. ALL FACULTY MEMBERS ARE INSTRUCTED TO RETURN TO THEIR QUARTERS AND AWAIT FURTHER INSTRUCTIONS. THE PUNISHMENT FOR ANYONE

CAUGHT OUT OF THEIR ASSIGNED AREA WILL BE SWIFT AND SEVERE."

"There is no sign of him, sir." It was the same guard that Hersch had lifted into the air. Fortunately for him, Hersch was too preoccupied with the matter at hand.

"Search every possible room in this facility. There is no way for him to escape. Find him and bring him to my office." The guard nodded and used his comm device to relay the commands to the rest of the guards searching for Virgil.

They searched all of the areas that were not already being guarded, but they could not find him. After twenty minutes had passed, the guard went back to see Hersch. "There is no sign of him anywhere, sir." He gulped hard as the words left his tongue.

"Do a roll call. Check every single sleeping quarter in this place." He then turned to the head of his security detail. "There are only three exits from this facility…the elevator we came down on, and the two service shafts. Check them out and report back to me." Without a word, the guard turned and headed out.

An hour passed before a guard came to his office. "There are three missing, sir."

"What do you mean three are missing?" Hersch looked as if he were going to explode.

"Virgil, Haley Hawthorne, and Cameron Leah…those are the three are unaccounted for."

"Clearly, they are hiding in an area that you have overlooked. I suggest that you come back to me with good news…for your sake," Hersch said as calmly as he could under the circumstances.

Just as the guard nodded and began to walk away, the speakers above them began to ring. Hersch looked at the guard, "I did not authorize an announcement." The guard called the dispatch desk from his comm device, but did not receive a response. "You get them on your comms, I will let them know that I did not—"

"ATTENTION…ATTENTION…THIS IS INTERIM WARDEN HERSCH. ALL PUPILS ARE INSTRUCTED TO VACATE THEIR QUARTERS AND WAIT IN THE CORRIDORS UNTIL I GIVE FURTHER INSTRUCTIONS."

Hersch's eyes reddened, as he realized someone was currently in the main guard room, imitating his voice.

* * *

"Hurry," Virgil said, pulling Haley away from the intercom system microphone in the guard room.

"Just one more thing," she said, as she picked up the microphone and slammed it on the floor. "This will buy us a little more time."

He cloaked the two of them and lifted themselves in the air above the room. As a guard rushed into the room and saw his colleagues passed out on the floor, he headed for the microphone to give an announcement for the pupils to stay in their rooms. Virgil and Haley were out of the room before the door closed behind the guard.

They stayed close to the ceiling as they made their way down one of the corridors. They froze momentarily as Hersch walked in their direction. A guard came running toward him from the guard room.

"There was no one there," said the guard. "They also broke the microphone. There will be no way to make another announcement."

Hersch clenched his fists at his side, trying to stay calm. Rather than hit the guard, he grabbed the pipe next to him on the wall. He squeezed the pipe without turning his head from the guard. It crumpled in his hand like a piece of paper.

"I cannot stress to you the importance of finding those children. Your life depends on it." He let go of the pipe and kept walking toward the guard room.

"He's a dangerous man," whispered Haley.

"Come on, let's get out of here," said Virgil, as he moved them toward their escape point.

They reached it without issue and filled Cameron in on what had transpired. Just as they had finished their story, Hersch and several guards were standing directly underneath them.

"I want everyone to split up into two-man teams and perform a grid search of this facility." Hersch pointed to a floor plan that was projected on the wall. "As each section is cleared, you will contact the guard room to mark that area and move on. Does everyone understand?" They all nodded at once. He then looked up and was quiet for a moment. "Has anyone checked that vent?"

"It is twenty-five feet in the air, sir."

Hersch turned toward the guard who made the remark and said, "Get someone up there now to check it out." The guard complied and gestured to a couple of guards to find a way to reach the vent. With that, Hersch began to walk out of the common area.

"Ok, Cam, you're up." Haley was nudging him to get started.

"Alright…here we go." He closed his eyes and began to concentrate. He pictured the east and west corridors in his mind. He pictured himself sending out his boosting energy to everyone in the area. *I sure hope this works*, he thought to himself.

* * *

Hersch had arrived at the intersection of the east and west corridors. There had not been as many pupils as he would have thought. *I guess the drugs in their dinners kicked in a little sooner than expected.* He smiled and opened his mouth to bark orders at the pupils who were out of their rooms. But before he could get a word out, a fireball smacked the wall halfway down the west corridor. As he ran toward the source of the fireball, a loud clanging noise sounded behind him. He turned around to find one of his guards on the floor, made of solid gold. Each time he turned, there was a child who was unable to control their newly acquired powers. He knew he had lost the facility at that point. He reached into his pocket and pulled out his comm device. "Initiate Silent Night…I repeat, initiate Silent Night."

"Negative, sir…we need your key card to initiate the protocol," said a guard from the guard room.

"Roger that, I am on my way."

Hersch weaved his way through the maze of children in his path. He was not worried they would hurt him, as they seemed too preoccupied with themselves at the moment.

* * *

"Ok, I think it worked." Cameron opened his eyes and shook his head to return his focus to the vent he was currently stuffed in.

"I think you're right," Haley said. "It sounds like all hell is breaking loose." Just as she said that, Virgil looked over at her and put his finger to his mouth and pointed beneath them. A couple of the guards had found a modular ladder that would reach the vent atop the dome. The vent was several feet wide and could fit all three comfortably, but it also amplified their voices.

"Time to go," said Virgil, as he began to levitate them three hundred feet toward their freedom.

* * *

Hersch finally made it to the guard room. He grabbed the door handle and accidentally pulled the entire door from the hinges. He was taken aback, as he had been able to control his *Gift* since he was a child. He soon realized the cause of his lack of control. *One of these brats is an amplifier.* He dismissed the idea for the time being. He had more pressing matters at hand. He made his way carefully to the central command guard desk. "Is everything ready to go?"

"Yes, sir…it only requires your key card," said the head guard.

"Good…let's get started." He pulled out his key card from his jacket pocket and placed it near the card reader. Once the card was accepted, the screen prompted for confirmation before executing the protocol. The guard looked over at Hersch, who gave him a nod to proceed.

The guard looked around the room and said, "Once the protocol begins, it cannot be stopped. The only ones who will not be affected will be the ones in this guard room." He saw the look of concern on his coworkers' faces. They were friends in here. They had good working relationships with all of the faculty in the facility. Now he was being ordered to betray that relationship. "Sir, we still have men in the corridors…shouldn't we—"

"Proceed." Hersch did not make eye contact with the man when he gave his command.

"Yes, sir." The guard pressed the key on his console and the room immediately sealed itself. All ventilation into the space was severed.

In the vent above the dome, Cameron looked down and saw the vent that was still visible go completely dark. "Uh…I think we might have a problem."

Haley and Virgil both looked down and saw darkness where there was only moments ago light. "We need to move faster," said Haley.

Virgil looked up and saw a light, but it was still hundreds of feet away. "Let's go single file," he said. "We'll go faster if we go one at a time." They nodded in agreement. "Haley, you'll go first…and then you, Cam. I'll stay in the back to make sure I am guiding us straight."

He moved Haley above them, followed by Cameron. He looked down warily at the vent before turning and continuing their ascent. He doubled the speed at which they were moving. "If you get too close to the side, just tap on the side and straighten yourself out."

They did not respond, but he knew they heard him.

* * *

"Are they going to tell us when they initiate the protocol?" One of the numerous guards in the corridor attempting to corral the children was looking to his superior officer.

"Of course they will…now get back to…"

The guard turned his head in the direction in which his superior officer was looking. He watched in disbelief as a bluish mist was released from one of the vents. Knowing immediately what it was, he began to run in the direction of the guard room. He watched as children and guards alike were falling to the floor from the effects of the gas. He made it to the guard room, sweating profusely. He swiped his key card, but the door did not open. His eyes widened, and he began to bang on the window. A dozen guards and the warden stared at him. He felt his eyes getting heavy. His pounding all but ceased as his legs gave out on him. He collapsed to the floor with a thud.

"He'll be fine," scoffed Hersch. "This room will remain sealed for the duration of the protocol." He did not raise his eyes from the screen in front of him, knowing that there would not be any objections to his command. He watched as the animated graphics on the screen displayed the dispersal of the gas throughout the facility. The display showed that the process was ninety percent complete.

"Sir…the process is nearly complete," said the head guard. "Only the ventilation systems remain." Hersch nodded, finally turning his attention away from the screen. He knew there would be no way for any kids to get into the ventilation system, as all of the access points were guarded.

* * *

In the ventilation duct, Haley, Virgil, and Cameron had come to the point where the duct made a slight turn to the left. Before that point, they were not able to see the top of the shaft. Haley read a plaque on the vent wall, which was dimly lit by a red light, much like the one at the top of their exit. Now, as Virgil made the turn, he could see a bright red light approximately 100 feet in front of them. When he was about twenty feet from the turn, he looked down and thought he saw the red light darken slightly.

Terror filled him as he realized what was happening. He turned back to see their progress.

"What the —." Haley felt her pace quicken substantially.

"Move!" Virgil made sure Haley and Cameron understood the urgency in his voice. This prompted them to push themselves up, on top of the speed at which Virgil was raising them. Virgil looked down again and was expecting to see the unknown substance far from them. Unfortunately for him, that was not the case. It was only ten feet or so beneath his feet and rising fast.

"We're almost there," said Haley, reaching out her arms in preparation of arresting her ascent. "Ok, slow down…I don't want to eat this grate."

Virgil looked down once again before slowing them down. "Hurry…we don't have much time."

They reached the grate, where Haley quickly grabbed hold and tried to push it open. She propped her legs on either side of the now narrow shaft, trying to get a little bit of power to use on the grate. She pushed with all of her strength, but it did not budge. "It won't open," she said, now breathing heavily.

""Scoot over…let me help," said Cameron, as he moved up behind her. He was much stronger than Haley, but that did not help him in this situation. He yanked and pushed on the grate, but it did not budge. "Haley, put your back to mine and brace the side with your legs." She knew what he was thinking and quickly got into place. "At the same time, push as hard as you can." Haley nodded and pushed as hard as she could. Their combined strength was still not enough to make the grate move.

"It's no use, Virgil, we can't even make it budge." Cameron was breathing as heavily as they had ever heard him. Virgil wasn't sure if it was fatigue or fear.

Virgil looked down one more time before turning to his friends. "Get as close to the grate as possible without touching it." They weren't sure what he was planning on doing, but they quickly did as instructed. Once Virgil saw them in position, he said, "Ok, now hold your breath and cover your ears until we're out."

Cameron and Haley nodded and took a deep breath. As soon as they held their breath, Virgil positioned himself just underneath them and anchored his legs on either side of the vent. He put his head down and closed his eyes. He took as deep a breath as he could and looked up again, now staring at the grate, which separated them from their freedom.

He raised his right arm above his head, as if to slam it into the grate, which was still eight feet out of his reach. As his hand reached its apex, the grate was hit with such force that it exploded into the air and out of sight of the shaft. Instantly, the shaft was flooded with bright light. Without adjusting his eyes to the light, Virgil lifted his left hand and used his invisible force to throw his friends into the light. As he did so, the gas that was previously underneath him had now quickly enveloped his body. The light that was only seconds ago flooding the vent was obscured.

As soon as Haley and Cameron hit the ground, they quickly ran back to the shaft opening only feet away. They made it back to the opening at the same time, but were forced back by a blue gas that surged out.

"Virgil!" Haley tried to get back to the shaft, but Cameron grabbed her before she could get there.

Almost out of breath, Virgil put all of his strength into his legs and braced himself against the shaft walls, which were pushed outward with the force of his legs. He gathered all of the strength he could muster and pushed off of the walls with all of his force and flew toward his freedom. The obscure light quickly turned to an unbearable flash. He closed his eyes, knowing he was free of the shaft, but unable to see where he would be landing. He braced for what would surely be a hard hit. He hit the ground, but not quite as hard as he thought. To him, it had felt as if he landed on the padding in the dome that he used for exercising.

Hitting the ground knocked the remaining air out of his lungs. He struggled to catch his breath. When he finally opened his eyes completely, he saw Cameron standing over him, smiling from ear to ear. Still squinting his eyes, he looked to the right of Cameron and saw Haley still sitting on the ground. She was wiping away the tears on her face. Cameron noticed the expression on Virgil's face when he looked at Haley. He took the opportunity to get a laugh at Haley's expense.

"Don't worry about Haley," said Cameron, as he helped Virgil to his feet. "She's just upset 'cause I don't want to date her."

Haley squinted at the two of them, her breathing shallow. Virgil and Cameron looked at each other, wondering what she was thinking. Not being able to hold it any longer, she gave them a big grin. She started to laugh out loud and ran to them, jumping in the air. Virgil caught her in mid-air, bringing her into his arms. They looked at each other for a long moment and then turned to Cameron. The three of them hugged each other tightly, knowing that they had won their freedom.

Little did they know that this was only a taste of what was to come.

CHAPTER THIRTEEN

Out of the Night and Into the Light

"The protocol is complete, sir," said the head guard, as he began to make his way to the storage room to grab the breathers. He handed the small devices to each of the men in the room.

"Good," responded Hersch. "Were there any issues?"

"Just one, sir."

Hersch turned to face a guard sitting in front of a display. "What is it?

"It's nothing, sir…just an issue with a sensor from an exhaust vent."

Hersch shook his head slowly, then turned to his personal protection detail. "Get up there and take a look." The guard nodded and grabbed a breather from the counter. He pointed to another guard to join him. Without another word, the two men exited the space.

* * *

After a long hug, Virgil, Haley, and Cameron looked at each other, then to the environment around them. Cameron reached down and picked up a handful of what he thought was dirt. As he studied the substance, Haley and Virgil followed suit.

"Ash," said Haley. "The surface will be covered with it."

Virgil looked closer. "It shouldn't be much though. They geo-engineered IO before inhabiting it." He opened his fingers, allowing the ash to slowly escape his hand. "We should use the breathers, just to be safe."

He reached into his bag and pulled out three of the breathers and handed one to Haley and one to Cameron. The device itself was small and easy to use. It covered only their mouth and nose, leaving their vision unimpaired. They helped each other with securing the strap on the back of the breathers to fit comfortably.

After they were situated, they walked to a nearby rock formation. They stood on the top of the rocks and surveyed the valley in front of them. The area was barren and littered with rock formations, much like the one they were on. Virgil looked back to where they had come out of the shaft and had a sudden realization. "They're bound to know that this exhaust vent has been compromised." He looked around the area for some kind of maintenance door, but all he saw was other rock formations. "Haley…do you think you can use your *Gift* to find out if there is a door within any of these big rocks?"

She tilted her head to the side, thinking about how to go about doing what Virgil had requested. "Ok, I'll give it a shot." She closed her eyes and took a deep breath. When she opened them, she was looking at a world of shimmering colors. She looked at the numerous rock formations in the area, but was unable to see any difference between them. Then, as if by instinct, she whistled in short bursts in every direction. Then she watched as the colored sound waves bounced off of the massive rocks like water.

Her attention was drawn to one particular rock directly across from where they were positioned. The sound did not bounce off in the same manner as all of the others she had just witnessed. Testing her theory, she whistled loudly in the direction of the questionable rock. As it hit the rock, she saw it bounce off of most of it, with the exception of a rectangular area in the front. "There," she said, pointing at the hidden door.

"You're amazing," Virgil said, as he watched her focusing back to her regular sight.

She smiled as she joined them back at the top of the rock.

As soon as she was on the rock with them, Virgil raised his right arm so that it was parallel to the ground. The shaft cover slowly lifted off of the ground and then lowered neatly where it had been secured only moments ago. Then, all of a sudden, the entire area they had just walked and fallen on transformed into a mini dust storm. Haley and Cameron watched as the sand flew around, but appeared contained behind an invisible shield. Haley could now imagine what a large snow globe would look like. After a minute or so, Virgil lowered his arm, and with it the control over the sands and ash. The debris floated gently to the ground, erasing any evidence and making it look as if they were never there.

The three of them looked at each other, the tension finally easing in their shoulders. The moment was short-lived by a screeching noise coming from the area Haley had pointed out was a door. Virgil quickly cloaked the three of them and sat on the rock. Haley and Cameron quickly followed his lead. The maintenance door slid open and two men came out, weapons drawn. Haley gave a worried glance in Virgil's direction. He did not notice, as his eyes were trained on the two men sent outside to possibly kill them.

"Go check the vent," barked the large guard to his subordinate.

The smaller man did so, without saying a word. He looked down the shaft, and after a moment, continued to walk around the area.

"All clear, sir."

The man in charge nodded and took out his comm device. Just as he did so, he noticed something out of the corner of his eye. He looked up and thought he had seen a bit of ash fall from the rocks directly across from where he was standing.

Cameron looked over at Haley, who a moment ago had tried to reposition herself on the rock that was digging into her leg. They watched as the man in charge made his way slowly to their location. Cameron and Virgil were in great shape, but it was nothing compared to the house of a man who was coming toward them.

He came to a stop a few feet from the rock in front of him. Little did he know, he only needed to reach out his arm and he would have been touching Virgil's foot. He stood there for a moment, as if lost in thought. Then, he moved to the side of the rock to look at the valley below. He took out a pair of binoculars and scanned the valley in front of him for any life forms. He knew that nothing or no one lived out here, so it would be easy to spot someone if they were out there. After a minute, he put the binoculars in his pocket and reached for his comm device.

"Sir, it is all clear up here."

"Are you sure?" Virgil knew the voice belonged to Hersch.

"Yes, sir...the area around the shaft has not been disturbed. There is no evidence that anyone has been here."

"Very well...get back down here immediately."

"Yes, sir."

The three of them watched as the two men made their way back to the maintenance door and disappeared into the face of the rock.

They waited a few minutes after the door closed before they moved.

"Way to go, Haley…you almost got us killed," Cameron said, as he stood up to dust himself off.

She gave him an icy stare, and he thought better of his comment.

"Alright, we need to figure out where we are exactly," said Virgil, as he made his way in between Cameron and Haley.

He handed Haley one of the backpacks and she sifted through it, looking for a particular item. After a bit of searching, she pulled out what appeared to be a rolled up piece of plastic paper. She handed the pack back to Virgil, who quickly closed it and strapped it back onto his shoulders.

Haley raised the roll in front of her and slowly began to unroll it from left to right. The material was completely transparent and showed the terrain directly in front of them. Cameron and Virgil watched in silence, knowing full well what to expect. They had seen this device on many occasions in the videos they were forced to watch about the military and their conquests over the *Gifted* rebels.

Once fully unrolled, the plastic flickered for a second then quickly filled with words and various other symbols. As she moved her field of view to the left, the plastic screen adjusted accordingly, labeling the terrain as quickly as she moved. She was even able to use the screen as a telescope and zoom in to a specific area and see what they may encounter if they happen to head in that direction.

"Can you see anyone over there?" Cameron was in awe of their new toy.

"It doesn't work that way," said Virgil, leaning over to speak quietly to Cameron. "It's not a real-time view. It will only show us topographical and geological information about the area we are looking at on the screen." He shook his head and continued to watch Haley as she slowly made a complete turn in place to get a better idea of where they stood.

"We're on the Jupiter side," she said, still looking at the screen.

"Duh," Cameron said, as sarcastically as he could while pointing at the massive planet directly above the horizon.

Virgil gave his friend a cautious glance and slowly shook his head. Virgil knew that one of Cameron's many flaws was that he did not know when to not clown around.

He needed constant reminders, like the one Virgil had just provided. Cameron quickly shut up and let Haley continue.

"We need to head west," she said finally, lifting her arm to point in the direction they were to go. "I think that we should head straight for a couple of miles, then turn west. They wouldn't be expecting that."

Cameron and Virgil nodded in agreement and began to climb down off the large rock. Once down, Cameron helped Haley down in an attempt to have her forget his last comment. She squinted her eyes and gave him a thin smile. He smiled and scratched the back of his head as they made their way to Virgil, who was already looking down at the valley in front of them.

"That's quite a climb down," Cameron moaned, as he looked for the best way down. Then, without warning, Virgil lifted Cameron off of his feet and twenty feet in front of them. For a second, he hadn't even noticed. That is until he looked down and saw the valley a hundred or so feet beneath him. He turned as calmly as he could, only to see Haley and Virgil smirking.

Virgil shrugged his shoulders. "Sorry, dude…but what good is having all of these *Gifts* if you can't have a little fun from time to time?"

"Ha, ha, very funny...now put me down." Cameron wasn't able to muster his comedic side while at the same time staring at the space between himself and the ground.

Without saying a word, Virgil reached out his hand to Haley. She tilted her head sideways, not knowing what he was going to do. Nonetheless, she took his hand. She then felt herself light as a feather as the two of them floated over to where Cameron was.

"I didn't think you needed me to hold on to you while you did this," Haley said.

"I don't," replied Virgil, smiling as he continued to look straight ahead.

Haley tightened her bond as her chest began to flutter.

They reached Cameron and as they did so, Virgil began to slowly lower them to the ground. After only a minute, they landed softly. To Virgil's surprise, the physical toll of controlling their descent was not present. The feeling of exhaustion was replaced with invigoration. He wasn't sure if it was the adrenaline pumping or if this was the new normal. He pushed the thought from his mind. At this particular moment, he needed to have his full attention to the task at hand.

"Ok, Haley, your turn." Virgil stepped back to give her some space. She again pulled out the plastic sheet. Once unrolled, she pressed the top right of the plastic and it instantly went rigid. This gave her the ability to have a hand free to move around while she studied the topography. On the right side of the sheet, there was a globe that represented IO, along with a red dot that pinpointed their exact location.

Haley used three fingers and gestured on the screen as if stretching out the globe. This caused the globe to move to the center of the screen. She continued to move the image around as she spoke. "We're about ten miles inside the red zone." Cameron scrunched his eyes, unsure of what she meant. "It's the Jupiter side of IO that's uninhabitable," she said.

"So let me get this straight…they put us in the ground in a place that's uninhabitable?" Cameron could only shake his head at his rhetorical question.

"So, why isn't this place filled with ash? IO is supposedly the most volcanic body in the solar system." It was now Virgil's turn at the unknown.

"A bunch of scientists came here years before anyone else and began to terraform it." Haley always had a thing for geology and was more than happy to school

Cameron and Virgil with something they clearly had not paid attention to in class. "They figured out a way to make the volcanoes on the sun-facing side of IO dormant. They then created an artificial atmosphere that covers most of IO that faces the sun. But, in doing so, they made the volcanoes on this side of the moon hyperactive." She pointed to a volcano that was erupting in the distance.

"That still doesn't explain why we're not covered in ash," Cameron said.

Haley continued where she left off. "They also came up with a way of decreasing the pull of gravity on this side, so that most of the ash that would normally fall to the ground just floats into space. This also caused the perpetual hurricane force winds to nearly cease."

"That's why I don't feel exhausted," said Virgil, suddenly realizing that it was the lack of sufficient gravity that assisted him down the mountain.

Haley nodded in agreement. "We better get moving...we don't know how long these breathers are going to last out here."

They began walking away from their prison.

Virgil used his *Gift* and picked up the ash and dirt in front of them as they walked. Once they passed the ash above their head, he released his control over it and it floated to the ground, covering their tracks as he had done at the shaft.

"That's pretty clever," Haley said.

They walked for a couple of hours before they stopped for a break. Haley checked the map, but was discouraged when she saw that they had only walked a few miles. "We need to pick up the pace," she said, breathing heavily.

"We can't," said Virgil. "We'll use up the oxygen too fast if we exert ourselves."

She knew he was right, but wanted to be as far away as fast as possible.

"When are we going to start heading west?" Cameron's breathing was also labored.

Haley examined the map once again. "Now's as good a time as any."

They rested for a few minutes then got back on their feet. "Lead the way," said Cameron, as he stepped aside and let Haley get in front of him.

"We'll stop there for the night if we take too long," Virgil said, as he pointed to a large rock formation on the horizon. Cameron and Haley nodded as they plodded through the thin layer of dirt and ash. Even though they did not have much in the way of debris on the ground, their steps took some effort. Virgil felt as if he were carrying someone on his back.

Unfortunately for them, the ash was not their biggest concern. They had not noticed it on the first leg of their route, but the cold thin air was beginning to hurt them to the bone. At one point, they even went as far as to walk side by side, touching each other's shoulders as they walked.

"This is ridiculous," huffed Haley, coming to a sudden stop.

"We need to keep moving," said Cameron. The steam trailed his words as they left his lips.

"Not unless you want to give me your shirt," she said, speaking through her teeth with forced restraint.

"You'd like that, wouldn't you?" Cameron replied, looking up and away.

Virgil put the survival pack on the ground and began rummaging through it, hoping to find something that would ease their misery. Finally, he found the answer in the form of a bottle. "Here," he said, handing the bottle to Haley. She read the label for a moment, then popped it open. There were five pills in the little container labeled *Body Heat*. She handed them each one.

"Swallow the pill and wait until you don't feel cold," she said. They all swallowed the pill before even asking what it did.

After a few minutes, they began to feel their muscles warming up. After ten minutes, the involuntary shaking was gone and they did not feel cold at all. "This stuff is great...now let's go before I get too comfortable and take a nap on this rock," Cameron said, as he began walking west.

As they continued forward, they started to see what appeared to be sunlight on the tallest rock formation on the horizon. Seeing that their destination was so close gave them their second wind. They walked a bit faster than before, unconcerned with their dwindling supply of both oxygen and body heat.

Realizing that their supplies would run out faster at this pace, Virgil slowed them down. "Slow and steady wins the race," he said, as he had them slow their pace to match his.

"Not when you're running for your life," Cameron said.

"He's right, Virgil," Haley said, as she began to pick up her pace again.

Not wanting to argue, Virgil quickened his pace to keep up with them, even though he knew this would come back to haunt them.

After an hour of walking, Haley stopped to sit on a rock to rest. As she looked out, she saw smoke rising near some rocks to the north. "Hey, we should think about stopping there for the night." She started walking in that direction before giving them time to answer. Virgil and Cameron looked at each other, then back at Haley. With their long strides, they were next to her in no time.

After about an hour, they reached the formation of rocks that had been emanating the smoke. To their surprise, the smoke wasn't smoke at all. It turned out to be steam venting from a crevice on the left side of the formation.

Slowly, they approached the source of the steam, hoping to find a spot where they would be covered from the elements as well as heat to stay warm throughout the rest of the evening.

Virgil assessed the situation for a long while and said, "We can't stay here."

Haley and Cameron narrowed their eyes at his words.

"You see that," said Virgil, as he pointed to the narrow column of steam as it rose. "That's not steam…it's sulfur dioxide. If we breathe it, we're dead."

Cameron kicked a rock hard and watched it fly through the air as it collided with a much bigger rock a few feet in front of him. "Damn, we can't catch a break," he said, clasping his hands together and placing them on his head.

"Over here," said Haley, standing in front of a large rock near the vent. "We can use the radiant heat of this rock to keep warm while we sleep." She had them come over to where she was to put their hands on the rock.

The warmth was enough to bring a smile to Cameron's face. "This is more like it." He leaned his entire body on the rock, as if giving it a hug.

Virgil took his hand off of the rock and put it in the pack that he had been carrying. He pulled out a rolled-up blanket and some thin rope. "Here, grab this side." He unfolded the blanket and handed one side to Cameron. He reached as high as he could and jammed some of the rope in a crack on the massive rock. Cameron saw what he had done and followed suit. Once the top was secured, they attached the blanket at the corners. They then did the same on the ground, attaching the corners of the blanket to either side of the rope. The result was a lean-to that provided just enough cover for the three of them to fit shoulder to shoulder.

"You boys are pretty handy," said Haley as she made herself comfortable on one end.

"I call the other side," yelled Cameron, raising his hand as if he were in class.

Virgil shook his head as he found his spot in between Haley and Cameron. "If you wanted to sleep next to me, all you had to do was ask," Virgil said, as he began to run his fingers through Cameron's hair.

Cameron did not move a muscle. "Dude, if you don't get your hand out of my hair, I'm going to throat-chop you."

The three of them got as comfortable as they could against the rock and proceeded to fall asleep.

Virgil saw himself in the air, then falling uncontrollably back down. Fear gripped him, as he realized he could not control his descent. Suddenly, a pair of hands reached out and caught him. The fear immediately turned into elation. "Again...again," he said, laughing as he patted the man's arm.

"Ok, ok," said the man, tossing Virgil even higher into the air.

"*Come inside...it's getting cold.*" Virgil looked over the man's shoulder to see where the voice was coming from. He saw the silhouette of a slender woman with the sun setting behind her.

"*Awe...one more, Daddy, one more.*" Virgil did not want to go inside just yet.

"*You heard your mom...now go wash up for dinner.*" The man put him down and he ran toward the open arms of his mother. As he got closer, he began to see her more clearly. He was now almost to the point where he could see her completely. Virgil reached out his arms—

"Virgil...wake up, man."

He opened his eyes to see Cameron standing over him.

"Seriously?" Virgil let the air out his chest as he slowly began to stand up.

"What?" Cameron did not realize that he had just ruined the best dream that Virgil ever had.

"Nothing," said Virgil, as he brushed the dirt and ash off of his shoulders.

He and Cameron both turned to see Haley standing on the top of a rock near the sulfur-dioxide vent.

"What are you doing?" Virgil made his way to Haley's side with a few steps.

When she turned to face him, he was momentarily taken aback. He couldn't help but to notice the light purple in her eyes swirling about. He hadn't realized that it was an effect of using her *Gift*.

"I'm scanning the surface for any clues on which route to take," she said, bringing Virgil out of his thoughts. She tilted her head to the side. "Are you ok?"

"Yeah…your eyes just caught me off guard."

"Awe, that's so sweet," said Cameron, as sarcastically as he could.

"No, you idiot…look at her eyes." Virgil helped Cameron up to where he and Haley were standing and motioned for him to look at her eyes.

Cameron responded with the same reaction as Virgil. He flinched backwards, but then came in closer to examine her eyes more closely.

Their sudden interest in her eyes started to make Haley uncomfortable. She reached out her arms, gently pushing the two of them out of her personal space. "Ok, I get it…my eyes are hideous," she said, as she turned back to face the barren landscape in front of them.

"You got it all wrong," countered Virgil, as he grabbed her arm to turn her back to face them. He reached into the bag and pulled out a small mirror. "Look for yourself." He gave her the mirror and watched as a look of horror washed across her face. After a moment, her expression changed to one of amazement.

"How is this possible?" She didn't take her eyes off of the mirror as she asked the question.

"Here...see if it happens to me when I use my *Gift*." Cameron turned to face them and took a deep breath. Once he opened his eyes, the purple in his eyes was swirling.

Virgil following his lead, slightly levitating himself. "Are my eyes having the same reaction?" Haley and Cameron nodded, and he lowered himself back to the ground.

"It must be an effect that we all get when we are using our *Gifts,"* Haley said, as her eyes went back to normal.

"But if that's the case...why did we never see it happen to you?" Cameron's question was aimed directly at Virgil, who had most of his *Gifts* for years. A shrug of Virgil's shoulders was the most appropriate answer he could think of at the moment.

"We'll have plenty of time to figure all of this out later," said Haley, waving away their concerns.

"She's right," Virgil said, as he began to walk down and disassemble their makeshift shelter. He rolled up the blanket and placed it, along with the other supplies, back into the pack.

Haley took the opportunity to nudge Cameron on his arm. "You notice that Virgil's been saying nothing but 'She's right' since we left Purgatory?"

Cameron rolled his eyes and walked over to Virgil to assist him with the last of the cleanup. He leaned over and whispered to Virgil, but loud enough where Haley could hear. "Dude, you need to tone it down with letting her think she's always right. Next thing you know, she'll be thinking she's in charge."

"She is in charge," said Virgil, smiling at Haley and giving her a wink.

She returned the smile with one of her own. "Ok, now that we've established that I'm always right and—"

"We will agree to disagree," blurted Cameron, crossing his arms across his chest and smirking at her.

"Fine," she said. "How about we follow me because I know which way to take that won't end with you falling down a volcanic vent."

Cameron was quiet for a moment. "Fine…but just this once."

"And every subsequent time after this," whispered Virgil.

The three of them made their way just outside of the rock formation. Haley pointed them to the west and began walking. The sky was just as lit up as when they had gone to sleep. They had learned in class some years back that even though this side of IO never faced the sun, it was always well lit by Jupiter, which was all that could be seen from any direction. Unfortunately for them, they were not able to regulate their sleep time to reflect day and night. They knew that this would only be the case until they traveled west enough to make it to the eastern side on the sun-facing side of IO.

"How much farther to the sun side?" Cameron asked, even though they had only been walking for a few minutes.

Haley held up the map as she walked. "At this pace, we'll be getting to the sun side by the time the sun rises."

"Cool…'cause we're almost out of water," said Virgil, hoping that his nonchalant tone would be enough to not worry them. This turned out not to be the case.

Haley and Cameron stopped immediately, as they watched Virgil continue walking.

"What do you mean we're almost out of water?" The trembling in Haley's voice was enough to make Virgil stop and turn to face them.

"These packs," he said, as he held one up in front of them, "were only designed for a single person for one day. As you can see, there are three of us, so the water will last for a third of the time." He let the words sink in as he swung the bag back over his shoulder.

"We just have to hope that there's some sort of outpost when we cross into the sun side," said Cameron, hoping to calm Haley down.

She took a deep breath and began walking again. She knew that worrying about it would not make their situation any better.

The three of them continued their journey to the light. Shortly after leaving their rest area, Virgil had decided against using his *Gift* to cover their tracks. He felt that he may need to conserve whatever energy he had for their trek. He slowed his pace ever so slightly, making it so that Cameron and Haley were a few feet in front of him. He looked at them and had a flashback of a time some years ago when they were very young. He longed for the times when life was simpler. When they were not on the run for their lives. He longed for the times when they knew nothing of the world, only of the bonds of friendship that they shared.

Cameron turned back to see Virgil. "You alright, dude?"

"Yeah," said Virgil. "Just thinking about when we were kids."

Cameron was quiet for a moment, remembering some of his best times from their childhood. "Hey, you remember the time when—"

"Hide!"

Cameron and Virgil turned to see Haley making a run for some nearby rocks. Without questioning, they ran to the rocks.

"What is it, Haley?" Virgil was still not sure what was going on.

Without saying a word, Haley pointed to the horizon.

At first, Virgil and Cameron didn't see anything. Then, as if at the same time, they saw a black speck in the sky that appeared to be growing larger by the second. Virgil's eyes widened, realizing that the rocks would not provide enough cover if the thing coming toward them went over their heads. He searched for the tallest rock he could see, which he found was just barely as tall as he and Cameron.

"Quick," he said as he reached for Haley's arm. The three of them made it to the rock and he motioned for Haley to get in between himself and Cameron. The rumbling from the flying machine grew louder and louder. He used his *Gift* to camouflage them to the rock.

"That won't be enough Virgil," said Haley. "That thing is going to have infrared on it. It's going to see us, even if we're cloaked."

"How could you possibly know that?" Cameron's tone was neutral, knowing that now was not the time to annoy anyone.

"She feels it," said Virgil, suddenly realizing that Haley was much more powerful than he had initially thought.

"How did you know that?" Haley openly stared at him, trying to figure out how he knew.

"It makes perfect sense," Cameron said. Virgil and Haley looked at him, their foreheads wrinkled. "If she can see and hear frequencies...she must be able to feel the vibrations and frequencies on the visible spectrum, even infrared waves." Their jaws gaped as they stared at him.

"What?" Cameron shrugged his shoulders. "You two think you're the only ones who pay attention in class?"

"Uh, yeah," said Haley. "Wow, Cameron, I didn't know you had it in you."

Their amazement was short lived, as the aircraft was nearly on top of them.

"Stay very still," Virgil said, as he took a deep breath and shifted his focus to his *Gifts*. Slowly, the sand and ash at their feet began to rise. It began to envelope them, much like a cocoon. Haley smiled as the blanket of dirt and ash rose above her head, only inches from her face. She knew that behind this curtain, they would be invisible to any instrument on the aircraft approaching them.

Cameron looked back just as the blanket went over his head. He saw the aircraft right above them, about thirty feet off the ground.

* * *

"The tracks stop here, sir." The guard turned around to give the warden an assessment of the situation. On the screen was a display of a video feed from a camera mounted on the bottom of the drone that had taken a hover position just above the escaped pupils.

"Very well," said Hersch. "Deploy the probe."

"Yes, sir." With that, the guard pressed a button on his display.

* * *

"What's that sound?" Haley began to breath rapidly.

"It sounds like a door of some kind," Virgil said.

"Can't you use your sonar or something to see through our cover?" Sweat began to build on Cameron's forehead.

Haley shook her head. "Sonar requires me making noise…and if I make any noise, that thing will find us."

* * *

The warden watched as a small craft exited the bottom of the drone, making its way to the surface below. It circled the entire area of rocks, then landed on the very rock that masked the targets of its hunt.

"Anything?" The warden was now standing over the guard's shoulder.

"The tracks appear to stop just outside of the rocks." He pointed to the screen and the readings taken by the probe.

"Are there any heat signatures?"

"No, sir...we thought there were when the drone was on approach, but we were mistaken."

"No," said Hersch. "You weren't mistaken. Perform tests of the area and move on. We're getting close." He walked away from the guard and sat in his command chair.

* * *

Cameron and Virgil looked at each other, eagerly waiting on the craft to leave the area.

WHAM!

Virgil and Cameron watched in horror as a metal rod smashed through their blanket of dirt directly in the middle of them. Haley looked up to see a piece of metal an inch from her head. She bit her lip to keep from screaming. The bitter taste of blood flooded her taste buds. It took everything in her not to gag. As they stared at the piece of metal, Virgil was struck by the thought that if the probe had come down only a few inches in either direction, he or Cameron would be dead.

After what seemed like a lifetime, the metal rod retracted. They heard a small humming noise and then heard it disappear over the sound of the other aircraft. Shortly after the small craft was gone, they heard the larger craft begin to rev its engines. After a minute, the aircraft flew away. They remained hidden until they could no longer hear it.

Excited to be free of detection, Virgil obliterated the blanket of dirt that was hiding them into a million pieces. He hugged Cameron and Haley as the dirt and ash rained down on them like snow. Cameron climbed to the top of the rock to get a better look. Virgil stared at Haley as he gently wiped the dirt from her face. Slowly, he brushed his hand on her cheek, using his thumb to wipe the tears from her face. He leaned forward to kiss her, but she put her hand on his chest to stop him.

"That wouldn't feel too pleasant right now," she said, as she pushed out her lower lip to expose the gash she caused when she bit into it.

"I can kiss it and make it feel better," he said, moving his eyebrows up and down.

"Really?" She squinted her eyes and smiled as she stepped back.

"Or…Cameron can heal it for you and we can be on our way."

"Cameron can do what exactly?" He climbed down to join them on the ground. Virgil pointed to Haley's lip as he dusted himself off.

"Piece of cake," said Cameron, as he took her hands into his and closed his eyes to concentrate. He opened his eyes and brought his attention to her lip. Haley stared at the swirling purple in his eyes, attempting to take her mind off of the pain on her lip. She squinted as she felt the split in her lip begin to seal as if it were being sewn back together. After a few seconds, the pain was gone and her lip was healed.

"I don't care what they say about you, Cameron, I think you're alright." Haley smiled as she rubbed her finger across her lip, feeling the spot where the gash once was.

Cameron stuck out his tongue and shook his head at her.

"Hey, come take a look at this," said Virgil. He was standing with a small pair of binoculars that he pulled out of the pack.

He handed them to Cameron and pointed in the direction that they would be walking. "What am I looking at exactly?"

"Do you see that tall structure that's perpendicular to the horizon?"

"What the heck is that?" Cameron still did not understand what he was looking at.

"Let me see." Haley took the binoculars and studied the object. "It's an environmental tower," she said. "They encompass the entirety of the sun-facing side of IO." Virgil and Cameron remembered hearing about them in class. "They work off of line-of-sight," she continued. "They work to create an artificial atmosphere."

Virgil squinted his eyes. "I thought that each colony had an artificial atmosphere around them."

"They do," she said. "But that is only until the terraforming is complete in another few years. Until then, they need to create an atmosphere around each colony so that the people can breathe and work outside."

"As much as I hate to interrupt your science class…I would really like to start moving." Cameron was already walking away as he spoke.

Haley and Virgil looked at each other then caught up to Cameron.

* * *

Meanwhile, back in Purgatory, the warden had made his way back to his office. He pressed a button on his desk and the holographic screen appeared. A man appeared and faced the screen.

"What is it?"

"We have a problem," said Hersch.

"Yes, I have been briefed," responded the man.

"No, Father, you have not been told everything."

"Which is what exactly?"

"One of the pupils who escaped is Raine's son," said Hersch, as he rubbed the back of his neck.

"That's impossible," scoffed the man. "His family was killed in the revolt."

"Apparently, that is not the case. I found his file in Numeyer's personal safe."

The man was silent for a long moment. "You must not let them get away. This is no longer a mission to capture them. You will kill him, and his friends. Is that understood?"

"Yes, Father."

CHAPTER FOURTEEN

A Change in Atmosphere

After a few hours of walking, the distant pillars were now towering in front of them, only now the true structure was visible. The tower they had been walking toward was in fact an obelisk. Not knowing what to expect, Virgil had been concealing their movements for the last hour, in an attempt to not alert anyone to their presence. This strategy paid off, as Virgil watched a guard at the base of one of the pillars pacing side to side.

"We have company," said Virgil, pointing in the direction of the obelisk. He then raised the binoculars to the top of the pillar, which did not appear occupied. "It looks like we only have the one to deal with." He handed the binoculars to Cameron. Virgil crouched back down behind the rock that was shielding them from sight. It was barely enough to cover the three of them, and he knew that they would need to be on the move sooner rather than later.

"I say we casually walk up to him like we're lost, then take him out." Cameron did not look at Haley and Virgil when he spoke. If he had, he would have seen their blank stares.

"That would be fine...if we hadn't just escaped from a maximum security kiddie prison," retorted Haley, with as much sarcasm as she could muster. "They probably have our faces plastered on every guard screen on IO." She snatched the binoculars from him and motioned him to sit back down next to Virgil.

"No need to be rude about it," Cameron said.

Haley ignored his response, choosing to concentrate on the situation at hand. "Ok...these obelisks are spaced out every seven miles or so. What if we make our way to the middle of two of them and go in from there?"

"But isn't the field between the obelisks energized?" Virgil was thinking back to their science classes about IO.

"The obelisks are energized, but not the field that connects them." By the looks on their faces, Haley knew she would have some more explaining to do. "Imagine that IO is one big over-sized battery. Each of these pillars are buried twenty feet or so beneath the surface. Below that, there is a steel cable that goes down an additional three hundred feet." She gave them a second to catch on.

Virgil nodded, finally remembering their lessons. "The steel cable takes that energy and directs it toward the obelisks." Haley nodded at his correct assertion. "The pillar then takes the charge to power the generator inside of it, which then releases an energy wave that connects to the next pillar." It had all come back to him now.

"Right...clearly you two know what you're talking about, but I don't. Can we walk through it or not?" Cameron's tone was growing anxious.

Virgil shook his head, "We can't take the chance that it sets off an alarm or something when we break the energy wave as we pass through it."

Cameron nodded as he looked to Haley to see how she would weigh in. "Great," said Cameron. "So how do we get past the guard?"

Before he could answer, Haley moved her head from behind the rock. She was now exposed to the guard, should he happen to turn in her direction. She was hoping that they were far enough away that she would look like part of the rock.

She closed her eyes and took a deep breath, giving herself to her *Gifts*. She opened her eyes and looked at Virgil and Cameron. "Be ready to move when I say so." They nodded as they stared at the swirling purple in her eyes. Then, she moved from behind the rock completely and sat with her legs crossed, seated on the ground.

She put her lips together and whistled an almost inaudible tune. Right away, she put her hands out in front of her. They could not see what she was doing, but they made sure to not interrupt her.

Haley concentrated as she used her hands to corral the rainbow of colors in front of her eyes. Once she amassed the sound waves into a ball, she began to push on the sides of the wave, making it narrow. After several seconds, she had transformed the sound waves in the shape of a small spear. She placed her hand gently under the sound wave and began to raise it. As she did so, she began to stand up. She came to a stop once she was on her feet and the audio spear was chest level. She turned her body to the side, pulling her right hand back as she turned. With all her might, she smashed her hand into the wave, sending it hurling toward the unsuspecting guard.

At that moment, the guard turned as he saw the silhouette of a person in the distance. He reached for his comm device on his hip. Just as his finger was about to touch the call button, an ear-piercing high-pitched ring went through his head. He fell to the ground and began convulsing. As he lay on the ground, just before his eyes glossed over, he saw the silhouettes of three people standing over him.

"Is he dead? Did I kill him?" Haley felt dizzy, as if in a dream. She never thought she would be responsible for anyone's death.

Virgil leaned over and put a finger on the guard's neck in an attempt to find a pulse. Unable to settle in one place, Haley paced as she waited on word from Virgil. He let out a huff as he stood back up. "He's alive...barely," he said, as he gave Haley a comforting hug. He lowered his head so that he was eye level with Haley. He met her gaze and smiled. "He won't be getting up anytime soon," he said, as he cupped her face with his hands. He gently wiped the tears from her face.

She felt an overwhelming sense of comfort and protection at that moment. Almost as if nothing and no one else but them existed. She reached out her hand and placed it on his cheek. "Thank you," she said, as she leaned in to kiss him.

"Ok, that will be enough of that," interrupted Cameron, as he squeezed in between the two of them before their lips touched. Haley pulled away from Virgil, lowering her chin and looking up at Cameron. He waved her off, knowing that there immediate situation trumped her puppy love.

That however, did not stop Haley from sucker punching Cameron in the stomach as she walked past him. "Was that really necessary?" Cameron did his best to pretend that the hit did not stun him.

"Oh, I'm sorry…I didn't see you there." She brought her right hand up to her face so that her fingers were covering her mouth.

He rolled his eyes and looked over to Virgil. "Come on, let's get him inside and get out of here."

Virgil slid his hands underneath the guard's armpits and waited until Cameron had a firm hold of his ankles before he picked him up. They quickly moved him to the tower. "Wait," Haley said, as she examined the tower wall. They stopped to see what was getting her attention. "What do you guys notice about that wall?" She didn't point to any particular area in front of her.

"Ugh," huffed Cameron. "Enough with the riddles...let's just get him in the door and..." A wave of stupidity rushed over him, as he now knew what she was asking. He turned his head and squinted in Virgil's direction. "Dude...aren't you supposed to be a genius or something?"

Virgil's eyes moved up to the sky, not having a proper excuse for missing the fact that there was not a door visible anywhere on the wall. "Listen...if you have a complex mathematical equation or a question with regards to logic and reason, I'm your guy." He used his head to point over to Haley. "If you want common sense, that's all Haley."

Haley's thin smile was hidden from their view, as she now was touching the surface of the tower in an attempt to find a hidden entrance. Instinctively, she changed her visual perspective and was now seeing the world of color around her. She stepped back several feet until the entire wall was in her field of vision. She then brought her lips together and whistled an inaudible tone. She watched as the color vibration rippled out and collided with the surface in front of her. The sound predictably smashed into the wall and was reflected off, in all areas but one. "There," she said, pointing to the left side of the wall, only feet from the corner. She took a breath and was back to her normal eyesight.

Virgil and Cameron put the guard back on the ground and made their way to the wall. They slid their hands along the surface, hoping to find the edge of the door and pry it open. As Virgil's hands passed over the surface, he noticed something out of the corner of his eye. At that moment, he knew what had to be done. "Hey, Cam, come pick up his feet," he said, as he reached down and picked up the guard's upper body. Cameron did as he was asked. He tilted his head to the side, unsure of what Virgil had in mind. "Move him in front of the door, with his right hand closest to it."

They carried the guard to the door, but nothing happened. They stood the guard up so that his full weight was now on their shoulders. Virgil took the guard's right arm and waved it from side to side, hoping to activate a proximity sensor. They heard a loud beep and quickly stepped back. The area where they knew the door to be started to shake, while the rest of the wall remained still. After a moment, the door disappeared, giving splashing light onto the floor at their feet.

"It's a holo-door," said Virgil, answering the unasked question on Haley and Cameron's faces. "They can mold it to any shape they like. It's not visible from this side, but once we're inside, it will appear to us as a glass window." He waited a moment for them to comprehend what they were seeing. As they gained their bearings, he reached down and pulled the proximity band from the guard's wrist. "Leave him here," Virgil said, motioning Cameron to lay the guard down.

"We can't just leave him here to die," Haley said, biting her lip.

"Don't worry," Cameron said, as he gently placed the guard on the ground. "When it comes time for him to check in, they will realize he's missing and come looking for him."

"But what if they don't get to him in time?"

"Don't worry, Haley, he'll be fine." Virgil had come to her side and placed his hand on the middle of her back. That slight touch was enough to make Haley calm down and relax.

"You're right…I'm just afraid that if we got caught that they would add murder to our list of crimes." She looked up at Virgil, then made her way into the tower. Cameron and Virgil followed her in. Once the three of them were inside the obelisk, they turned to watch the door close. They heard a slight hissing noise, but nothing else happened.

"When's it gonna close?" asked Cameron, tilting his head to the side and pursing his lips.

"It's already closed," Virgil said. He picked up a small rock and threw it what looked like an open door. It bounced right off and hit the ground. "Someone could've been standing here the entire time we were out there and we never would have known."

"That's pretty cool," said Cameron. "Now, where do we go from here?" He began to look about their surroundings.

"Up," replied Haley, as she walked toward the center of the space. The inside of the tower was the size of the Dome in Purgatory. All four walls were lined with bulky electrical and power systems. Haley instinctively walked to the center of the structure, as there was a thin white light that came from the top of the tower straight to the floor.

Once all three of them were inside of the beam of light, Haley motioned Virgil to place the proximity band near the small console next to her, just outside of the light. Once he did, they began to be lifted off the ground. As they rose, Virgil kneeled down and touched the invisible platform that was raising them to the top of the tower. "Now this is pretty cool," he said, as he stood back up.

As they neared the ceiling, a circular portal opened to exactly the size of the beam of light around it. The lift came to an abrupt stop just as their feet cleared the opening. They were now in a space half the size of the one they had traveled up from. The space was dimly lit, making it hard for them to get their bearings. Virgil was the first to leave the platform, making his way over to a console near the far wall.

He smiled when he reached the console, realizing what he was now able to do. "Watch this," he said, as he swiped the proximity band over the console, making the screen light up. He touched the screen toward the top and began to slowly drag his finger downwards. As he did so, the pyramid-shaped walls began to appear translucent. The more he moved down, the lighter the panels got. He completed the movement on the screen and a moment later, the entire space was filled with light. The walls now appeared as windows.

"It's the most beautiful thing I've ever seen," said Haley, slowly shaking her head in disbelief.

They fanned out, each taking a side to look out of. Virgil saw the energy barrier that connected this obelisk to the next some seven miles away. From his vantage point, he was now able to see the barrier not only extend outward, but upwards as well. Haley was seeing the same on opposite side, but in much more detail. She focused her vision on the barrier and was surprised to see subtle pulses of energy only she would be able to see. They reminded her of the lightning strikes she studied in her science class, and for that brief second, she actually missed her studies. Her thoughts were quickly squashed, as Cameron yelled for them to come to his side.

"You guys need to see this," he said, without taking his eyes away to look at them.

Haley and Virgil joined him and were momentarily in a state of shock. As they looked in the distance, they saw what appeared to be a city. It spanned most of the horizon. Taking turns with the binoculars, they saw buildings several stories tall and small white domes they assumed were homes. Encircling the colony, they saw luscious green vegetation and trees.

"What is that place?" Cameron directed his question at Haley, who was in possession of their map. He nudged

Haley with his elbow, trying to get her to focus on his question.

"Oh...sorry," said Haley, shaking her head and pulling out the map. She pointed the map directly at the city in front of her. "That is the colony of Zal. It is the easternmost colony."

"Eastern? We've been heading west this entire time. How could this possibly be east?" Cameron scratched his head. "I'm so confused."

Virgil patted him on the shoulder. "You're not going crazy. We were on the backside of IO. As we arrived here, we crossed from the dark-side to the sun-side, at the easternmost point," he said, pointing to Zal.

"Let's get going," Haley interrupted. She did not want to wait on Cameron to figure out what Virgil had just explained. "Let's get whatever supplies we can from here and get moving."

Cameron and Virgil were all business again. Virgil went back to the console and slowly adjusted the pyramid walls back to their original setting. The three of them then made their way back to the lift. Shortly after the floor opened underneath their feet, they were descending.

Virgil caught sight of a door on the western wall that read *Storage*. "Jackpot," he said, pointing to the door.

They were on the move as soon as the platform touched the ground. Seeing no knob, Virgil lifted his wrist to the plaque that was mounted in the middle of the door. It gave a low beep, then dissolved into thin air. They made their way inside and began to look around.

"The breathers are on empty...we should grab a few more." Cameron was reaching for the box labeled *Breathers* just above his head.

"We won't need any once we're on the other side of this tower," said Virgil.

"That's not entirely true," Haley said, thinning her lips as she turned to face Virgil. "When we were upstairs, I saw a dome around Zal."

"What?" Virgil tilted his head to the side. "But you said—"

"I know what I said earlier, but that was before we were up there." She took a breath and continued, "I guess they aren't done with the artificial atmosphere yet. We can probably breathe on that side, just not very well. Especially if they have a dome over the colony."

"So...more breathers?" Cameron still had his arm raised, waiting for the go-ahead. He grabbed the box once he saw Virgil nod his head. Once he put the box on the ground, he reached for a survival pack from a lower shelf.

Haley followed suit. They spent the next few minutes stuffing their three packs with as many supplies and rations as they could fit.

"Make sure everything is spread out equally," said Virgil. "Just in case we get split up in there."

As soon as they were all packed up, they exited the space and made their way toward the wall opposite from which they entered. They put the backpacks on their shoulders and used the waist strap to secure them properly.

"You ready?" Virgil had finished fitting his breather and was now looking to them, waiting for their response. They nodded, as he moved his wrist to the panel next to the door. With a click, the door was gone. In front of them, some ten feet, was another door, separating them from their new environment. They made their way to the second door and again, he lifted his arm until he heard a click. When the door disappeared, they stepped out onto the sand. Once they were clear of the door, it solidified once more.

As they began to walk, a small flash caught Cameron's attention out of the corner of his eye. He stopped to look in the direction of the flash, but only saw a big pile of sand.

"What's wrong?" Virgil saw that something was bugging Cameron.

"I'm not really sure," Cameron said, as he walked over to the source of the flash. "Hahahahaha…" He turned, smiling at Haley and Virgil.

They looked at each other, then back at Cameron. They figured he was beginning to lose his mind.

Seeing the look on their faces, he lifted his left hand, as if to ease their concern. "Today, we are riding in style." With his right hand, he grabbed at the pile of sand and pulled hard. The next second, there in front of their eyes, was what appeared to be a hover cycle.

Cameron let out a loud laugh, followed by Haley and then finally by Virgil.

"Looks like our luck is starting to change for the better," said Virgil, making his way to the cycle.

"I'm driving," yelled Cameron, as he leaned over to grab the handle.

"Maybe next time," Virgil said, as he waved his wrist in front of Cameron's face. With a smile, Virgil sat down and put his hands on the handles, instantly powering the cycle on.

"You suck, dude." Cameron stepped back, allowing Haley to get in the middle behind Virgil. Once she was seated, she wrapped her arms tightly around Virgil's stomach. He turned and gave her a smile, gesturing for Cameron to hop on. Before sitting down, he lifted part of the seat, which then acted as a backrest. This way he wouldn't have to hold on to anyone.

Once the three of them were ready to go, Virgil pressed the green square button near his right thumb. Suddenly, a digital display similar to the one on Haley's map appeared. He tapped the area on the map that said *Zal*. The cycle then gave a low hum and lifted from the ground.

"Here we go," said Virgil.

Within a few minutes, the obelisk was no longer visible. The colony of Zal was now directly ahead of them.

CHAPTER FIFTEEN

Zal Penitentiary

As they neared the outer perimeter of Zal, Virgil cloaked them, as to not be seen by anyone on patrol or on the lookout for them. He eventually brought them to a stop one hundred yards from the gate. From there, they would be able to get a good view of the patrols and formulate a plan.

"I say we go on foot from here," said Virgil, examining the entrance through the binoculars.

"I was afraid you were gonna say that," said Cameron, shaking his head.

"There…look," interrupted Haley, as she pointed to a group of settlers who were walking along the perimeter a couple hundred yards from the gate. "We can make our way in with them." She looked over at Virgil. "You just have to cloak us long enough to get to those buildings past the crops."

He gave her a nod and quickly cloaked them. They paced themselves enough so that as they were arriving to the gate, so were the group of settlers. As they came closer, they realized that everyone in the group, except for the man pulling the wagon, was old. The young man had broad shoulders and stood a full six inches over Cameron or Virgil. He appeared chained to the wagon that had only two wheels. He looked to be wearing a harness, breathing calmly as he pulled. The three of them slowed down slightly, trying to get a look in the back of the wagon.

They were shocked to see several more settlers, even older than the ones walking alongside. As they looked about, a very old woman gave a warm smile in their direction. Virgil was momentarily stunned. He knew there was no way she could see them. He dismissed it as a smile meant for another in her party.

The well-built man at the helm of the wagon came to a stop just in front of the gate. Two men wearing breathers came out of their guard shack, fitting their breathers as they walked. They had both of their hands on their sonic rifles, ready to fire at a moment's notice. "What is your business here?" The guard on the left addressed his question to the man leading the wagon.

"The same business we have every day," said the large man, wiping the sweat from his brow.

Virgil was intrigued by the fact that the man, along with all of the elderly in the wagon, did not require a breather. His pondering was quickly replaced by a whipping noise. WHACK!

"You will address me correctly, convict, or so help me…" The guard stretched the metallic whip out once again, ready to strike.

The man did not flinch when he was hit, instead looking over to a woman directly behind him. She took a tired breath and softly closed her eyes. The man turned back to face the guard. "Prisoner 61224 returning from the mines, sir." His jaw tightened as his eyes found the guard's face.

"See, was that so difficult?" asked the guard, as he pressed the whip's handle into the man's chest. He looked to the other guard and motioned for him to open the gate. He obliged and spoke into a comm device that was built into his wrist band. After a moment, the area in front of the gate dissolved away, leading into another area the size of their dining hall. This area was meant as the buffer between Zal and the outer elements.

The three of them kept pace just behind the wagon as Prisoner 61224 pulled it in. Again, Virgil caught sight of the old woman smiling.

Once inside the buffer zone, the gate behind them solidified, followed by an opening of the area in front of them. Once they exited the buffer zone, there was a guard waiting to escort the prisoners to their quarters. As the barrier solidified behind them, the three of them quietly let out the breath they had been holding for the past minute or so.

As they were regaining their composure near the rear of the wagon, the elderly woman who had smiled earlier was now seated at the edge, her feet hanging over the moving wagon. She smiled once again. "That's a clever trick, young man." She said it so softly, that Virgil nearly didn't hear it. Once he realized she was looking directly at him, he tripped. He quickly caught himself and due to his momentum, was now only a few feet front the wagon. He looked over at Haley and Cameron, but they did not seem to notice.

The old woman reached out her arm right in front of Virgil. She then threw herself forward, falling out of the back of the wagon. Without thinking, he reached out his hand to grab hers and prevent her from being hurt. She grinned, as she looked from Haley over to Cameron. Their eyes opened wide, thinking that they were no longer cloaked. It took all of Virgil's energy to keep concentrated enough to keep them cloaked while at the same time freaking out.

The woman used Virgil's hand as a cane, making sure not to fall behind from the wagon too much. "It's ok, child...they can't see you," said the woman, as she continued slowly forward. She squeezed his hand tight, not taking her eyes off of the road. "This is a dangerous place for your kind. You'd best to get out of here as fast as you came in."

"We can't," whispered Virgil. "We have nowhere else to go." His eyes darted from side to side, making sure no one else noticed that this woman appeared to be talking to herself.

The woman said nothing as they walked. She turned and looked up at Virgil. "Follow us into the prison compound, then meet me behind building two."

He looked over at Haley for reassurance, but she looked as confused as he did. Cameron was no help either. He just shrugged his shoulders, deferring to Virgil's judgment. Finally, Virgil gave in, looking at the old woman and nodding.

She gave him one more smile, then motioned him to the wagon. "Now help me back up there before I throw my back out." He gently put his head under her arm and lifted her back onto the wagon.

The three of them spent the next fifteen minutes walking well behind the wagon, out of range of anyone listening. "Do you think we can trust her?" Haley fidgeted with her hair as they walked.

"I don't think we have a choice," said Virgil. "She saw us, and she could've told someone, but she didn't." He looked over to Cameron. "At this point, I think we take our chances."

As they talked, they hadn't noticed that they were clear of the crops and approaching a wall some twenty feet high. From their point of view, they were far enough back to see three of the four walls of the compound. No buildings were visible from outside. Further down the semi-paved road, they saw the city. The closer and closer they went to the compound, they more nervous they became.

They quickly made their way to the wagon just as the compound gates were opening. Once the gate was open, the wagon moved forward. The guard manning the gate began to close it, even before the wagon was clear. The three of them had to rush to the side of the wagon, just missing the gate closing behind them.

Virgil raised his left arm, motioning for Haley and Cameron to stop. They let the wagon continue forward as they stayed back, assessing their situation. Sadly, there was not much to see in the compound. It was approximately the size of two football fields, with buildings lining either side of the road. At the end of the short road, there stood a building marked, *Administration.*

The wagon made it half way down the road before coming to a stop. A guard appeared from one of the buildings and walked over to the man pulling the wagon. He appeared to have unlocked the man, who then dropped the harness to the ground. The guard grabbed the reins and motioned for another man to grab the wooden bar of the wagon to keep it steady.

The man who had pulled the wagon was now assisting the elderly with exiting the back of the vehicle. Once he was finished, he again grabbed the wagon, this time moving it to the back on the building that the guard had exited from. Once everyone was cleared from the road,

Virgil cocked his head to the right, signaling Haley and Cameron to follow him behind a building.

Once they were behind the building and safely out of sight, Virgil removed the cloak. "Ok, I'm going to track down that old lady…you two wait for me here." He put his hand on Haley's shoulder as she shook her head in disapproval of his idea to separate.

"Don't worry…I'll be fine," he said, looking her in the eyes. "Just stay out of sight and I'll be back as soon as I can."

"Don't worry, dude," said Cameron. "I'll take care of her."

"In that case," Haley interrupted, "I'm going with you, Virgil."

Cameron's smile turned into a scowl. Haley backhanded him lightly in the chest, making sure he knew it was only a joke.

Virgil cloaked himself and began walking toward the road. He stood in the middle of the road, trying to remember what building the old lady mentioned. He looked at the administration building and then to the buildings on either side of the road. Each building had a number written in black paint. The odd number buildings were on the left side and the even number buildings were on the right. He then remembered that she said building two.

Virgil quickly walked up the road until he was in front of the building. He quietly walked to the open door and found that this was their dining hall. The food had a foul odor, but this did not bother him. He felt as if he hadn't eaten in days. His only source of nutrition since escaping Purgatory had been emergency rations.

Distracted by the smell of food, he neglected to hear a pair of guards approaching from behind him. By the time he did, it was too late. He had no time to move out of the way. The only thing he had time to do was position his body sideways, minimizing the area he took up in front of the door. Unfortunately, this was not enough to stop the guards from running into him. The right shoulder of one guard, followed by the left shoulder of the other guard hit Virgil at nearly the same moment.

"Hey, watch where you're walking," barked the guard on the right.

"My apologies, sir," said the guard on the left. He stood there for a moment, scratching his head and staring at the area in front of the door. Unbeknownst to him, Vigil was already gone from that spot and near the back door of the building.

That was close, thought Virgil, leaning against the wall, wiping the sweat from his brow.

* * *

Three buildings back, Cameron and Haley waited patiently for Virgil's return. Cameron watched the side of the building, while Haley kept an eye on everything behind the building. Cameron caught sight of two guards on patrol on the road. He quickly pulled back from his position, thinking he may have been spotted.

"Hold up," said one of the guards. "I thought I saw something back there." The two guards turned and began walking in the direction of Haley and Cameron.

"I think they saw me," said Cameron, running over to Haley.

Haley put her finger to her mouth, signaling him to be quiet. She closed her eyes and listened for movement. To her horror, she heard what Cameron had suspected. Without thinking, she ran up to Cameron, hugging him tightly. She again closed her eyes and began to vibrate. Surprised by her sudden shaking, Cameron flinched. This only caused her to hold him more tightly.

The guards round the corner, weapons drawn. Cameron's eyes opened wide, as the barrel of the guard's rifle was only inches from his face. Instinctively, he hugged Haley tighter in an effort to shield her from what was certain pain. The second guard walked around the first, looking around for any other sign of movement.

"There's nothing here," said the second guard. He lowered his rifle and began walking back to the road. The guard with the rifle to Cameron's face took one final look around, then lowered his weapon and walked off. "I could've sworn I saw something," he said, quickly making his way back to his partner.

Once Haley heard them walk away, she slowly loosened her hold on Cameron.

He grabbed her by the shoulders and held her at arm's length. "What the hell was that?" He was sweating heavily and breathing rapidly. "Those guys had us," he said.

"I phased us out of their vision," Haley said, shrugging her shoulders. She appeared calm, but inside she was shaking like a leaf. She couldn't believe she was able to do that. However, she did not want to make the situation worse by losing control like Cameron. She caught her breath and said, "Normal people can only see about one percent of the light spectrum."

"So…you just put us in a range that they couldn't see?" Cameron began to pace back and forth. "How did you know what they wouldn't be able to see?"

Haley opened her eyes wide and shrugged her shoulders. "Your guess is as good as mine."

* * *

Unaware of what was happening not far from him, Virgil sat on a metal container in the back of the dining hall. He was taking deep breaths, attempting to regain his composure from the incident at the entrance only moments ago.

CLICK…

He tensed up and rose to his feet as the back door cracked open just enough for a small person to squeeze through. After a moment, a small frail old woman appeared out of the entrance. She cleared the door and quietly shut it behind her. She looked around, as if unable to see Virgil fifteen feet in front of her.

"Step forward, child," she said, slowly walking away from the door.

Keeping himself cloaked, he slowly began to step forward.

"Ah, there you are," she said, stopping once she caught sight of him. She took a labored breath and motioned him over to assist her with standing. He obliged and made it to her in two strides. He took her by the arm and led her to the spot he had just vacated. He sat her down and waited for her to speak.

"Thank you, child...my strength isn't what it used to be."

"Of course," said Virgil, taking a seat on the ground next to her. "I have so many questions...I don't even know where to start."

"That will have to wait, I'm afraid...you don't have much time," she said, looking around to make sure she was not being seen. "It is only a matter of time before they catch you. You need to make your way to Euboea Montes."

"But, that's heading northwest...we were going to head west to Pele."

The woman shook her head. "You need help first. You need to find people like yourself who know the ins and outs of the colonies."

"My friends are never going to go for that," he said, scratching the back of his head.

"Your friends? I thought you were by yourself?"

"Oh, my apologies…I thought you saw them."

"Son, I barely saw you and you were right in front of me."

They shared a laugh, then quickly returned to planning. "Well, now that I know it's more of you, then you are really going to have a hard time not getting captured." She began to stand up. Virgil assisted her to her feet. "You know…all of this secrecy and law breaking is making me think of the good ole days." Her gaze strayed from Virgil to the empty sky behind him.

Virgil moved his head so that he was making eye contact with her once more. This snapped her out of her brief trip down memory lane. "Right," she said, bringing herself back to their conversation. She reached out with her left hand, "My name is Maggie…Maggie Hawthorne."

Virgil stepped back slightly, increasing the space between them. "Do you know someone named Haley Hawthorne?"

Maggie moved her hands to her mouth, nearly unable to stand. After a moment, her eyes welled up with tears. No longer able to stand, she sat back down. "She's my granddaughter."

CHAPTER SIXTEEN

On the Road Again

"Your granddaughter?" Vigil placed his hand on Maggie's shoulder. "This is great news," he said, kneeling down to look her in the eye.

"No," she said, sobbing uncontrollably. "She can't know that I'm alive...not right now." She stood up and made her way back to the door.

"But, I can't keep that from her," Virgil said, this time not following her. "She would never forgive me."

She reached the door and lightly knocked three times. "I've arranged for a guide for you, but you won't have much time." The door opened and the huge man who had pulled the wagon was now standing in front of them.

The man's face was unreadable. Virgil didn't know if he was going to help him or kill him. Then, the man smiled big and grabbed Virgil's hand.

"I'm Yuri," said the man, with a thick Russian accent. Virgil had recognized it from the countless videos they sat through in history class.

"Pleasure," said Virgil, trying his best not to wince at the pain the Russian giant was inflicting on his hand.

Seeing his discomfort, the man released his grip. "Sorry, I don't know my own strength sometimes."

With a renewed sense of purpose, Maggie touched both of them on the shoulder. "Yuri will get you and your friends to Zal. He has family there who can get you safely out of the city and on your way to Euboea Montes."

"My family run Zal," said Yuri, as he smacked Virgil square in the back. "I get you there, and you get me out of here." He looked over at Maggie, as if confirming the deal she made with him. Maggie nodded and Yuri stepped back, waiting on her to finish her conversation with Virgil.

"Now go and get your friends. You don't have much time." She turned and motioned Yuri to open the door.

"Wait," said Virgil. "When do I tell Haley that I found and abandoned her grandmother?" He spoke the words with as much dry humor as he could muster.

Maggie took a deep breath. "Once you find Marcus Raine in Euboea Montes, then you can tell her." She grabbed the door and walked in. Before closing it, she turned to Virgil and said, "Thank you for taking care of my Haley. It means more than you know." A tear ran down her cheek as she turned and let the door close behind her.

"Come...we don't have much time," said Yuri, looking around to make sure they weren't seen. Virgil nodded and took a breath. He then cloaked the two of them and headed back to where he had left Haley and Cameron.

When they arrived, they found Cameron pacing back and forth and Haley sitting quietly on the floor.

"Time to go," said Virgil, surprising the two of them.

"It's about time, dude," Cameron said, walking over to Haley.

He and Haley both abruptly froze in place, as Virgil reappeared, this time with company.

Sensing their anxiety, Yuri quickly stepped forward to introduce himself. "I am Yuri...I will help you get to Zal."

Haley eyed Cameron, then they both eyed Virgil.

"He's cool," said Virgil.

"Can we talk to you for a sec?" Cameron gestured for him to the corner with himself and Haley.

Haley was the first to speak. "Seriously, Virgil…we don't know anything about this guy." She looked to Cameron for support.

"She's right, dude," Cameron said. "How do you know we can trust him?"

"Maggie said—"

"Who's Maggie?" Haley abruptly cut him off, feeling as if she and Cameron were out of the loop.

"She's the woman I met from the wagon. She said Yuri could help us…and I trust her."

"We must go now," interrupted Yuri.

Virgil nodded and turned back to Haley and Cameron. "He's from Zal…he knows how to get us in and out without being caught."

They finally relented and made their way to where Yuri was standing.

"Ok, we wait for guards to open gate and we go." Yuri had already planned on how they were getting out of the prison.

"That won't be necessary," said Haley, looking over to Virgil.

Without a word, Virgil cloaked everyone and began to lift them off of the ground. Yuri's eyes opened wide, realizing that he was floating in midair.

They traversed the wall with ease and landed gently on the other side of the wall. The road was to their right and Zal was straight ahead.

"Come," said Yuri. "We stay off road."

Virgil kept them cloaked as they put more ground between them and the prison.

They walked in silence for most of their trek through the barren fields. It was Yuri who broke the silence. "So…you guys prisoners too?"

"Sort of," said Virgil.

"What means this?" Yuri did not know how someone could sort of be held against their will.

"We didn't know we were prisoners until a short time ago." Haley was eager to clarify their position, as she did not want to come across as weak. "But we escaped…and now we need to figure out our next move."

"You come with Yuri…I take care of you." He gave her a big reassuring smile as he kept walking.

"How about you Yuri? What's your story?" Cameron took the opportunity to gain some knowledge on their new companion.

"I big man in Zal," he said, poking his thumb into his chest as he spoke.

"Duh," Haley said, poking her finger on Yuri's massive arms.

He laughed. "Ha…no, I can make people do what I want."

Cameron cocked his head to the side, hoping he would elaborate.

"I have power to get into someone's mind and make them do what I want."

"Can you also read their thoughts?" Virgil was intrigued by their new comrade. He initially figured that Yuri's sheer size would mean that his *Gift* would involve his strength.

Yuri shook his head. "Nyet."

"Can you show me?" Haley jumped in front of Yuri, hoping to see what he could do.

He shook his head. "I took shot today," he said. "I cannot do mind trick until tomorrow."

"Jedi mind trick," said Cameron, waving his hand from side to side.

"I do not know this Jedi," said Yuri, in an uncertain tone.

"Don't worry," laughed Cameron. "These aren't the droids you're looking for."

"Anyways," said Virgil, attempting to bring the conversation back to Yuri's abilities. "Is there anything else you can do?"

Yuri shook his head. "I did not know we could do more than one thing."

Virgil discreetly looked over to Haley and Cameron, hoping they would understand what he was wanting them to do. He wanted to make sure that Yuri knew as little as possible about their *Gifts* until they knew more about him. "So, you pretty much know what we can do," he said. "I can make us invisible, Cameron can levitate us, and Haley can see frequency waves."

"Like Maggie?"

Virgil gulped hard, afraid that his secret would show all over his face.

"You ok?" Haley saw the uncomfortable look on Virgil's face.

"Yeah, I'm ok. I just felt bad leaving all those people behind." All he could do was look at the ground, hoping that Yuri would not let out any damaging information.

Yuri looked at the two of them and continued, "I was caught three years ago and sent to the prison. My brothers try to free me, but they fail." Yuri picked up a rock and threw it to the side. "They are not special like me, so they leave me there. They give up on me."

Making it to the city wall was enough to bring Yuri out of the past. "We are here," he said, looking up at the wall, eager to get back home.

"Should I lift us up over the wall?" asked Cameron, eyeing Virgil.

"This will not be necessary," Yuri said in his heavy Russian accent. He walked over to what appeared to be a very large boulder near the wall a few feet away from them. He leaned forward and spoke a few words in Russian that they could not understand. A moment later, the entire rock dissolved away, revealing two very large tattooed men pointing rifles at them.

The two men began shouting in Russian, but did not lower their weapons. Yuri raised his arms, gesturing at the three of them and speaking very fast. Virgil was on edge, not realizing he kept rubbing his sweaty hand on his pant leg. He was prepared to throw the men into the air should Yuri's fast talking not work.

The two men suddenly lowered their rifles, yelling something to Yuri, then picked him up and hugged him.

"It is ok…these are my comrades," said Yuri, smiling as they loosened their grip on him. He walked past the men to an opening in the ground. "This tunnel will get us into Zal. From there, we go see my brothers." He waited for them to nod before climbing down. He was followed by Virgil, then Haley, and finally by Cameron. As Cameron turned to climb down, he noticed the two men return to the post and reactivate their optical illusion.

The tunnel was a short walk, then up another ladder. It appeared just long enough to get from one side of the wall to the other. As Virgil climbed out of the hole, he saw Yuri talking to another two men with guns. He watched as Yuri exchanged hugs and pleasantries with the men. He looked around as he helped Haley and Cameron out of the hole. They were between two small buildings.

Yuri walked back over to them. "This is supply route we use to smuggle…things." His vague answer was enough to keep the three of them from asking questions.

"Fantastic…what now?" Cameron was eager to get off of the street. One of the men nudged Yuri on the arm, squinting his eyes and pointing his chin at Cameron. Yuri uttered something to the man, prompting him to laugh. "What's so funny?"

"Nothing," said Yuri. "I tell him that you are girl pretending to be boy."

Haley snorted, unable to get a laugh out fast enough. "I like him," she said, looking over to Virgil. "Can we keep him?"

Knowing that they did not have much time, Yuri cut them off. "We go to center of city. There, we see my brothers and we get you going to Euboea Montes...ok?"

Haley and Cameron snapped their heads toward Virgil.

"I'll explain later," he said.

"Good," Yuri said. "If you girls are ready, we leave now."

CHAPTER SEVENTEEN

All In The Family

The group emerged from the vacant alley. The three of them stiffened their posture, looking at the city in front of them, then glancing at each other, wondering if they were all feeling the same thing.

"Look at that," said Haley, reaching out, as if able to touch the buildings in the distance.

"We go there," said Yuri, pointing to the center of the city. There, rising high above any other structure, was an obelisk. It was much like the ones they saw at the border. However, this one worked slightly different than the ones encircling IO. The buildings got smaller and smaller the farther away they were from the tower.

"That tower," explained Yuri, "it make shield for all of Zal. It sends energy into the air, then it creates dome that covers eight miles."

"Is this how all of the colonies are set up?" Haley asked her question while at the same time adjusting her sight to see the dome in all of its radiant colors.

"Da," he said. "All except the colony of Pele. That one is twice size of all others. You can see dome, yes?"

Haley nodded.

"Ok, let's get moving," interrupted Virgil, patting Yuri on the shoulder.

Haley returned her sight and joined the group.

As they walked, Yuri gave them more information on how the colonies were arranged. "All of the colonies start with the crops." He turned and pointed as they walked. "That is for about a mile. Then, there are homes for people who take care of crops. After that, there are homes for normal people." He waved his finger around, showing them that this was where they were currently walking through.

"So what do people do here exactly?" Cameron had no idea what kind of work could be found in such a small city.

"They build things," he said. "Everyone has job or responsibility in colonies. There is no room for parasites. If you do not work, you do not survive." He looked sternly at each of them, making sure his point was acknowledged.

"But what about the children and the elderly?" Haley was astonished at his statement. Surely, the elderly would not be forced to work.

He calmed her nerves, speaking softly and reassuringly. "The children have job in schools. The old work until they cannot work no more. Then, family take care of them."

There was a question that was nagging at Virgil. "So what about all of the elderly in the prison? What was their crime?"

Yuri's voice went flat. "Their crime was being special…like us. They are sent to the mines just outside of the barrier. There, they are forced into the mines."

"That's terrible," said Haley, shaking her head as she walked.

"That is the way of things," said Yuri.

They walked for a long while in silence down the deserted alleys. Occasionally, they would have to be cloaked by Virgil, as to not been seen by the authorities.

The silence was broken once again by the curious Russian. "So, how old are you kids?"

"We're not kids," snapped Cameron.

Yuri put his hands out, gesturing for Cameron to calm down. "Ok, ok…how old are you non-kids?" He smiled and smacked Cameron in the back, sending him a few steps forward.

"They're seventeen," said Haley, pointing at Virgil and Cameron. "And I'm sixteen." She rolled her eyes, almost imperceptibly, as if she was being mocked for her age.

Yuri stopped walking, as if surprised by her response. "You guys are not eighteen yet? But your power…"

Collectively, they gave him a questioning stare, wanting him to elaborate further.

"When people like us turn eighteen, their full potential is unlocked in their body. But you three," he said, moving his eyes from one to another. "You are already powerful."

"What do you mean?" Haley moved closer to him.

"We can only do a little before we are of age. Before I was eighteen, I could only make suggestion in someone's mind. Now, I can make them do whatever I want."

"So you're saying that as soon as we turn eighteen, we will be able to do even more than we can now?"

Cameron was now in Yuri's face, making strong eye contact.

"Da. Your power will increase tenfold."

They gulped hard, realizing the enormity of the revelation. Now, more than ever, they needed to keep the full extent of their abilities a secret.

Seeing the looks on their faces, Yuri asked, "Who are your parents?"

"We don't know," answered Virgil, shrugging his shoulders. "We were taken from our families at a very young age."

Yuri thought for a moment, nodding his head. "Yes, I have heard of kids being taken. No one ever knows where they go."

They continued their trek toward the tower. They had passed the homes and were now walking in between two and three-story buildings. They made their way to the end of an alley. Yuri stood at the corner with his hand out, motioning for them to get against the wall. They moved to the wall and waited while a group of people walked by.

"Ok, we go now." Yuri waved them over to where he was standing. "We cross road to that building," he said, pointing to a small shop with plastic windows. It had a sign that read, *BORSCH.*

"Soup?" Cameron asked, in an uncertain tone.

"It belongs to my family. We get food and eyes for you guys."

"Uh, yeah…we already have eyes," said Cameron, opening his eyes wide, pointing to both with his fingers.

"Nyet," responded Yuri. "If you are seen with those." He pointed at each of their faces. "You have more trouble than just the authorities."

As they crossed the small road through the crowds, a large man, looking much like Yuri, appeared in the doorway of their intended establishment. Yuri stopped when he reached the man, speaking Russian and explaining their situation. After a moment, the Russian man reached out and gave Yuri a massive bear hug.

Yuri turned to his traveling companions. "Come, we go inside now." He walked into the building without turning to see if they were following him.

"I don't know about this, guys." Haley's voice crackled and her hands tightened at her sides as she spoke.

"We have to play this out," replied Virgil. He walked toward the entrance, turning his head as he entered. He knew they would follow him, but he wasn't quite sure of what he would be walking in to. The last thing he wanted was to put his friends in harm's way, but he knew that they did not have many options at the moment.

As the three of them stood in the entry of the restaurant, they saw only a handful of people sitting in the mostly empty tables. A short overweight man with a large bald spot stood behind the bar, wiping it with a towel as they walked by. His eyes never left them as they walked by, stalking their every movement. They reached Yuri in the back of the room, holding a door open, motioning them to enter.

"Do not worry about Oleg," he said, seeing the concern on their faces. "He is big teddy bear."

As they walked past him, Yuri nodded to the bartender, letting the door close behind him.

Oleg took his hand off the trigger of the gun under the bar that was tracking his new guests as they walked past him. He put down the rag and readjusted the gun on the swivel to face the entrance of his fine establishment. Once set, he turned and pulled a comm device from behind a bottle of vodka. "We have guests...Yuri is with them." He snickered and rolled his eyes as he placed the device back where he had retrieved it.

In the room behind the restaurant, the group walked to another door on the left, where the large man escorted them through. It took the three of them a moment to realize that they were now in the building next to the restaurant. Once inside, a large bookshelf was moved into the place of the door, hiding any evidence of their entry.

The space appeared to be a small warehouse, filled with liquor and all kinds of contraband. At the opposite wall stood a man behind a desk. Yuri straightened his back and walked toward the man.

The man raised his hands, prompting Yuri to stop. "I should kill you now where you stand." The man leaned forward, placing a gun on the desk.

"But..." Yuri began to walk again. "What would you tell Mama?"

The man's tight jaw eased, slowly turning into a weak smile. "I tell Mama you go crazy." The man came from behind the desk, hugging his brother tightly. "We thought you were dead," said the brother, holding Yuri's face in his hands, looking into his eyes. "What happened to you, Yuri?"

"Later, my brother." Yuri put his hand on his shoulder and turned to his guests. "Everyone...this is my brother Mikhail."

Mikhail turned to the three of them, methodically making eye contact with each. After examining them, he turned to Yuri. "Why have you brought outsiders into my place of business?"

Yuri rolled his head, knowing that this was against their rules. "They save me from prison…I owe them."

"Please," said Virgil, stepping forward. "We just need to get to Euboea Montes."

Mikhail moved his brother to the side and walked up to Virgil. "Da…this is no problem." He nodded as he smacked Virgil in the back. Suddenly, he pulled a gun from his back and pointed it squarely in Virgil's face, inches from his eyes. "You interrupt me one more time, and I put bullet in your skull."

Virgil said nothing, but nodded in obedience as he tightened his fists at his sides.

"Calm down, Mikhail," said Yuri, reaching up to lower the gun from Virgil's face. "They are like me, brother."

Mikhail turned his body so that he was not facing the three of them. He made some type of gesture to Yuri that they could not see. They saw Yuri look down and nod his head. "It is settled then," he said, turning back to face his guests. "You free my brother…we take you to Euobea Montes. A deal is a deal." He slapped Yuri on the chest as he walked back to his desk. He picked up a comm device and said something to someone in Russian.

Virgil couldn't help but watch Yuri as his brother spoke into the device. He recognized the blank looks. The dropping of one's chin to their chest. These were looks that he had come to know quite well in his years in Purgatory. It was a look of betrayal.

"Be ready for anything," he whispered.

Haley and Cameron hadn't seen what he saw, but they would heed his words regardless. They nodded their understanding.

Mikhail placed the comm device back in a desk drawer and walked back to the group. "Come. We get you eyes and some food." He pointed to the back of the space where another man sat drinking vodka. "ChtO eta?" The man quickly rose to his feet. "I need eyes," barked Mikhail.

The man opened a box to his side and pulled out a smaller box. He handed it to Mikhail and stepped back, putting his hands together and looking down. "Sorry, boss."

Mikhail handed the box to Yuri. "You in luck. I have for you and for your friends."

Yuri handed each of them a small container filled with liquid. He opened his and showed them what they needed to do. He placed his finger in the liquid and pulled out what appeared to be a small contact lense. "You put on your eyes…make you look normal." He placed the first lens and then the second. "This is how you stay hidden."

Cameron was the first to try. Virgil and Haley watched as he fumbled with the first lense, struggling to even get it on his finger. "Can I use that mirror?" He pointed at the wall, hoping it would alleviate his annoyance.

The three of them got to the mirror and after some initial issues, they were able to place the lenses on their eyes. It took them several minutes to get used to the feeling of a foreign object in their eyes. As the sensation became more comfortable, they stared at the mirror. They could not fathom that such a small change in their look could have such a profound impact.

"You see," said Yuri. "New eyes."

"Good…now we eat," said Mikhail as he walked toward the room they had previously come from. "Oleg makes the best borsch on IO."

They followed their host to a table at the back of the restaurant. Mikhail sat facing the door while Yuri sat to his left. Haley sat across from them, with Virgil and Cameron on either side of her.

Oleg arrived shortly after with a pitcher of water and a bottle of vodka. Yuri picked up the vodka and poured himself and Mikhail a generous serving. "You kiddies get the water," he said, pointing his chin toward the pitcher.

Virgil poured a glass for Haley and Cameron. "So, what's the plan?" He got straight to the point.

"The sun is almost down," replied Mikhail. "We take you to train first thing tomorrow morning." He gulped down a shot of vodka and gestured to Yuri to refill his glass.

"Tomorrow? Can't you just take us now?" Cameron clenched his jaw.

"Nyet. No trains run in the dark."

"Then we'll walk," said Cameron.

"There are things outside of the colonies that would eat you in an instant." Yuri nodded in agreement with Mikhail's statement.

"My brother is right, my friends. These creatures are not afraid of the dark. We leave at first light on the train. Tonight, you stay in safe place," Mikhail insisted.

"Ok," said Virgil reluctantly.

Oleg came back to the table with several bowls in tow. He placed one in front of each person. He handed a spoon to Mikhail and dropped the rest on the table. Yuri quickly grabbed a spoon and began to go to work on the borsch. He ate is if he hadn't eaten in years.

Haley and the boys picked up their spoons, unsure if they should eat or not. Cameron thought for only a moment, then began to devour the meal. He was so hungry for food that he did not think too long about the fact that it may be poisoned. He finished his bowl before Haley or Virgil even started.

Seeing their friend scarfing down his meal only made their hunger worse. Finally, Virgil gave in and stuffed a spoonful into his mouth. The flavors were like nothing he had ever tasted. He savored the bite just long enough to fill his spoon with another.

After all was said and done, they had each consumed three full bowls of borsch. Virgil looked over to Oleg, who was tapping his finger on the bar, opening his mouth to say something but stopping short.

Realizing that they had most likely eaten his profits for the day, Virgil reached into his bag and pulled out a coin. He walked up to the bar and placed the solid gold coin in front of Oleg. "That was the best meal I have ever had." He smiled and walked back to his table.

Oleg's eyes went wide, catching Mikhail's attention. "What did you give him?"

"I paid him for our meal." Virgil poured himself another glass of water.

Mikhail leaned forward, resting his hands on his chin and elbows on the table. "So tell me, how did you find Yuri?"

Virgil looked over to Haley and Cameron to make sure they were alright with him telling their story. Once he saw their approval, he said, "We escaped from one prison, only to find help in another." He went on for the next thirty minutes explaining their journey and how they got to Zal.

Mikhail and Yuri said nothing, occasionally nodding their heads and glancing at each other. "And that's it," Virgil said, conveniently leaving out the part about where they had more abilities than they were letting on.

"So, what is in Euboea Montes?" Mikhail leaned back in his chair. The effects of the vodka were starting to kick in. He picked up another glass to take a gulp.

"Marcus Raine," responded Haley.

Mikhail nearly choked on his vodka. Yuri shifted uncomfortably in his chair. Mikhail wiped his mouth and said, "How do you know him?"

"We don't," said Virgil.

Haley leaned forward in her chair. "We were told he could help us get safely to Pele."

Mikhail persisted, "Why we cannot take you there?"

Virgil was sensing that there was something wrong. "What are you not telling us?"

"Marcus Raine is very powerful man." Yuri did not look up as he took another shot.

Mikhail shook his head in agreement. "Marcus can destroy whole colony if he wanted to. He is number one enemy of the authority."

"So why doesn't he just destroy the colonies?" Virgil was not sure if he could trust what Maggie said.

"He is afraid his wife and son might die if he does this."

"So why would Maggie send us to someone who could kill us?" Haley too was now questioning what Virgil was told.

"He does not kill his own kind," said Yuri. "He goes from colony to colony, always searching for his family. He has been doing this for years." He looked over at Virgil and said, "He has gone mad."

"Great." Cameron threw his hands in the air, feeling defeated.

Haley had a similar response. "Let's just go straight to Pele and forget that guy. If he's —"

"No!" Virgil slapped the table, suddenly defensive.

Haley and Cameron were caught off guard. They had never seen Virgil overreact to anything. He was always the calm and calculating one.

After seeing the surprise, Virgil realized what he had just done. "I'm sorry...I don't know what got into me." He looked at his hands on the table, almost as if he were willing them to stay still. "We're going to Euboea Montes to find Marcus Raine." He looked to Cameron and then to Haley. "If you two want to go to Pele, then you're going to do it without me." He leaned back in his chair and exhaled deeply.

"Take it easy, man," responded Cameron, scratching the back of his head. "We just don't want to be killed by a crazy person."

"He's not crazy," snapped Virgil.

Cameron put his hands up, signaling to his friend that he was not his enemy.

Haley gently placed a hand on Virgil's shoulder. "How do you know?"

"Maggie."

"But you barely knew her either," said Haley.

"She is good woman," Yuri said, as he took another shot.

Virgil motioned to Yuri, hoping the Russian would make his case. Unfortunately for him, those were the only comments of Maggie that Yuri was willing to provide.

"What if she lied to you? Have you thought about that?" Haley was unwavering.

"Because I just know, ok." Virgil's tone softened, not wanting to argue with her. He knew that if she knew what he knew, she would not question him. *Because she's your grandmother!* He had the words at the tip of his tongue, but he did not have courage to utter them.

She gazed with focus at her friend. He was keeping something from her, but she hadn't the slightest idea what. "I won't stop until you—"

"Enough!" Mikhail slammed his glass down hard on the table, silencing Haley immediately.

"You children bore me," he said, waving over Oleg for another bottle. "In the morning, we go see Vladimir." He glanced over to Yuri, giving him a look that only they understood. "He will know what to do with…your friends."

Virgil looked at Yuri and thought he saw shame in the Russian's eyes, but before he could process his thought, the look was gone.

Slowly, Yuri stood up with the help of the chair. "Come, my friends," he said, slapping himself lightly on the face in an attempt to sober himself up. "I give you tour of Zal." He headed toward the front door.

"We don't have time for sightseeing," complained Cameron.

Haley interjected, "We still have a few hours of daylight left and nowhere to go."

With a huff, Cameron gave in.

The three of them exited the bar behind Yuri and stood at the entrance, taking a moment to examine their surroundings. They noticed much taller buildings only a few blocks away.

"The closer we get to the tower, the higher the buildings get." Yuri pointed from the edge of the dome to the tower.

As they walked, he pointed out that even though they were in a city, there were few electronics and even fewer vehicles. "There is no oil, so there are no cars from Earth. Everything here runs on solar or thermal power." They had trouble paying attention to their tour guide, as their senses were being assaulted like never before. Foods they had never smelled. The noises of a bustling city that they had never heard.

"How was all of this possible?" Cameron stared at the tall buildings in front of him. Each appearing to be housing of some kind. Very few looked to be purposed for anything else.

"Each ship that came from Earth had enough people and raw materials to build an entire city. Pele had two ships, which make them biggest."

"How long did it take to build all this?" asked Haley.

"It was built before I was born," said Yuri. "For thirty years they built. Each year making the tower a little higher. Each time the tower was built higher, the dome grew larger. Now, they do not have more supplies to make bigger."

Seeing a logical fallacy, Virgil asked, "If Zal's growth is finite, how does it control the population growth?"

"Every woman is only allowed to have one child," said Yuri. "After that, they are sterilized." His tone was indifferent.

"Then how does that explain you and your brothers?" Haley got her answer in the form of a smile from Yuri.

"My father is not good with rules. When doctor tried to sterilize my mother when Vladimir was born, my father shot him in the head."

Haley lost her breath momentarily, unable to comprehend such wanton violence.

Seeing the color drain from her face, Yuri jumped to defend his father. "You think my father is bad man?" Haley stared at him, afraid to answer. "That pig tried to sterilize my mother. They are the monsters." His drunken demeanor helped only to fuel his anger. He raised his arm as if to strike Haley. As it came down toward her face, she instinctively put her arms up to cover her face. Knowing that the blow should have come already, Haley opened her eyes.

She saw Yuri on his back with Virgil's foot on his throat.

"You try that again and I will end you." Virgil dug his foot deeper into the Russian's throat, making sure he understood.

Two of Mikhail's men who had been following them had popped out of the shadows and headed straight for Virgil.

Seeing the men racing toward Virgil, she closed her eyes and shifted her focus. The men were now only a few feet away. As if in sync, the men threw themselves toward Virgil. At the same moment, Haley slammed her foot on the ground. The almost imperceptible vibrations under her feet were exponentially increased instantly. Once the vibratory waves made it to her waist, she slapped her arms outward, hitting the wave. Just as the men were inches from Virgil's throat and legs, they were thrown backwards by the invisible force.

One of the men hit a nearby wall with a thud. The other was not so lucky. He hit a light pole ten feet away, appearing to break his ribs. Haley refocused herself, taking stock of what she had done. The feeling of remorse was nowhere to be seen in her eyes. She did not feel sorry for defending her friends.

"Are we clear?" Virgil asked Yuri again.

Yuri nodded and was freed from Virgil's boot.

The three of them watched as Yuri staggered to his feet. He stumbled over to his comrade at the pole. He cursed Virgil and his friend in Russian.

He reached down to pick up his friend, but the large man winced in pain. Seeing the agony in the man's face, Cameron walked over to him. He put his hand on the man's shoulder and closed his eyes. "He has a ruptured spleen and internal bleeding. He will die very soon if I don't help him."

"How do you know this?" Yuri said, crossing his arms as he observed Cameron.

Cameron looked over to Haley, knowing that Virgil would tell him not to show his *Gift*. To his surprise, Haley shook her head from side to side. She did not want to risk their safety by revealing his *Gift*. He then looked over to Virgil, hoping that his compassion would trump his fears at that moment. However, this was not the case. Virgil shook his head in concern as well.

"Screw it." Cameron placed his other hand on the man's side. He would ask his friends for forgiveness after he saved the man's life.

Haley started to walk toward him, but Virgil put his hand on her shoulder, "Just wait."

They watched as Cameron began to heal the man. Yuri's eyes opened wide, realizing what was happening.

Yuri looked over at Virgil. "Did you know he could do this?"

Virgil nodded, not taking his eyes off of Cameron.

After a minute, Cameron stood up and took a deep breath. It wasn't until he opened his eyes that he noticed a small crowd around him. He looked over to his friends who were pursing their lips, trying to figure out their next move. He avoided making eye contact with Yuri as he helped him pick the man off of the ground.

Once they helped the man to his feet, Cameron turned to walk back to Virgil and Haley. He stopped walking as he saw Haley's bulging eyes. Cameron watched as Virgil's hands rose, almost as if in slow motion. Then blackness. Cameron had not seen the pistol as it bashed him in the back of the head.

Paralyzed by fear, Virgil and Haley watched helplessly as several of Mikhail's men carried Cameron off through the crowd.

Mikhail stood in front of his men, broken bottle in hand. He waited while the crowd parted and closed behind him. "I take your friend to see Vladimir. He will be most pleased." He took a step toward them. This prompted Virgil to step back and usher Haley behind him. This did not sit well with Mikhail. He took another step forward, cracking his neck form side to side in an attempt to intimidate them. "Come with me now, and I promise you will not be harmed."

"Maybe next time," replied Virgil.

"Very well." Mikhail looked to either side and said, "Bring them to me."

In an instant, four very muscular men wearing tight shirts emerged from behind him. They made their way slowly toward Haley and Virgil.

Haley got on her toes and whispered into Virgil's ear. "Cover your ears."

Without a second thought, Virgil ducked and covered his ears. As he went down, Haley opened her mouth wide and let out an ear-piercing shriek. Everyone within fifty feet was brought to their knees, with the exception of Yuri and Virgil. *That's strange.*

She was pulled from her thought instantly as Virgil grabbed her wrist and began running in the opposite direction down an alley.

"Get them, you idiots!" Mikhail was the first on his feet. His men followed shortly thereafter. They attempted to follow them, but they were barely able to walk. The effects of Haley's shriek were profound.

Shortly after getting around the corner, Virgil camouflaged the two of them and they walked quickly toward the more populated areas, hoping they would get lost in the crowds. After walking for quite some time, they turned a corner and found themselves in a huge square. At the northern part of the square rose the Zal Obelisk. It rose twice as high as any building near it. Directly south of the tower on the opposite side of the square was the capital building.

"What the hell just happened?" cried Haley.

"I don't know," said Virgil. "But right now, we need to disappear until we can figure out how we're going to get Cameron back."

Haley nodded as he led them through the square.

The center of the square was packed with people. Some were walking through, while others were shopping at the dozens of stands lining the square. Anything and everything that they could ever need was for sale around them. They soon found that each side of the square was designated for a certain type of item for sale. On one side, there were vendors selling fruits and vegetables. On another was clothing and on another was home goods. Splintering off the main square were alleys that had even more vendors selling their wares.

Virgil led Haley directly to the side of the square that had clothing. He quickly grabbed two pairs of pants and some shirts and paid for them without even trying them on. He was not so fortunate when it came to Haley. She picked out several outfits, all of which required her trying them on. After what seemed like a lifetime, Haley settled on a couple pairs of pants for their journey and a nice red dress.

"What could you possibly need that for?" Virgil handed the vendor a golden coin from his pack for their garments.

"It's a girl thing," she replied. "You wouldn't understand."

"Thank God."

She crumpled her nose as she looked at him, then made her way to where the shoes were on sale.

"We don't have time for this, Haley." Virgil pointed to the small bit of sunlight still in the sky.

"We'll get where we need to get to a little faster with better shoes."

He couldn't argue with her logic. Their shoes from Purgatory were of poor quality and they would benefit from better footwear. He picked out the most expensive pair of hiking boots he could find. He waited patiently while Haley tried on numerous pairs. She finally settled on a pair that were much like his. As he handed the vendor a gold coin, she snuck another two pairs of shoes on the counter.

"We'll take these as well." She smiled at Virgil, watching as he shook his head and pulled out another coin.

"Trust me, these will come in handy." She held up a pair of red heels that conveniently matched her newly acquired dress and a pair of black dress shoes for Virgil.

They changed their outfits and stuffed the rest of their purchases in their bags. After discarding their Purgatory clothes, they went off in search of answers. As they shopped in the square, they asked the vendors for information regarding Vladimir and a useful guide.

Each time they inquired about Vladimir, they were asked to leave. It seemed that everyone they spoke to was too frightened to say anything. At the edge of the square, where it turned from market to back alley, a small man hid in the shadows. He overheard two young kids asking about a mob boss and found himself now following them. He puffed on his pipe as he watched them make their way toward him.

"How are we going to find him if no one is willing to help us?" Haley seemed to be at her wits' end. She sat on a small dividing wall near the edge of the market.

"Don't worry, we'll find someone who will help us."

"One hundred credits." The voice came from behind a building next to them.

They looked at each other, then walked in the direction of the voice. They were halfway to the other side of the building as the person spoke again.

"That will be far enough," said the person.

Haley and Virgil stopped and looked to the area in front of them that was covered in shadow. They could see the silhouette of a man, but nothing else.

"Show me the credits, and I'll tell you how to find Vladimir."

Virgil reached into his bag and pulled out one of the solid gold playing cards. "We don't have credits, but we have this." He held out his hand, holding the card out so the man could see.

"Throw it over here," said the man.

Virgil did as he was asked. He threw the card into the shadows and waited for the man's response.

After some time passed, the man finally spoke. "The man you seek is in Pele." He waited for a response from them, but when none came, he continued, "He is a very dangerous man. Are you sure you want to find him?"

They both nodded.

"Very well. He owns a club called The Bardo. It is near the tower square."

"Do you know how we can get to Euboea Montes?" Virgil knew that the only way to find Cameron was with a little bit of help.

A puff of smoke appeared from the shadows, followed by a small man. He looked fragile enough that he would break if he walked too fast. "I can take you there," he said, smiling big and showing the deep yellow tinge on his teeth. "For a small fee of course."

"Deal," said Virgil, reaching out his hand to shake on it. The man came forward and grasped Virgil's. He barely squeezed, as he was afraid to hurt the frail little man.

"But we need to leave tonight," said Haley.

"This is not possible," replied the man. "No one travels outside of the city at night."

"We'll pay you double." Virgil reached into his bag and pulled out three more gold cards. The man nearly fell over at the sight of the cards. Virgil knew that this was probably more money than the man had ever seen.

"You have got yourself a deal, my friends." The man smiled big once more, then took a puff from his cigar. "My name is Yoshiro."

"I'm Virgil...this is Haley." He handed Yoshiro one of the cards. "Half now...half when we get there."

"You are very clever, Mr. Virgil."

"It's just Virgil."

"Whatever you say, Mr. Virgil." The sickly looking man took another puff on his cigar. "So, what are we looking for in Euboea Montes?"

Virgil looked to Haley, then at their new guide. "We're looking for Marcus Raine."

Yoshiro coughed up the half-inhaled puff of his cigar and looked at his clients. "That's going to cost you triple."

CHAPTER EIGHTEEN

All Aboard

SPLASH!

Cameron's eyes flew open, followed instantly by a jolt to his body. He felt as if a thousand needles had pricked him all at once. The rush of fear he felt moments later was enough to look past the ice cold water that was thrown on his face. He attempted to stand, but found that his hands and feet were bound to the chair he was sitting on.

"You are very powerful, my friend."

Cameron recognized Mikhail's thick Russian accent. "Hmm hmm, hmm hmmm." Trying to speak with a rag in his mouth was not as easy as he had hoped.

Mikhail stepped into the light just in front of Cameron. He grabbed the corner of the cloth in Cameron's mouth and yanked it out.

Cameron leaned forward, doing his best to minimize his gag reflect. "What do you want?" He coughed several times to clear his throat.

Mikhail reached behind his back and pulled out a gun. He repositioned it on the front of his waist, making sure that Cameron got the message that they weren't fooling around.

The message was received loud and clear. Cameron's heart began to race as he shifted in the chair.

"Yuri...come." Mikhail did not turn around, as his brother came up to his left. He leaned forward, getting only a few inches from Cameron's face. "I want you to heal him."

"But there's nothing wrong with him," replied Cameron. He looked over to Yuri, who was sharing his look of befuddlement.

Just then, Mikhail pulls his gun from his waist and pointed it at Cameron's head. "You will heal him, or I kill your friends."

"But he's fine," said Cameron, now taking short staggered breaths.

"He will make you all better, Yuri," Mikhail said.

"But I do not have anything—"

BANG!

Before Yuri could finish what he was saying, Mikhail had shot him in the stomach.

Gasping for air, Yuri reached over and grabbed Mikhail's shirt, refusing to let go. "Why you do this, Mikhail?" His breathing became labored as he fell to his knees.

Mikhail again pointed the gun in Cameron's face. "You heal him now or I kill you."

Cameron bit his lip, accidentally drawing blood. "If you kill me, he'll die anyways." He licked the blood from his lower lip, feeling the cut already healing.

"This is true," replied Mikhail. He looked to his side and signaled one of his men. A moment later, the light in the room in front of Cameron lit up. Through the opaque window, he could see the silhouettes of Virgil and Haley.

"No!"

BANG!

The flash in the room was immediately followed by a spatter of blood on the window. Virgil then fell to the ground.

Cameron jerked violently on his restraints, trying to free himself. He jerked so hard that he knocked the chair over, sending his head crashing to the floor.

"You heal him, or I kill your girlfriend next." Mikhail picked Cameron back up so that he would have a good view of the next execution.

Cameron knew he wouldn't be able to live with being responsible for the death of his friends. He gritted his teeth and closed his eyes hard. *When this is done…I'm going to kill him.* He cleared the thought from his mind. "Ok, I'll do it."

Mikhail reached down and felt for a pulse on Yuri's throat. "You better hurry, or you will both be dead." He reached over to untie Cameron's hands.

"Don't touch me." Cameron took a deep breath and focused on Yuri. He felt his healing energy leaving his body. Subconsciously, his *Gift* knew exactly what needed to be done and went to work.

Mikhail watched in awe as the gunshot wound he had just inflicted on his brother began to close up. Just as the hole was closing up, a small metal slug slid out. A few seconds later, Yuri responded with a loud cough.

"I never see anything like this." Mikhail was running his hand on Yuri's stomach, not quite able to believe his eyes.

Cameron took a moment before opening his eyes. "Now let go of Haley."

"Haley?" Mikhail turned his head sideways.

"Don't play games with me!" yelled Cameron.

He smiled wide, turning to one of his men to open the door. There, on the ground lay a large bald man with a black and red star tattoo on the crown of his head. Next to him, stood a woman matching Haley's build.

"These are people I find in the street." He turned around and pointed the gun at the woman. All she could do was watch helplessly as he pulled the trigger. He planted three rounds in her chest before she hit the ground. He then walked over and put two additional rounds in the chest of the man on the ground.

"That is just in case you try to bring them back." He holstered his gun behind his back. "We can't have any witnesses." He walked over to Yuri and tried to help him up. Yuri promptly smacked his hand away, getting to his feet on his own.

"Don't be such cry baby, Yuri," said Mikhail, as he gently tapped Yuri's cheek. "He heal you without even touching you."

Yuri stood quiet for a long moment. Then, he burst out with spontaneous laughter. "Mikhail, we are going to be rich!"

Cameron sat quietly staring at the two people who had been killed in front of his face. His fear of what they would do to him kept him from trying anything stupid. That feeling however, was lost when he turned to see Mikhail and Yuri smiling and drinking as if they had not just murdered two people.

"Where are my friends?" asked Cameron.

Mikhail laughed. "Don't worry, my friend…all you need to know is that they are safe."

Cameron calmed himself and closed his eyes. After taking a breath, he imagined his healing force taking the life force from Yuri and Mikhail.

"Wait until Vladim—"

Cameron opened his eyes to see Mikhail and Yuri with their hands on their chests, falling to the ground.

"What is happening?" Mikhail coughed up blood as the words came out. His eyes were wide open as he looked at Cameron.

The roles had been reversed, and Cameron saw an opportunity to escape.

WHAM!

Darkness.

Cameron was knocked unconscious yet again. This time by one of Mikhail's men who was behind him.

It took twenty minutes for Mikhail and Yuri to get back on their feet after nearly dying at the hands of their prisoner.

"Yuri…he is the most powerful *Gifted* I have ever seen."

"No," said Yuri, rubbing the back of his neck. "He is strong…but no one is as powerful as Marcus."

Realizing his brother was right, Mikhail did not argue. "We must be careful with him, brother."

"Agreed. We must be able to control him before we take him to Vladimir. If he kills Vladimir, Mama will kill us." They smiled as they left the room. Cameron lay unconscious on the ground.

* * *

"You know," said Yoshiro, taking short puffs of his cheap cigar. "I heard it from a little birdie that there were some escaped fugitives on the loose in the city." His eyes darted back and forth between Haley and Virgil. Haley had her arms crossed, refusing to make eye contact. "Haha," he laughed. "Don't worry, my friends, I would never turn you in. I give you my word."

"Of course," responded Virgil, nodding his head, but also refusing to make eye contact. He knew now more than ever that they would need to guard their true identities. He reached over and put his arm around Haley. "From now on, you can refer to us as Chris and Heather Stevenson." He looked to Haley, hoping she would understand what he was doing. It took her only a moment, then she smiled.

"Yes…we are brother and sister and traveling from Telegonus Mensa." She placed her hand on his stomach, causing him to flinch involuntarily. He tensed his stomach muscles, making it seem as if he were naturally that defined. This made her chuckle, which in turn made him laugh.

"Right…" Toshiro stared at them blankly.

"Now, how do two siblings go about getting to Euboea Montes without raising any suspicion?" Virgil fashioned the fakest smile he could muster.

"Oh, Chris," laughed Haley, smacking his chest.

"Ok, stop it or I'll quit right here and now." Whatever humor the frail man possessed was nowhere to be seen. "We can't travel out of the city during the day. Facial recognition would catch you at the train or any of the other exits out of the city."

"We thought trains were the only way to get around," said Haley.

"They are...between the colonies. But there are countless service entrances around the dome." He stroked his goatee, trying to find a resolution to their predicament. "I think I will need to smuggle you out." He turned and began walking away. He stopped after several feet, realizing that they were not following him. "Are you coming or not?"

They looked at each other, then caught up to Yoshiro. "Smuggling us out will not be necessary. We can easily get on the train."

"Unless you can disappear, that will not be possible."

Virgil ignored Yoshiro's condescending smile and looked him in the eyes. "I said it won't be a problem." He kept his eye contact until Yoshiro looked away.

"Very well," responded Yoshiro. "If we go to the train station now, we can catch the last train out to Euboea Montes."

"But it's going to be dark in a couple of hours," said Haley, narrowing her eyes.

"We are heading northwest, toward the sunlight. It will arrive at Euboea Montes just as night falls."

"How far is it from here?" Haley remembered from her studies that all of the outer eight colonies connected together to Pele. What she did not recall was that four of the colonies not only ran to Pele, but their neighboring colonies as well. Fortunately for them, Zal had a route that would take them to Euboea Montes.

"It is approximately 500 miles," said Yoshiro, stopping at a street vendor for a change of clothes. "It will take a little more than an hour to get there." Yoshiro knew that right about now, his new companions would be asking him a couple of questions. He spoke as he stepped behind a barrier and threw off his old smelly pants. "The train that will take us travels over three hundred miles an hour." He slid into the new pair of pants, then a nice cotton shirt. He finally turned and faced the two of them, pointing to the merchant with his eyes.

"Oh…right," said Virgil, pulling a small gold coin out of his bag and handing it to the vendor. "Wait a minute," snapped Virgil. "Why are we buying a new outfit?" The vendor bit the coin, making sure that it was real, then quickly turned and walked to the other side of his tent. He did not want his customers to have a change of heart and ask for the coin back.

"You can't expect me to buy three expensive train passes dressed like a vagrant, do you?" Yoshiro reached for a pair of shoes, knowing he would not get any resistance from Virgil. He slipped on the shoes and thanked the vendor. "You can keep my old clothes," he said, making his way to a nearby alley.

The three of them made their way west through a series of back alleys behind buildings. In the areas that were not well covered, Virgil cloaked himself and Haley. He did not want to take the chance that they would be seen. After a ten minute walk, Virgil could see a high flag pole with the logo of a train. "There it is," he said, leaning over to tell Haley.

Yoshiro stopped abruptly ahead of them. "Ok, from this point on, there are cameras everywhere. If you get spotted when we turn this corner, you will be picked up before we make it to the train." He looked at each of them, still unsure how they would hide from the cameras. Their entire walk up to that point involved Yoshiro walking very fast and having them keep up. Not once had he turned around to see that his companions were invisible.

"Ok, lead the way," said Haley.

Yoshiro put his arm out. "Wait…didn't you just hear me?" He cursed under his breath in what they could only assume was Mandarin. The language was forbidden in all of the provinces, with the exception of Hi'iaka. His English up until that point had been perfect. Clearly, the prospect of being arrested for aiding fugitives was beginning to affect the man.

Without a word, Virgil closed his eyes and began to disappear. Yoshiro's mouth fell open as he watched a smiling Haley disappear with Virgil. There was a long silence, as Yoshiro stared at the area they had previously occupied.

"Ready when you are," said Haley.

Not being ready for the abruptness of her voice, Yoshiro shuffled back a step or two, again cursing under his breath. Once he regained his composure, he pointed his head toward the corner. "Let's go," he said as he walked away, not knowing if they were in front or behind him.

They made their way to the train station, where Yoshiro proceeded alone to the window to buy the passes. Only moments before, he had instructed Haley and Virgil to wait near platform two.

"Where are you headed, sir?" The cashier behind the booth spoke through a small speaker in the glass window.

"Euboea Montes," replied Yoshiro, as he wiped the sweat from his brow. "I require three passes." He caught sight of an authority officer through the reflection of the glass. He looked down as he reached into his pocket to pull out a gold coin.

The cashier couldn't help but to notice that the man standing in front of him was extremely nervous. His assumptions were verified as soon as he saw the man lay a gold coin on the counter. "I do not have change for that, sir." Doing the math in his head, the cashier knew this coin could pay to get them around to any colony four times over.

"It's ok," responded Yoshiro, not making eye contact with the man. "I won it in a game of chance."

"Of course, sir." The cashier took the coin and inspected it. Once he was satisfied of its authenticity, he signed his ledger and pulled a slip of paper with a barcode on one side, and the number three on the other. He placed it on the counter and began to slip it under the opening. "Wait," said the cashier, pulling the paper back just as he was about to hand it to Yoshiro.

Yoshiro's breathing began to quicken. "Please, sir, we don't want to miss the train."

"Where are your riding companions?" The man looked over Yoshiro's shoulder, but he could not see anyone.

"They are waiting for me near the train." He wiped the sweat once again from his brow and pointed to the clock on the wall. "If I don't get back soon, they're going to start to worry about me."

The cashier stared at the man for a long moment. "My apologies, sir," he said, as he slid the passes under the opening.

"It's quite alright, young man." Yoshiro took possession of the passes and quickly turned and walked away.

What he was not able to see as he walked away was the cashier's hand. As the man handed Yoshiro the passes with his left hand, his right hand was underneath the counter, pressing the button that summoned authority officers.

"I got them," whispered Yoshiro, as he waved the passes over his head as he approached the terminal. He quickly put his arm down, not wanting to draw any unwanted attention.

"We're right behind you," whispered a voice directly behind him.

Yoshiro's posture stiffened as he clenched his jaw. He was still not used to the idea that they could become invisible. He took a breath and walked toward one of the ushers near the front of the train. He kept his head down as he handed the man the pass.

"Where are your other two companions?" The man wore no expression on his face.

"They...they decided not to come with me," replied Yoshiro. He lifted his hands and shrugged his shoulders. "I mean honestly, who wouldn't want to travel with a man as good looking as myself?"

The usher's blank look was now replaced with a smile. "You have yourself a nice trip, sir." He scanned the pass and waved him to board.

Yoshiro gave him a nod, and then boarded the train. Unbeknownst to the usher, the old man's companions had boarded just before he scanned the pass.

Once on board and safely in the aisle, Yoshiro turned and whispered, "Ok, we are good now." Out of the corner of his eye, he noticed a woman looking curiously at him. He smiled, not knowing what to say. Until that moment, he hadn't realized that he looked like he was talking to himself.

"Are you ok, sir?" He turned around to see Haley and Virgil standing in front of him.

"Ah, yes…I'm fine," he replied. He held out his hand and said, "Would you help an old man to his seat?" He scowled at them as they led him into the next cabin.

He stopped walking and snatched his arm back as the door slid closed behind them. "Are you two crazy!" He put his hand to his chest and began to breathe heavily.

"Calm down, Yoshiro." Virgil had his hands out trying to calm their guide down. "You're going to give yourself a heart attack."

"That would be better than what would happen to me if we got caught." He ran his hands through his hair, trying to calm himself down.

"Don't worry," said Haley. "They have no idea you helped us."

This did little to calm the old man down.

Yoshiro opened his mouth, as if to yell at them, when suddenly, the door to the cabin behind them slid open. He quickly closed his mouth and composed himself. "Tickets please," said the train employee.

Virgil and Haley moved aside to allow the man to reach Yoshiro, who was holding out the pass.

The man scanned the pass and handed it back to Yoshiro. He smiled and said, "Enjoy your ride." He opened the next door and was gone.

"We should head to the back of the train," said Yoshiro. Haley and Virgil nodded and motioned for the man to lead the way.

As they walked, Virgil couldn't help but to notice the softness of the seats on the train. He had never seen such craftsmanship in Purgatory. Haley looked back at him and smiled, as if she was thinking the same thing as him. They struggled to keep up with Yoshiro, as they continually slowed down or stopped to squeeze the headrests on the seats, or run their hands across the silk curtains.

When they finally made it to the final compartment, they saw Yoshiro already seated. He looked as if he had aged ten years. Virgil and Haley took the seats to either side of him, hoping it would ease the man's tension.

"Have you two never been on a train before?"
Yoshiro couldn't help but notice their fascination with
everything they touched.

"Nope," replied Haley.

"Where we grew up," said Virgil. "Let's just
say…you wouldn't wish it on your worst enemy."

Yoshiro did not seem to understand. He looked to
his left and saw an ordinary, yet very pretty teenage girl.
And to his right, he saw a very handsome well-built young
man. Neither seemed to be malnourished or abused. *These
kids look like they grew up in the suburbs of Pele. They
must be hiding something.* "But I don't understand," he
said, shifting in his seat to face Haley. He knew if he were
going to get any answers, it would come from her. Over the
years, living on the streets, the old man developed a talent
for reading people. This allowed him to more easily pick
out the people in the crowds who were subject to his
various cons. During their short trip, he watched as Virgil
would look to Haley, ever guarded of his words. He knew
answers would not be forthcoming from him. "You two
look as if you've never gone hungry a day in your life."

"We were fed three meals a day," said Haley, as
she leaned forward to look at Virgil. Reluctantly, he
nodded his head, giving her the ok to tell their tale. She

went on to explain to Yoshiro where they had come from and what had transpired before meeting him.

Virgil was stuck by the relief on Haley's face and her body language. The more she spoke about their ordeal, the more at peace she seemed. He, on the other hand, remembered Yuri's betrayal of them only hours earlier. Haley was far too trusting of people, and as such, would force him to be even more vigilant of their associations.

"Kidnap, imprisonment, escape, and kidnap..." Yoshiro looked up, trying to piece together everything Haley had just said. She had spoken so fast that she had to catch her breath when she finished. "Got it," he said finally.

"That's why we need to find Marcus Raine," said Haley.

"But that's the thing," responded Yoshiro. "You never said *why* you needed to find the most dangerous man on IO."

Virgil straightened in his chair. He did not want Haley to accidentally volunteer any information that Yoshiro didn't need to know. "Someone like us told us that we need to find him." He raised his chin slightly, wanting Yoshiro to understand that he did not want to be questioned on this particular issue.

"Ok, calm down," said Yoshiro, leaning back toward Haley. "I just think your friend is not much of a friend if they want you to go looking for Mr. Raine, that's all."

Seeing Virgil tense up, Haley reached over and put her hand on Yoshiro's shoulder. "Why is everyone so afraid of that guy?"

"I heard that during the war, he decimated an entire legion of authority forces all by himself." He let the words sink in before continuing. "When they took his wife and child, he went mad and nearly leveled the colony of Catena."

"What is his ability?" Virgil couldn't imagine the kind of power it would take to raze a city to the ground.

Yoshiro shook his head. "No one knows…at least no one who's still living." He reached for Haley's hand and held it in his. "Are you sure you want to find this man?"

At this point, Haley wanted nothing to do with Marcus Raine. She always trusted Virgil's judgment, but felt that he was blinded by what Maggie told him in the penitentiary. *I don't understand the blind faith he has with that woman.*

"Haley?" Virgil looked curiously at her, wondering what she was thinking about.

She shook her head. "Sorry." She cared for Virgil and knew he would never knowingly put her in harm's way. "Absolutely," she said, looking Yoshiro right in the eyes. She then sat back in her chair. *God, I hope you're right about this, Virgil.*

* * *

Meanwhile, not far from the train, several authority officers converged on the ticket booth. The cashier quickly rose to his feet as he saw the men approaching. All three of the men wore all black uniforms, distinguished only by the colors on the armband. He looked directly at the officer with the green armband as they reached the window. The other two men with red armbands remained a step behind.

"What seems to be the problem here?" The officer's eyes appeared cold to the cashier. The man looked to have as much emotion as a robot.

"I…someone came through here and paid with this." He held up the coin to the glass. The officer motioned for him to slip the coin through the opening. The cashier did as he was instructed. He did not want to provoke the officers. He knew their reputation for brutality and was going to make certain he would not be the subject of it today.

"Who gave you this?"

The cashier turned and pointed to a frozen video frame on the screen behind him. "That man...he bought a ticket for three, but was by himself when he purchased it."

The officer turned to his subordinates and said, "Get the ushers over here, now." They saluted and walked away toward the train. The cashier and officer waited several minutes for the ushers to arrive.

"Have any of you seen this man?" The officer pointed to the monitor behind the cashier. The ushers studied the picture for a moment, when one said, "Yes...I scanned his pass in cabin two before I exited the train."

"Was he with anyone?"

The usher thought for a moment "Yes, he was with a boy and a girl...maybe his grandchildren."

"Did he say they were his grandchildren?"

The usher shook his head from side to side.

"Then don't assume anything." The officer's words sent a chill down the usher's back. He bowed his head and stepped back.

The officer again turned to his subordinates. "You two, remove them from the train and bring them to me."

"That won't be necessary, Officer."

"Excuse me?" barked the officer, as he turned around. He spotted the man walking toward him and quickly stood at attention. "My apologies, sir." He stood at attention until the man raised his hand to signal him to stand at ease.

The cashier looked over the officer's shoulder to see a man dressed in an all-black uniform with blue encrusted armbands. The name on his uniform said, *Hersch.*

Behind him were several elite officers dressed in black with the special forces insignia of an eagle on their armbands. They each sported an assault rifle and a hand gun fastened to a holster on their thigh.

"We'll take it from here," said Hersch, smiling wide, knowing that his quarry was in his sights. "When does the train depart?" he asked the cashier without taking his eyes off of the train.

"Five minutes, sir."

"Good," he said, clasping his hands behind his back. Let them go."

"Let them go?" The guard with the green armband tilted his head to the side.

Hersch turned and looked directly at the officer. "Is there a problem?"

"No, sir, it's just..." The man did not dare to look up, as he knew he was already in enough trouble for questioning a superior officer. "We have them now...why not take them?"

"Kindly explain to our friend here why we are letting them go." He waved one of his elite officers over to speak with the officer.

"Commander Hersch knows that if the train is moving, they will have no possible way of escaping. We will board the train as it departs and then take them before reaching Euboea Montes."

The officer stared at the ground as he nodded to the elite officer. He knew all too well what would come next. Another elite officer stepped forward and the two began beating the man.

"Any more questions?" asked Hersch, as he turned back to the train.

CHAPTER NINETEEN

Next Stop: Nowhere

"ALL ABOARD!"

The abrupt announcement from the overhead speakers was enough to make Haley flinch. She turned to see Virgil staring out of the side of the window. With her *Gift*, she was able to see the city barrier not far from the station. Beyond that, all she saw were wide open spaces of nothingness.

Feeling that someone was looking at him, Virgil turned to meet Haley's gaze. "I was just curious how a train can even work in such a hostile environment."

"What do you mean?" She got out of her seat and walked to the window. "It looks pretty simple to me."

"Levitated tracks," responded Yoshiro.

"You mean levitated train?" Virgil was sure that the train they boarded resembled the bullet trains he read about.

"Both," replied Yoshiro.

It took only a moment for the answer to come to Virgil, at which point he nodded with understanding.

"A little help here," said Haley, raising her eyebrows.

"The ground is constantly shifting on IO," said Virgil. "To compensate for that, they have a magnetic levitating track." He looked over to Yoshiro. "I bet they even have some type of map that they can use to manipulate the course of the tracks any time they wish, huh?"

"You are pretty clever," said Yoshiro, as he shook his head. "Who taught you this?"

"No one…I just figured it out." He shrugged his shoulders as if it were nothing to him. In truth, Virgil never came across a problem for which he could not find an answer.

"So then how long will the trip actually take if the tracks can be changed anytime they want?" The doors began to close and once again, Haley flinched.

"NEXT   STOP…EUBOEA   MONTES. APPROXIMATE TIME OF ARRIVAL IN ONE HOUR, THIRTY MINUTES."

Virgil smiled as he pointed to the speaker closest to him.

"On a good day," explained Yoshiro, pointing to a map of the train routes on IO. "We could make it there in less than an hour."

"Over five hundred miles in an hour?" Virgil was sure the old man was mistaken.

Yoshiro ignored Virgil's condescending tone and said, "Because the gravity on IO is not what it was on Earth…this train can travel at nearly twice the speed as the ones you read about." He raised his eyebrows and crossed his arms as he looked at Virgil. He knew the boy would not be able to rebut his argument.

Virgil smiled at Yoshiro, then caught a glimpse of something over the man's shoulder. Knowing that Virgil had just noticed their movement, Yoshiro stepped aside, allowing the entire window to be seen by Virgil and Haley.

While discussing their speed, they had not noticed that the train had already left the station. They stared blankly out into the vast open space, not knowing what to say.

Yoshiro saw their reaction to the view and took the opportunity to provide an even better view. He moved back to his seat and pressed a button on the panel on the right side. Slowly, the caboose ceiling and back faded away, leaving a full 180 degree view.

Haley and Virgil turned slowly in place, taking in the views as they went. "This is amazing," said Haley, smiling as she took Virgil's hand in hers.

"Agreed," replied Virgil. He squeezed her hand then motioned for her to sit down next to him.

They sat down and leaned their heads back, taking in the view of the sun setting overhead. In the distance, they were able to see what they knew was Europa. They watched as the neighboring moon slowly made its way across the sky. A few minutes later, they both closed their eyes.

Yoshiro narrowed his eyes as he watched his companions. He could not understand how two young kids could be so tired. He smiled as he paced the compartment, clutching his golden payment in his hand. He decided he would let them sleep until they reached their destination while he figured out the best way to make contact with Marcus Raine.

* * *

At the front of the train, another plan was being discussed. "Is everything set?" Hersch examined the blueprints of the train as he spoke with his second in command.

"Yes, sir," replied the soldier. "We are ready to go as soon as you give the word."

"Good," said Hersch, nodding his head as he paced the compartment. He knew that his targets were in the next cabin. What he did not know was the extent to which their *Gifts* had developed. He did not want to take the chance that he would lose them again. "Change of plans," he said, walking back to the blueprints. "We will pump sleeping gas into the compartment from the space just underneath the compartment door."

His second in command nodded to his subordinates and they unpacked the requested equipment without a second thought. They learned long ago that your health depended greatly on your ability to follow orders.

Two of the soldiers made their way to the door and slid a small tube under it. Once the tube was secured into place, one soldier sealed the bottom of the door while the other connected the hose to a small canister that held the gas. They nodded once they were ready.

"All set, sir."

Hersch nodded. "When we are at the halfway point, you can begin." He motioned the men to stand around him. "Two minutes after that gas is released, everyone in that compartment will be out cold. You will identify the targets, bind their hands and feet, then inject them with the serum. Is that understood?"

The men acknowledged the orders in unison.

Hersch looked at his watch, knowing that it would not be long before his prey would fall victim to his trap.

* * *

"Wake up," whispered Yoshiro, as he shook Haley and Virgil's shoulders. Virgil quickly jumped to his feet while Haley slowly opened her eyes.

"Are we there yet?" Haley yawned as she rubbed her eyes.

"Not quite," replied Yoshiro. "We're about halfway there." He pointed to the side opposite of him and said, "I wanted you two to see that." In the distance, there was what looked to be a huge metal mountain.

"Is that…" Haley wasn't sure what she was looking at.

"An ark," said Virgil.

"Very good," Yoshiro said. "It was one of the seven original ships used to bring us to IO. Now it's used for spare parts and salvage for the various colonies." All that remained of the giant ark was the shell. It spanned several miles in either direction. It looked as if it could take up an entire colony by itself.

"What happened to the other six ships?" Haley knew this was something that was never mentioned in their studies.

"Several years after colonizing IO, the ships were re-tasked with salvage missions to Earth. They're due back in a few months."

"I thought the entire planet was uninhabitable," said Haley.

"It is," responded Yoshiro. "But there are still countless subterranean cities that have an untold amount of equipment and supplies that can be brought here."

"It's been decades though," said Virgil. "I can't imagine there would be too much left."

"That's right," agreed Yoshiro. "In fact…I heard that this may be their last trip there. Earth has nearly been picked clean."

* * *

Meanwhile, only four compartments away, a strike team was getting ready to storm their known location.

"On my mark," whispered the soldier. He raised his hand and stuck out three fingers. "One…two…three!" They quickly slid the door open and flooded the compartment, guns at the ready. They swept the cabin, checking every person that they passed. "All clear." The soldiers lowered their rifles as Hersch entered the cabin. "They're not here, sir."

"What do you mean they're not here?" Hersch's anger began to rise as he rubbed the back of his neck.

"They must have moved back after boarding the train."

"Follow me," said Hersch, baring his teeth. He walked to the next compartment door and threw a punch. The metal door nearly split in two. Several of the passengers jumped out of their seats, as they were not sure what had just happened. Hersch ran into the space, pistol in hand.

"What is the meaning of this?" A well-dressed man in a suit stood up and blocked the walkway between Hersch and the next compartment.

Hersch raised the gun to the man's head. "You have about two seconds to get over it before I pull this trigger." The man thought better of his actions and sat back down. Just after Hersch passed the man, a soldier approached him and slammed the butt of his rifle to his head. The man was left unconscious and bleeding while the soldiers ran into the next compartment.

* * *

"Did you hear that?" Haley looked over to Virgil and then looked to the door.

Yoshiro's calm demeanor instantly changed to one of fear. He swallowed hard and ran to the door. He quietly slid the door open enough to peek through. After a moment, he slowly turned his head toward Haley and Virgil. "Quick...hide yourselves," he said, whimpering uncontrollably.

Virgil positioned himself in front of Haley and cloaked the entire back of the compartment.

Yoshiro had already closed the door and was barely clear of it when it came down. The door slammed to the ground with such force that it knocked the old man off his feet.

Haley moved to help the man, but was held back by Virgil. He looked at her and shook his head. Her eyes opened wide at the sight in the doorway, prompting Virgil to turn from her and see the man they had been running from.

Knowing that this was the final compartment, Hersch stalked into the space. His eyes examined the entire compartment, seeing nothing but the man at his feet. He reached down and grabbed the old man by the back of his shirt and picked him up. "Where are they?"

"Who?" murmured Yoshiro. He did not want to look the man in his eyes, as they would give him away.

Hersch turned to one of the officers, then backhanded Yoshiro across the face. "Three kids...two boys and a girl."

They still think the three of us are together, thought Virgil. He looked at Haley, who appeared to be thinking the same thing.

"I did not see three kids," replied Yoshiro, as he spit a wad of fresh blood from his mouth. Sadly, he was telling the truth about not traveling with three kids, but he knew that no longer mattered.

Without a word, Hersch threw the man like a rag doll into a row of chairs. The old man screamed in pain as he hit the seats and then the floor. "You have three seconds to show yourselves before I shoot this man." He stepped next to where Yoshiro was on the floor, tapping his gun on his thigh and smiling. "One…..two…..three."

BANG!

A single shot was fired, followed by a shrieking cry from the old man on the ground.

Haley squeezed as tight as she could around Virgil's waist, digging her face into his arm. She knew that if they showed themselves, it would be a death sentence. But she also knew that Yoshiro could be killed just as easily because of them.

Virgil's posture stiffened as he watched thick red blood begin to pour out of a wound in Yoshiro's stomach. He had read enough books to know that the old man would not live through a shot like that.

"Next time it will be his head," Hersch said, baiting them to show themselves. He lifted the gun once again. "One....two....thr—"

"Wait!"

Slowly the invisible curtain at the back of the train disappeared.

"Well, hello there," said Hersch, lowering his gun.

"Please, don't hurt him," said Virgil, pleading with Hersch to show mercy.

Hersch turned his head to the side. "Who, him?" He pointed his gun at Yoshiro and pulled the trigger. The old man went still in an instant.

"You bastard!" Virgil stepped forward, but was stopped short by Hersch's gun as it was pointed at him.

Hersch looked over the barrel of his gun to Haley. "Where's the other one?"

"Dead. He was killed by the Russian mafia," she said, hoping she was lying.

"That's a shame," he said smugly. "I was hoping to take care of the three of you myself." He turned and began to walk out of the compartment. "I was supposed to bring you back alive, but...." He shrugged his shoulders and smiled at Virgil and Haley. "Take care of them and put their bodies on the transport when we arrive at Euboea Montes."

As soon as he cleared the doorway, the soldiers lifted their rifles to fire.

"Haley, now!" Virgil moved swiftly to the side, then directly behind Haley.

Hersch turned to see Haley whistling and Virgil covering his ears behind her.

"No!" As Hersch lifted his arm to warn his soldiers, Haley was in the process of throwing a punch.

As soon as Hersch stepped forward, he was immediately thrown backwards by an invisible force. As he stood up, he saw Virgil raising his arms in the air. As he did so, Hersch's men began to slide toward him from the caboose. *He's lifting the train!* As he began to walk toward the door, he heard a crackling noise under his feet.

He jumped backwards just as the steel floor connecting the caboose ripped apart. At the very last moment, he grabbed hold of the door frame of the compartment and watched as his best men were sucked out of the hole and thrown into the air. The speed at which the train was moving had created a vacuum that would continue until it slowed down or stopped.

It was not until his last man was ejected from the train that he noticed the caboose had straightened itself out and was slowing considerably. He caught one final glimpse of a smiling Virgil before it disappeared into the sunset.

"Stop this train!" Hersch had managed to pull himself safely back into the train. His targets had eluded him, but he would make sure they could not get far. "Reverse this train," he said, making his way to a call box on the wall.

"Negative," said the voice on the other end.

"Stop this train now, or so help me I will —"

"Negative, the train is automatically controlled. I do not have the capability to override the system."

Hersch ground his teeth as he made his way back to the cabin near the front of the train. He sat down, going over in his head how he was bested again by a couple of kids.

* * *

Several miles behind the train, Virgil gently lowered the caboose to the ground. Once it touched down, he turned to make sure Haley was alright. "Are you hurt?"

She shook her head as she massaged the back of her neck. "Just a bit shaken up."

Virgil stepped out of the compartment and climbed to the top, hoping to get a better view of their surroundings. After a couple of minutes, Haley joined him.

She made her way to the edge of the caboose and sat down. "How did you do that, Virgil?"

"What do you mean?" He knew exactly what she meant, but he didn't have an answer for her.

"I mean…you broke this caboose off at several hundred miles an hour, while at the same time not letting us fly uncontrollably through the sky before plummeting to our death."

He took a seat next to her and exhaled loudly. "I don't know…it felt different this time. It didn't feel like telekinesis. It felt like I was controlling gravity."

"That is because you were, young man."

CHAPTER TWENTY

Close Encounters of the Third Kind

Haley and Virgil froze instantly. Neither was sure if the other had heard the voice in their head.

"I am speaking to the two of you."

"Who are you?" Haley stood up and looked around. "Show yourself."

"Yes, of course," said the gentle voice. *"My name is Xenex."*

The dirt in front of the sunset began to swirl. A moment later, a figure appeared and the dust settled.

"My apologies for the theatrics," said the being. *"I do find all of this dirt rather distasteful."* The silhouette could be seen wiping the dust off of his arms.

As he came closer, they realized that the man stood nearly ten feet tall. Virgil made his way to the ground, then helped Haley down.

"There is no reason to be afraid, Haley."

"How do you know my name?"

"I know everything about you...as well as your friend Virgil."

Instinctively, Virgil positioned himself so that he was between the being and Haley.

"My, my, aren't we untrusting," said Xenex, as he transitioned from a silhouette in the sunset, to a tall blond man only feet from the two of them. "Would you prefer if I spoke out loud and not telepathically?"

"That would be a start," replied Virgil. Seeing the man standing before them, Virgil couldn't help but ask, "Are you human?" The man spoke very proper English, but stood taller than any human was ever capable of. His golden robe looked to be something out of Ancient Rome, and yet his long flowing blond hair and pale white skin made him appear to be Scandinavian in origin.

"Yes...and no. I will explain all of this in due time, but for now, we need to leave." He stepped aside to reveal a black oval that was his exact height. As they peered inside, they could see only darkness.

"We're good here," said Virgil.

"You don't seem to understand," responded Xenex, as he walked up to them, hands behind his back. He seemed to almost glide across the ground, making no sound as he stepped. "If I leave you out here, you will be dead in an hour, and it is not your destiny to die in this desert."

"You can see the future?" asked Haley.

"Yes, but —"

"Then why not tell us what will happen to us?" said Virgil.

"That is not how it works, young one. If I tell you the future, I have in essence already changed it for you. You must find the path for yourself."

"If that's the case, then why are you helping us now?" said Haley. "By helping us, aren't you already changing our future?"

"You are very smart, Miss Hawthorne," said Xenex, as he began to pace in front of them. "You are correct. It is this exact moment that I have seen in my mind for the last 7000 years. Since the moment we gave the knowledge of farming and cultivation to the Sumerians."

"That's impossible," murmured Virgil.

"I have been witness to the numerous iterations of the human species on Earth and other worlds. For some reason, you can't seem to get it right."

"Get what right?" asked Haley.

"Peaceful existence," replied Xenex. "Mankind evolves and eventually finds evermore inventive ways to kill each other as well as the planet. I and others like me were tasked long ago to look over mankind's progression and eventual enlightenment."

"How's that working out for you?" jabbed Virgil.

"Touché," said Xenex, as he bowed his head. "But that will not be the case for long." He turned back to face the two of them. "I will teach you how to harness your *Gifts*, then you will find Marcus Raine and retrieve your friend Cameron from Pele."

"How do you know all of this?" Virgil stared in awe at the man in front of him. Even he couldn't deny the power and authority the man exuded.

"As I said, young man…I have been waiting for this moment for quite some time. Now come, we must go before your pal Hersch descends upon us." He began walking toward the portal he had created.

Haley looked Virgil in the eyes and nodded slightly, then began walking with Xenex. Knowing that he would never leave her side, Virgil followed her to where Xenex was standing.

"How do we know we can trust you?" said Virgil.

"Because, my dear boy, you and your friends are destined to save the world."

"Come again?" said Haley, putting her hand to her ear.

"The sons of IO are going to be responsible for saving the world."

"The sons?" muttered Haley, looking up in the air.

"Ahem," said Xenex. "My apologies…the sons AND daughters of IO will save the world."

"That's what I figured," said Haley, as she smiled and stepped into the void.

"Wait!" shouted Virgil. He knew she had done that on purpose. He'd have gone first to make sure it was ok.

"You must trust me, Virgil, you will be safe with me."

Virgil nodded and turned to walk into the portal. He stopped suddenly and turned to Xenex. "You said the sons of IO were destined to save the world, yes?"

"Correct."

"So if I and my friends are going to save the world, what does that have to do with Marcus Raine?"

"I did not say it would just be you and your two friends saving the world. Marcus Raine is the key to everything. Without him, you cannot hope to succeed."

"What makes him so special?" Virgil said, turning and placing half his body into the void.

"His *Gifts*, along with yours, will bring Earth back to life."

"I guess that's a good reason, but aren't you afraid he'll kill us? We heard he's gone mad."

"Don't worry, the last thing he will do is hurt you." He placed his hand on Virgil's shoulder, nudging him into the void.

"How can you be so sure?"

"Because he's your father."

"Wait...what?"

Before Virgil could say another word, Xenex pushed him into the void.

CHAPTER TWENTY-ONE

Epilogue

"Как Вы знали, что он излечит меня?"

"English, Yuri…"

"How did you know he would be able to heal me?" Yuri looked down as he spoke with his brother.

"That's easy…I threatened his friends and boom, he heals you." Mikhail had his hands out; unsure as to why his brother would not come to the same conclusion.

"You idiot," said Yuri, shaking his head. "Our powers do not work on people like us."

Mikhail squinted his eyes at his brother. "But you are healed, yes?"

"That's not the point."

"Then what is point?" Mikhail rolled his eyes, inhaling exhaling deeply. "I shoot you…he heals you…everything is ok."

"Do you understand what this means?"

"No, baby brother…but if you do not tell me I will be getting very annoyed with you."

"It means that he is very powerful."

"And we are going to be very rich, yes?"

Yuri nodded. "Da."

Just then, Cameron began to moan softly. He slowly opened his eyes and saw Mikhail and Yuri looking down on him. He attempted to lift his arm, but found that it was tied down. His feet were also bound.

"It is ok, my friend," said Mikhail, as he patted Cameron on the chest.

Cameron acted as if the man was not there and faced Yuri. "Where are my friends?"

"Safe," replied Yuri.

Cameron let out a sigh of relief. He knew his situation was dire, but as long as his friends were ok, he would deal with it.

Mikhail leaned down, blocking Cameron's view of Yuri. "Your friends will be safe as long as you do what we tell you."

"Ok, dude, I will work for you as long as I have your word that you won't hurt my friends...deal?" Cameron opened his hand to shake on the deal.

Mikhail grabbed Cameron's hand and agreed to the terms, even though his captive was unaware that he did not have his friends. That secret would be conveniently left out. He cut the restraints on Cameron's arms and legs and helped him to the seat next to Yuri.

He knew they were in some kind of vehicle and that they were moving very fast, but he was not sure where they were going.

"Where are we headed, dude?" he asked, as he rubbed his sore wrists.

Mikhail squinted his eyes, "Pele. You are going to meet Vladimir." Cameron nodded and sat back in his seat. Mikhail leaned forward and looked at Cameron for a long moment. "What is this "dude" you speak of?"

For that brief moment, he forgot that he was being held against his will. He leaned forward and placed his hand on Mikhail's shoulder. "Dude, if I'm going to work for you, you're going to need to learn a little bit of slang."

ACKNOWLEDGEMENTS

First and foremost, I would like to thank my beautiful wife Alba and our two amazing children, Gabe and Jazmyn. Without them, this idea of being a writer would've been just that, an idea. I can now happily say that I have written my first book!

We always stressed to our children that in life, you should find what you love to do and then find someone that will pay you to do it. I decided to take my own advice and become an author at age 35. It still amazes me how the universe works things out once you figure out your true path in life.

Many thanks to Danny Ayala for creating the perfect cover for this book. You took the ideas in my head and translated them perfectly on the page.

Special thanks to my editor, Tracy Seybold

And finally...you the reader. My utmost thanks and appreciation for taking the time to read my very first novel. I hope to gain your attention once more in the sequel to this novel.